Falling Feathers

The Sunflower Beach Series

Dolores Puterbaugh

Contents

To Gerry, always.

Special thanks to Gerry, for patient reading, listening, encouragement and thoughtful feedback.
Thanks to Dora Campbell for guidance and encouragement on the writing and publication process.
Thanks to Betty for reading, proofing and encouragement.
Thanks to Savannah Grace for guidance on designing the cover and selecting the artwork.
Thanks to Dolores and Doe for encouragement and help on cover art and design.

Preface

When I was a child, I created an imaginary monster to scare my siblings – tales of a slimy beast that lived beneath the house and could emerge, wet and terrifying, from the sump in the darkest, dampest corner of the basement. Naturally, I scared myself more than anyone else and, as helping with laundry was one of my chores, I ended up spending a few years racing up the stairs, heart pounding, several times each day, hoping to lurch out the basement door into the warm kitchen before The Sump Pump monster could get its terrible webbed grip on me. Going downstairs was even worse, and it didn't take long before even the flap of the door of the laundry chute in the bathroom could trigger a surge of adrenaline as I rushed out before that terrible, scaly arm could reach me.

That being said...the people and situations in this book are the fruits of my regrettably over-active imagination. Except, of course, for the animals: some of the animals memorialize much-loved and much-missed animal companions.

Chapter One

Relentless pain. Throbbing, really. Alex rubbed her jaw and glanced at her watch. The dentist's waiting room was quiet: The television set was turned on to a talk show but had been muted by a prior patient. The walls were full of posters of beautiful, smiling people of all ages, their teeth gleaming. Perhaps they were smiling because they were done with the dentist. She hoped to be smiling when she left, too. She shifted, and the olive vinyl seat squealed softly.

Behind the window separating the reception desk from the waiting area, the staff were talking about their weekends and complaining about the hold time at insurance companies. "This is ridiculous," one said, holding the phone away from her ear for a moment. "It's some sort of instrumental version of 'Material Girl' for the third time."

Her coworker laughed, shaking her head. "Seriously?"

It was another quiet time of waiting. There was little to read except pamphlets advertising dental services. Alex always had a book with her, so boredom was seldom a problem. Which was a good thing, she thought, considering how many hours she had clocked waiting.

Waiting in pediatricians' offices, waiting at dentists' offices and the orthodontists', the teacher conferences that inevitably ran long, the bus stops on rainy days, and the long evenings waiting for teenagers to sneak in after curfew, trying to be furtive but too awkward to pull it off, always crashing into something in the dark hall on their way up the stairs. She'd spent years carrying books for the children, and still always had something for herself.

Today, however, the pain was distracting and the usual relief of diving into a book didn't help. She fidgeted with her jacket, pulling absent-mindedly at loose threads around the button holes.

The door to the treatment area swung open. "Mrs. Bonhall! Good to see you!" It was Francis, the same cheerful dental assistant who had been there for her cleaning two weeks ago. Francis was tall and thin, with springs of dark hair that bounced when he walked. Francis liked to talk. He was a dental assistant by day and working on his master's degree in library science at night. Upon learning that Alex was one of the librarians at the state college in town, he assumed it was perfectly fine to ramble on about his classes, his projects, and his intention to work at the very same library someday. Alex wondered if he would talk less when he was a librarian. Having to think about her work while in a dentist's office was surely some sort of penance.

Francis was relentlessly buoyant. "How's the library?" he asked, clicking at the computer in the exam room. "I've been going crazy with end of term," he continued, not waiting for her to respond. "My portfolio for how I would promote student services in the online platform is due in two days. Super-exciting stuff but constantly changing." He squinted at the screen. "So, what brings you here today?"

"Pain," Alex answered, pointing, but Francis was typing, not looking at her.

"Cold sensitivity? Heat sensitivity? Pain when you chew? When tapping?"

"No, no, no. I don't know. I don't tap my teeth."

"Mm-hmm." There was a brief silence while Francis typed about her failure to tap at her teeth, nodding at the screen.

It was odd for Francis to be quiet for more than a few seconds. Alex felt awkward in the silence. *Maybe I was rude, the way I answered about tapping my teeth.* She cleared her throat.

"So, Francis ... how did you decide on library science?"

Francis sat up straighter, turned toward her and tilted his head. "Huh. I don't think anyone's ever asked me that before."

"And?" She smiled encouragingly.

He nodded slowly, thinking. "I don't know, it just seemed ... peaceful. Secure. You never hear about librarians being suicidally depressed. Like dentists get, for example. I mean, not Dr. Quinn or anyone here," he added quickly, glancing at the doorway. Francis paused. "I love reading. I enjoy just being around books. Walking into the library, from when I was a kid. Remember Mr. What's-his-name? The head librarian in the children's section, the guy who made marionettes and put on puppet shows to go with the story hour on Saturdays?" Francis stared into space, shaking his head. "It was magic. Just magic. I'd like to be able to do that, make books come alive."

"Mr. Carmetto? Yes, he just retired last year. He volunteers at the children's hospital now." Mr. Carmetto had been with the public library for years, and was a master puppeteer, making his own marionettes and adapting them to all sorts of stories.

"Oh, see, that's cool." Francis looked closely at Alex. "What about you? What made you decide to be a librarian?"

Alex took a deep breath. "Well, it's kind of a long story. I double majored in wildlife biology and fine art in undergrad, and then we moved here for my husband's work, and I was class mother for our son, and then our daughter, and spent a lot of time with the kids at the school's library. And I really liked the librarian. Evelyn. Evelyn Cooley."

"I think she's still there," Francis said. "At least, she was a few years back, when my youngest sister finished elementary school."

"Maybe she'll stick around long enough for you to take her job," Alex suggested. "Would that work for you?" *And then you won't be at the college, talking at me all day.*

"Yeah, that would be cool. Lots of vacation time, too," Francis remarked. "Art and wildlife bio? What was up with that?"

"Oh, I guess I liked both and couldn't decide. And truth be told, I had this crazy idea that I would do scientific illustrations. You know, like those 'Snakes of North America' and 'Butterflies of the Eastern Seaboard' laminated brochures you see around. Or maybe textbooks."

"Oh, sure. I get it." Francis nodded, but Alex doubted that he did get it. She knew she didn't look like either an artist or a wildlife biologist. She had at one time. She had the pictures to prove it—long, wild hair and the kind of legs earned by honest hiking, miles at a time, through all kinds of terrain. But now, pudgy with a sensible, shoulder-length bob, she didn't think Francis, or anyone else, would mistake her for either a wildlife biologist or an artist.

The dentist came in. "Hi, Aunt Alex," he said cheerfully. "How are you?"

"Fine, Dr. Quinn."

"Please. It's Cody." He pulled down his mask and grinned. He was her friend Gloria's son, and she'd known him since he was nine. Seeing his whole face made it easier to call him Cody; the splash of freckles that matched his bright hair gave him the appearance of never having quite grown up. Of course, he was a grownup—he was a professional, the new head dentist at this clinic, and raising the twins by himself.

"Francis, did you find Mrs. Bonhall's latest X-rays?"

"They're pulled up for you."

"Thanks. I'll let you know if I need anything. Could you check on the patient in exam room four, see how the numbing is going?"

Francis left them, and Cody, taking a seat, asked again, "So, Aunt Alex, what's going on?"

"Cody. Sorry. The pain is terrible. Right here. It's so bad I've been worrying about a root canal."

"Let's have a look." He tapped at her teeth—nothing; not the lightning bolt of pain that would indicate a wakened, cranky root. Poked at them—still nothing. He turned to peer at the computer screen. "Aunt Alex, you were here two weeks ago—X-rays, a cleaning—there's nothing here." He turned back to her. "If you needed a root canal, you would have gone through the roof when I tapped the tooth with this." He wiggled a metal probe menacingly.

"So, what's with the pain? Cody, I'm telling you, it's horrid."

Cody leaned toward the computer, tapping at the keyboard. "It seems like you were here about the same time last year with the same symptoms, when Dr. El-Sharif took care of you. She recommended a mouth guard, at least at night."

"Yes, I use one. Most of the time." She paused. "Well, actually, I'm on the second one. I chewed the first one up pretty badly. I guess I'm hard on mouth guards."

"Use it all the time—every night, anyway. It's bruxism—you clench your jaw and grind your teeth. It's bad for your teeth and causes headaches. The rest of the time, try to remember: lips together, teeth apart." He tilted his head. "You're clenching your jaw right now. Are you annoyed?"

Her eyes flew open. "No—no, not at all. Relieved, actually."

Cody hesitated and took his mask off, combing the other hand through his bright hair. It was what he did when he was just Cody and not Dr. Quinn. "Bruxism has a lot to do with stress. Maybe you should talk to someone." He wrote down a name and a phone number. "Dr. Sam helped me a lot the last couple of years. She's really good with stress."

"She's nice?" Alex was worried. She trusted Cody, but she'd never gone to a therapist. It seemed to her that her coworkers who had therapists all ended up doing something that no one expected. Aribeth had taken up pottery and in short order had evicted her two adult children so she could have the pottery wheel installed in one's room, and use the other for meditation and yoga. She had a kiln put in the backyard and disconnected her satellite television service. Chen had thrown out all her conservative clothes and taken to wearing long, flowing vests over slacks, lots of bracelets and large hoop earrings. She was learning to play the hammered dulcimer. George had decided he needed to hike the Appalachian Trail and was fifteen months into a grueling training program in preparation for his hiking sabbatical in two years. Seeing a therapist seemed like risky business, the first step toward a descent into chaos. Alex took the paper and held it gingerly. "A therapist. Do you think?" and she paused.

Cody smiled, shaking his head. "No, I do not think you're crazy. And no—I don't think you think I am, either."

"Oh, I wasn't going to say crazy. About us. I wondered about her. I mean ..." She took a deep breath and sighed it out, louder than she expected. "I mean, everyone I work with who has been seeing a therapist has done things that seemed a little odd. Surprising. Well, crazy, actually. One or two might have actually gone off the cliff, so to speak. I wondered if she was safe."

"Hmm." Cody paused. "What sort of crazy?"

Alex shrugged. "Well, you know. Building an art studio in the house. Throwing out the adult kids. Planning a sabbatical to hike the Appalachian Trail ..." She trailed off, realizing none of it sounded so crazy when she said it aloud.

Cody nodded. "Sounds like people having a life. Not too crazy."

Alex examined her fingers, grimacing. She felt the pain move, ever so slightly, to the center of her jaw. "It seems risky, that's all, making lots of changes. Things could happen." She sighed. "Well, you know Sandy. Imagine dealing with that."

Cody grinned. "Yeah, well, Sandy's a grownup." He paused. "But as far as Dr. Sam being safe, it's more like C. S. Lewis's Aslan, you know, when Mr. Beaver tells the children, 'Of course he's not safe! But he's good.'"

Alex thought that sounded dangerous. "Comparing a therapist to a lion is not helping." She sighed. "But a therapist, for my teeth?"

"I think you are very, very stressed. More stressed than you know. The body doesn't lie, and that includes your teeth."

"But, counseling? For bruxism?"

"Not for bruxism directly, no. For stress. For whatever's causing the stress. Seriously, Aunt Alex. If you're grinding your teeth, something's grinding at you. Better to deal with it sooner than later." He frowned at the computer screen. "Well, it's kind of already 'later,' isn't it? Since you're here for the same thing as last year." He looked at her sideways. "And maybe the year before that ...?"

She shrugged. "Maybe." Cody nodded and seemed to be waiting. "Okay, I will," Alex promised flatly. She folded her hand around the paper. "Thanks, Cody."

"No problem. Seriously, Dr. Sam's great. You'll love her." He put his mask back on and called in the assistant. "All done here, Francis, thanks. No charge for today—nothing to see here. Thanks, Mrs. B. Let us know if you need us before that next cleaning scheduled for March."

"Thanks, Doctor," she said, and put the paper in her pocket. She thought about how the past few years had been for Cody, raising the twins mostly on his own, with his mom's help, since Jenna left them. It made sense he'd have needed to talk to someone; best friend or not, Alex couldn't imagine getting a lot of comfort out of Gloria under those circumstances.

Alex shook her head, remembering how young and sad Cody had looked during those first long months, clinging to the hope that Jenna would turn back into her sweet, thoughtful self and rejoin their little family. He had struggled to care for the children, who were toddlers when their mother left them. It occurred to Alex that Cody had only begun seeming like his old self in the last two or three years.

She drove back to the college, reminding herself to stop clenching her jaw. *Lips together, teeth apart*, she thought. *Make that the mantra.* Lips together, teeth apart. She glanced at the dashboard clock—fifteen minutes until research desk duty. She promptly felt a lightning bolt of pain as she kept lips together and slammed teeth together, too.

Think happy things, she told herself. *Imagine being on sabbatical next year!* No research assistance desk duty, no endless meetings about outreach and cross-subject integration programs and online interactive chats with students, and all the things that were never part of library work when she'd earned her master's degree. She passed the entrance to one of the county parks and briefly imagined being there, walking, sketchbook in her bag, just strolling without any responsibilities. Waiting for the left turn arrow at the intersection for the college, she imagined herself sketching the path that wound along the creek, the Spanish moss hanging soft gray-green in the morning light. She started a bit at the honk behind her; the light had gone green. She gave a sheepish wave to the person behind her and pulled into the college parking lot, hurrying to get to the library in time.

The research assistance desk was her least favorite duty. It was the entire library staff's least favorite duty, and so Dr. Greene, the head librarian, had decided they would all share it in equal, short shifts—three shifts, two hours each, every week. It was so no one would be tempted to start drinking on the job, Dr. Greene had asserted, grinning, but no one really believed it was a joke. "We don't want any vodka and tonics behind the research assistance desk! Ha!" Dr. Greene had a habit of reinforcing attempts at humor with a loud "Ha!" just to be sure everyone got it. The entire staff had smiled the same weak smile and avoided making eye contact with one another for the rest of the meeting.

Alex went into the back office where the librarians had their desks and small lockers. Suzanne Barnaby was there, taking a break. She was about Alex's age, and had about the same length of service with the college. She was taller and quite thin. She claimed her physique and energy were all due to healthy food and a dedicated yoga practice. She made a point of bringing vegan, gluten-free treats to every staff meeting and tried to convert the rest of them to healthier habits. Today, however, she was sitting cross-legged on her desk, holding a large bowl of miniature chocolate bars. There was a pile of crumpled wrappers on the desk beside her. She grinned at Alex and held out the bowl. "Want any? There are a few dark chocolates left. And a milk chocolate peanut butter." Suzanne eyed the contents and gave the bowl a shake. "I'm afraid the dark chocolates with almonds are gone. Sorry."

Alex shook her head as she peeled off her jacket. "Thanks, but no, just came from the dentist."

"Ugh, my condolences. Bad news?" Suzanne carefully peeled the wrapper off another chocolate, closed her eyes and smelled it.

"No, just the same thing as last year. Apparently, I grind my teeth so badly that it hurts like I need a root canal. Second year in a row. Maybe the third. Despite a mouth guard at night." Alex grimaced. "Stress! Imagine that." She watched Suzanne holding the chocolate like a bottle of fine perfume. "What's up with the chocolate, anyway?"

Suzanne shook her head wryly. "You forget I had research desk for the morning shift, and we're almost at end of term."

"Ah. Stress."

Suzanne lifted her candy bowl as if she were making a toast. "Stress!" she echoed. "Hence the chocolate overdose ... and the pain in my upper back." She twisted and tilted her head around in a way that seemed disjointed. "What I need is a long soak in a hot bath."

"And a break," Alex finished. "Well." She glanced at the clock. "I've got research assistance desk duty."

"Ah, your turn. My condolences, again," Suzanne said kindly, popping the chocolate into her mouth. She closed her eyes, smiling a gentle, yogic smile of contentment. Alex wondered what that would be like, to be so relaxed around people that she could sit like a child on the desk and eat chocolates without reservation. It occurred to her that if she were thin, like Suzanne, maybe she wouldn't feel self-conscious about eating fattening foods in front of other people. Maybe, on the other hand, Suzanne just didn't care what people thought, because otherwise she'd be eating the healthy stuff in public and sneaking the chocolate. Alex frowned and rubbed her jaw as she headed toward the research assistance desk.

There was a line of about ten students, some standing, a few sitting on the floor, in the vicinity of the research assistance desk. Alex tried to smile broadly and warmly at all of them. "How good to see you all! Thanks for coming!" She sat down and beckoned the first student.

The first student in line had a draft of a paper in her hand that her instructor had returned with all sorts of marks for suggested improvement. She sat down in the chair facing the desk, drawing up her legs into a cross-legged position. While Suzanne had managed to look like an adult attempting to relax, this young woman seemed like a five-year-old at story time. She shoved a purple lock of hair behind her ear as she thrust the paper across the desk at Alex and announced, "I need help with this."

Alex glanced at the paper. A research paper for Dr. Ambrose in the English department—a lot of his students had shown up this week. He always insisted on a hard copy draft so no one could deny seeing the feedback. The first comment, scrawled on the cover page, was a suggestion to please review the syllabus for the required format and types of sources for this assignment. Dr. Ambrose was always polite. "Sure. Do you have the syllabus with you?"

"Huh?"

"The syllabus. It's in the online portal for the course and you were supposed to print it out. Dr. Ambrose usually asks that of his students."

The girl just stared at her, so Alex turned to her computer. "We have most of the instructors' syllabi on file. Let me find this one and print it out—Comp 2, right?" There was no response. When she looked up, the girl was tapping away at her phone. Alex felt the pain start in her lower right jaw and tried deliberately to relax her face. She hit print for the Comp 2 syllabus and put it on the desk facing the student. "Here we go,"—she glanced at the draft—"Karma." She wondered what kind of parent named a child Karma. Was it cultural, or some sort of vague, hippie notion of a cool name? Of course, maybe it had nothing to do with the parents; a lot of students seemed to adopt names to express themselves, which only caused difficulty when they changed them midsemester and expected faculty to adapt instantly. She wondered if Karma was really someone's little Mary Margaret or Jennifer Marie, rebelling in this small way.

"Just a second," Karma mumbled.

Alex started speaking in a firm, neutral tone, just as if Karma had said, "Yes, thank you!" "The first problem is that you seem to have used the wrong sort of sources, so the information you're providing isn't reliable. You need to use peer-reviewed articles, and it looks like you have a lot of blogs listed here."

The girl looked confused. "Those *are* peer-reviewed. They each had, like, at least five hundred followers and lots more likes."

The pain in Alex's jaw spread to her front teeth. She smiled and said, "Okay, usually students learn this in Comp 1. Peer-reviewed sources are—" She stopped her well-rehearsed mini-lecture. Karma was tapping vigorously at her phone again. Alex reached into a desk drawer and pulled out the three-page handout on types of sources and how to find them in the library's databases. She placed it on top of the syllabus, plopped those pages atop the girl's paper, and pushed them gently across the desk with a big smile. "Here you go. I think you will find that all your questions about source types and formatting are answered here."

Karma looked up. "Aren't you going to help me?" she asked with astonishment.

Alex smiled, folded her hands, and thought, *I just did*. What she said aloud was, "Please review the handout, the syllabus and your paper, mark any parts that you don't understand after that, and come on back. Thank you for visiting the library today." Then she turned to welcome the next student waiting. Karma unfolded herself, pushed back noisily, gathered her papers and stomped off. Alex shifted in her chair as the next student sat down and heard the rustle of the paper Cody had given her, tucked in her pocket.

The next student, an anxious-looking young man, sat down, clutching a folder full of loose papers. Alex smiled with an aching jaw and asked, "How can I help you today?"

Chapter Two

The Blue Jay

The blue jay, an intelligent and garrulous member of the Corvid family, will often steal other birds' food or monopolize feeders. It is quick to sound an alarm when danger approaches, a trait that benefits other birds. It will cooperate in groups to mob predators, and can even mimic their cries when they wish to drive competitor bird species away from resources. The blue jay can be aggressive when threatened, but is also capable of making a soft, pleading sound.

The kitchen was smallish, a modified galley design. It had a window opening to the living room and a broad archway into the dining area. It was an older home. They'd been there for twenty-five years, since Joe landed his full-time teaching position in the history department at the state college, and Jonah started kindergarten. It was just right for two people very comfortable with one another to collaborate on a meal, which Joe and Alex often did.

They had met at another state college, far away. Alex had been an undergraduate student, trying and succeeding in managing a bachelor of science in wildlife biology with a bachelor of fine arts, focused on drawing and painting. She was completing this in five years with heavy summer courseloads and a part-time job tutoring at the college library. Joe was an adjunct instructor in the history department—not one of Alex's professors, they were quick to point out when telling their story. Alex suspected most people didn't believe them. They probably thought it was some sort of forbidden romance turned disappointingly mundane and legitimate: long-married, two children, visiting family during the summer, driving sensible cars.

The truth of their meeting was far more interesting than the standard bookish-young-professor-meets-artsy-coed trope. One of the visiting art instructors was a famous Western landscape and wildlife painter, of the Navajo nation, and the college hosted a one-woman show for her. The opening included a buffet of Southwestern foods, one of the graduate students in the music department playing traditional instruments, the artist's own remarks on her work, and a guest speaker to discuss the history and significance of indigenous American artists. Alex came for the art and the free food, as all art students did if they weren't working during an opening, and Joe was there for the history. They met across a bowl of fresh salsa.

They had chatted about the show, the speakers, and the food. Alex had assumed it was the sort of polite small talk professors make with students and wandered off to study the paintings, hoping for a few words with the artist, but Joe kept popping up at her elbow. It took a few of those "pops" before she realized he was interested in her as much as, or more than, the art opening. It was nearly 9:00 p.m., and the college staff were gently encouraging guests to leave. The catering crew was wheeling out what little remained of the food.

"It was nice to meet you," Alex said, edging toward the door. Joe stepped along beside her.

"I'll walk you out to the car; the parking lot's already looking half-deserted." It wasn't, of course, and the security team, with their golf carts and reflective vests, were on the ready to escort anyone who wanted to their cars.

"Thanks." They walked along, Alex silent, Joe talking effusively about the historian. "Well, here we are. Thanks for walking me over." She felt awkward. *Should I just unlock the car and get in, basically slamming the door in his face? Why doesn't he just nod and say good night and walk off?* He just stood there with his hands in the front pockets of his jeans, looking intently at her with those oddly large, amber eyes.

Joe cleared his throat. "It was great to get to talk. Maybe we could keep the conversation going? Another time, I mean. Like over coffee? At the coffee shop on the quad?" He paused. "I'm on campus Mondays through Thursdays. My classes are nine to eleven and then one to three, so any other time ... if you're available to meet, that is." He stared just to the side of her face, as if there were something very interesting on the roof of her car.

He's nervous, Alex thought in amazement. It hadn't occurred to her she would make someone nervous. She pushed her hair behind her ear with one hand and said, "Sure, that sounds good. My bio class ends at three and that could work."

"Biology?" Joe's head tilted and the gaze was more intense. "I thought you were an art major."

"Art and wildlife biology. It's a long story." She started to open her car door. "I'll tell you about it on ..."

"Monday?"

He's in an awfully big hurry. "Sure, Monday at three thirty at the coffee place on the quad."

"I'll look forward to it." Joe just stood there. Alex got in, closed the door, fastened her seat belt and started the car. Joe continued to stand there, with a vague smile. She gave a little wave and drove off. When she glanced in the rearview mirror, she saw him still standing there, watching her drive away.

The oven door creaked open loudly, startling her out of her memory.

"How long until the fish is done?" Alex asked, chopping vegetables for a salad.

"Ten minutes. Maybe five." A pause. "How was the dentist?"

Alex pushed her hair out of her eyes with her forearm. "It was Cody today. Everything's fine. There's nothing wrong with my teeth, except they hurt."

Joe poked at the fish, grimacing, and said cautiously, "This happened last year. And the year before. Didn't Dr. El-Sharif recommend the mouth guard?"

"Which I wear religiously."

"And chew on all night." Joe put the fish back in the oven.

Alex shrugged and sprinkled cut up peppers on three plates of greens. "I know. I get a little stressed by this time of the semester."

"It's not a *little* stressed, honey. Maybe you should—"

Joe's guidance was interrupted by Sandy whirling into the kitchen, a bundle of energy. "That smells good! What is it?"

"Fish," her parents said in unison.

"Ooh ... farm raised or wild?"

"I don't know," said Alex, which was the truth. She didn't have the mental space to worry about how the fish grew up. She considered grocery shopping an extraction mission, not an environmental activism statement. She wished again they had pushed harder against Sandy's idea to major in environmental psychology, which seemed to be good only for a part-time tutoring job—not in psychology—and a lot of environmental protesting with her best friend, Rachel. Rachel was a school counselor and managed to squeeze her ecological concerns around a steady career, one with benefits and a retirement plan.

"It depends," Joe said cheerfully. "What's the right answer this week?" He turned, leaned back on the counter and crossed his arms, grinning. His hair was nearly all gray, and as usual, he looked rumpled and alert, his large amber eyes unwaveringly focused on whatever interested him at that moment. At this moment, it was Sandy, rested from a nap and bursting with enthusiasm.

Sandy rolled her eyes and tucked her long, light brown hair behind her ears. "You should care more about the environment. What kind of life do you want your grandchildren to have?"

"Our grandchildren are two greyhounds, a dachshund-Chihuahua mix, and a very naughty golden retriever. I hope to outlive all of them," Alex said drily.

Sandy started to say more but her mother handed her two of the plates and said, "Please bring these to the table for me, thanks."

Sandy kept gesturing with plates in her hands, explaining how important proper sourcing was. "We have to respect nature! How are we going to continue to have fish if the oceans are overfished?" Somehow, she managed to keep the food from flying off the waving plates. "You both just joke about this, as if the environment weren't important." She shook her head as she set the plates on the table.

"No one's arguing with you, Sandy, but you have to admit, the directions change pretty often. Last month, I believe, you told us we should avoid farm-raised fish because it was inhumane. They weren't allowed to swim freely and live as nature intended. And now it's something else. Maybe we could comply if the rules didn't keep changing." Joe somehow found all this amusing, always playfully taking the bait and enjoying the repartee. Alex stayed silent; she didn't enjoy the endless hectoring. *Let him handle the aggravation*, she thought, and then noticed her jaw aching.

"Dad. Seriously. We're overusing the earth's resources. If we eat everything, what about the rest of the food chain?"

Joe was having fun. "Hmm, do you think the mermaids are running out of food because of our supper not being properly sourced?" He took the fish out of the oven and slid it carefully from baking sheet to serving plate. "I'm sure the manatees don't care; they're vegetarians. Or maybe they do care, anyway. Friends being someone else's supper and all that."

Sandy scowled at him. "Dad, I'm not five. Stop treating me like I am."

Alex slipped toward the sliding glass doors. Every evening, just before dinner, Alex put out food for the birds on their back deck. Sandy regularly objected to this, asserting that it upset the balance of nature and led to overpopulation of certain species, learned helplessness, and other terrible things. Alex thought bitterly that Sandy always failed to notice the irony of a grown woman with an apparently useless degree who lived with her parents and worked part-time griping about learned helplessness and pathological dependency in cardinals and blue jays. Today, she was too busy debating her father about the environment to lecture her mother about fostering dependency in wild animals.

Alex was always happy to see the birds—and squirrels, and the occasional bold little fruit rat—enjoying the mixed seeds. The birds, especially, were entertaining. The blue jay parents were in the final stages of raising their young; the young were nearly the size of their parents and perfectly capable of feeding themselves, but occasionally feigned helplessness for a free meal. Sometimes the parent acquiesced and sometimes it simply hopped in a half-circle to face pointedly away from the begging fledgling. It seemed to Alex that this behavior was accompanied by a bit of a shake of tail feathers.

She imagined herself hopping around in a half-turn away from Jonah, Beth, and all their dogs, and from Sandy and her endless demands for ecological correctness. She wondered what that would look like—her slowly expanding middle-aged bottom wiggling like a jay's tail feathers at one of her squawking offspring—and smiled.

"What's funny, Mom?"

"Nothing—just thinking about my bird friends," Alex replied. "Let's have dinner, shall we?"

Settling in, after grace, Alex asked, "So, honey, any thoughts on that possible sabbatical?" She was willing to talk about almost anything besides Sandy's next harangue or Joe's advice about her aching jaw. Their pending sabbaticals were a safe bet.

Joe rested his elbows on the table, his forkful of food suspended. "I'm still thinking of tying two things I love together. Fishing and history. This sounds kind of crazy, but I'm imagining a trip up the Eastern Seaboard—from here in Florida to Maine—investigating the history of fishing from the indigenous peoples to the present day."

"And maybe get in a *little* fishing yourself, of course," Alex replied.

"Well, of course. That's the phenomenological aspect, truly understanding the lived experiences of fishermen ... and women"—he glanced over at Sandy, who was briefly preoccupied in examining a piece of fish—"over the years."

"It sounds like fun. I'm looking forward to a lot of time in nature, myself." Alex paused, preparing to broaden the conversation to her sabbatical. She hesitated, just briefly, and missed her chance.

"Understanding those who came before us." Joe drifted into a monologue about how numbers and facts were not real history but merely a way of attempting to quantify the lived experience.

"I was thinking, too, that I could get a little art in," Alex inserted, but Joe kept rolling on. Alex kept eating, nodding, and making occasional listening sounds. When Joe paused for a moment, savoring a bite of fish, she broke in again. "You know, I've been looking at some places in the mountains in north Georgia and the Carolinas," she said, but before she could finish, Joe picked up the thread.

"Interesting," he mused. "I was thinking of sticking closer to the coastline, but going inland a bit could be worthwhile."

"What I meant was," Alex began.

Sandy interrupted. "I don't suppose you're planning on using an electric car or a hybrid," she complained. "I mean, Dad, that's a lot of driving. You care about fish so much, well, what about all that pollution? It all ends up in the water."

"And do you and Rachel bicycle to all these protests?" he asked, grinning, and winked at Alex. Sandy rolled her eyes and poked at her salad. Alex wondered if he would ever pause to consider that they were both eligible for sabbatical next year and perhaps she would want to talk about her ideas. Joe was used to giving lectures in the classroom and fielding questions later. He seemed to slide into that mode easily at home and with their friends.

He had gone back to exploring the significance of understanding the lifestyles, including fishing methods, of the past. "Because it's not the events themselves, but often how people respond to those events, adapt to them, that make the real history."

"That's psychology," said Sandy. She was neither stifled nor impressed by her father's topical lectures; she jumped right in with questions and her own pronouncements. She had always been that way, ready to tell people what she thought.

"Philosophy and sociology, too," agreed Alex. "There's a lot of overlap because the main subject is the human person. But I think that just spending time in nature opens up a greater understanding of the human, too." She was hoping to keep the conversation from segueing into an argument between Joe and Sandy. She imagined she could find a gap in which to introduce her sabbatical ideas.

"Right!" grinned Joe. "That is what makes history interesting. That's what has to be brought to life for students."

"But that's everything, every day," Sandy said. "How we respond to what happens."

I'd like to respond to what happens, Alex thought, rubbing her jaw. *I'd like to respond to what's happening right here.* Instead, while Joe and Sandy had one of their regular debates on the degree to which psychology could take credit for everything, Alex cleared the plates and brewed decaffeinated coffee for her and Joe. Sandy wouldn't want any; Alex bought whatever was on sale, and this particular brand wasn't properly sourced. The argument continued behind her, a spirited exercise in playful debate.

Alex imagined herself slamming plates onto the counter and just roaring at them to listen, just shut up and listen. In her imagination, they sat there, their mouths gaping in astonishment. Then, after she'd had her say, they were full of encouragement and thoughtful questions. *Like that would happen*, she thought resentfully, and pushed a cabinet door shut with a slam.

"Mom? Is something wrong?" Sandy called in. "It's kind of loud in there."

"Sorry. Everything's fine," Alex said flatly. "You two kids keep having fun." Alex wondered what was wrong with her. Why couldn't she just talk? Why did she keep holding back, not just diving in over them the way they did to her?

Joe picked up the thread. "Sandy, no one's saying psychology isn't important. I'm saying all these things are intertwined and we only mark them in different columns as constructs to make organizing data easier."

And there they go. It could be another thirty minutes of arguing. Alex tried changing subjects. "Mimaw's planning on coming in the Sunday before Thanksgiving and leaving the Saturday after," she tossed over her shoulder. Sandy, will you have time this weekend to help me get the guest room set up?"

That stopped the argument between Sandy and Joe. Sandy turned toward her, perplexed. "Mom, that's over two weeks away."

"And time flies around here," Alex replied. "You're busy, I'm busy, and we both have been using Jonah's old room as a way station instead of putting things away. So please take care of your stuff this weekend. She'll be here for Thanksgiving and again over New Year's."

"What about Christmas?" Joe asked. "Is it Elsa's turn?" Alex's sister lived closer to their mother, Marlene, who tried to alternate holidays so no one was upset. Lately, she usually spent Christmas with Elsa and New Year's with Alex's family, asserting cheerfully that Christmas was a season and so she was technically spending Christmas with everyone.

Alex nodded. "Elsa's got this one, and that's fair. Benjamin's turning ten and this is probably his last magical year; Mom shouldn't miss it." Benjamin was Elsa's oldest grandson. She suspected he didn't really believe in Santa, entirely, but wasn't quite ready to give up the game.

"Oh, that's cool," Sandy said. "I remember how that was." She sighed and twirled a long piece of hair. "Sometimes I still miss it."

"Well, your aunt Gloria's grandchildren all believe. You and Rachel should soak some of that up while you can. I'm guessing Bobby will ruin it for everyone." Bobby was five, making him four years younger than Cody's twins, but he was not likely to keep secrets for the sake of other children. His grandmother described him as "challenging," but the school used other terms and kept recommending classes for the parents and all sorts of plans to help Bobby "make better choices."

Joe nodded in agreement. "I don't see Bobby taking pleasure in helping his little sister believe."

"He's definitely no Cody. Or Sandy, for that matter."

"Oh, please, don't talk about it." Sandy feigned embarrassment. Joe, rising from the table, kissed the top of her head and made his way to the living room and his favorite chair.

Sandy, at age ten, had still believed in Santa. Her brother's skepticism meant nothing to her, and his overt distress, eventually, that at eight, and then nine, and ten, Sandy insisted that Santa existed was a source of inspiration for her. The more Jonah criticized her for believing, the further Sandy dug in her heels. One day, Sandy announced to her parents that she had figured out her eventual graduate thesis project. It had surprised them, a bit, that she was aware there was such a thing as a graduate thesis in fifth grade, but they nodded and asked questions.

Sandy explained that she was going to have two graduate degrees, one in anthropology, and one in physics, and her combined thesis project would put these Santa doubters, including her brother Jonah, who thought he knew everything, in their place. They would see, finally, that Santa had to be real. She had vague ideas about quantum physics and science fiction. At ten, she was confident in how it would all work out. They never did sort out what anthropology had to do with it, but she seemed to know that anthropology had to do with studying people, and Santa being a person, well, it was a rock-solid plan to Sandy.

Joe and Alex agonized over what to do, and it was decided that Joe would handle "the talk," as they called it. They went over the talk themselves, or attempted to, but Alex kept bursting into tears and they never could work through what, precisely, Joe was supposed to say. After a week or so, he'd called Sandy over and suggested they go have a little talk. She asked if she was in trouble and he assured her she was not. "Then why does Mommy look upset?" she asked as they headed toward her room. "Mommy only looks that upset when someone's been bad or something bad happened. Did something bad happen?" Joe assured her everything was fine, Mom was fine, which was, of course, untrue. Alex stayed in the kitchen trying not to cry. She kept opening drawers and rummaging around, looking for nothing in particular. Everything she touched seemed to make the poignancy worse: the woven potholder Sandy had made in first grade, the keychain with a picture of Sandy and Jonah, years ago, at the zoo. They came out about ten minutes later, Sandy going quietly outside to the backyard and looking sidelong at her mother as she passed.

Alex looked up anxiously. "How did it go?"

Joe shrugged. "Pretty well. I explained. I asked if she had any questions."

"And?"

"She said she had two. Would she still get presents, of course." Joe hesitated.

"The other?"

He smiled wistfully. "She asked if you knew. About Santa. I said yes, Mommy knows, you can talk to her about it. And she said, are you sure?" Alex leaned into him and he hugged her tight. "It's going to be okay."

She nodded into his shoulder but she didn't believe it would really be okay.

That was years ago, and somehow Christmas had stayed wonderful, but it would be even more wonderful to have some of the magic back, just for a while. As she neatened up the kitchen and prepared their coffees, she wondered, for the thousandth time, if she would ever have human grandchildren to enjoy.

Thirty minutes later, Joe and Alex were ensconced in their living room with coffee, relaxing, and Sandy had left to meet Rachel. A cell phone made a soft pinging; Joe and Alex groaned in harmony. "Is that yours?" Joe asked. It was Alex's. She glanced at the message.

"Jonah is stopping by to drop off the dogs in a few. He's on his way. He can't stay long."

"*What?*" Joe leaned forward, closing his book.

"You remember ... they're going away for a long weekend and we've got the dogs."

"Can someone explain to me how two young professionals, each of whom out-earns the two of us together, cannot afford to kennel their animals?" Joe put his book down roughly on the coffee table; the bowl of polished rocks rattled. The top ones said "Peace" and "Tranquility."

Alex shrugged, then sighed. Her toothache had migrated from the lower right to the upper left. "Well, it's too late to deal with it for this go-round. Maybe we should have a chat when they get home."

"It's bad enough you've given in to spending your lunch break walking their dogs every day. Why do we have to have an invasion of four dogs every time they're bored and want to blow a few thousand dollars on a quick getaway? Where is it this time?"

"A jaunt to the Bahamas. They're feeling burned out, Beth said." Alex rolled her eyes.

Joe shook his head. "This isn't happening again. I'm telling you. I will have a talk with our son when this little jaunt is over."

Alex grimaced. "I hope it's enough time to reserve kennel space. They're going away all week for Thanksgiving." She picked up a pebble that said "Serenity" and sighed, rubbing it between her fingers.

Chapter Three

It wasn't that she didn't like dogs, of course, but after three days Alex was eager for Jonah and Beth to pick them up. The rescue greyhounds, Apple and Mac, were unhappy with being too sedentary. Anastasia, the dachshund-chihuahua mix, was incredibly needy, and the golden retriever—his name was Solar, but he was called Sol—had been chronically disobedient for so long that he was usually referred to as Naughty Sol.

Alex walked the dogs four times a day—usually in pairs. This ate up most of her weekend. And then they had three different foods: one for the greyhounds, one for Anastasia, and another for Naughty Sol. Naughty Sol, dissatisfied with the combination of buffalo-based kibble and veterinarian-approved food out of a pouch, lived up to his name.

He devoured Sunday's dinner—a roast—before it was fully defrosted, and then Apple and Mac ate the foam tray and vomited it all over the house. Joe was wiping off the dogs' paws and faces, and Alex was in the midst of mopping up bits of sticky foam off the kitchen floor when Sandy came home. Sandy tried to be helpful by using the occasion to lecture her parents on the wastefulness of Styrofoam packaging. Couldn't they be more responsible in sourcing their groceries? Joe invited her to take over the grocery shopping and its expense any time, which led to a further debate about money, regarding what Sandy asserted was the ridiculous expectation that she put money aside for her student loans before she had quite finished her dissertation. She couldn't even buy groceries on her income; who could reasonably expect her to save extra money, Sandy demanded to know.

"Maybe you could at least help out a little here if you can't pitch in for groceries?" Joe suggested. Alex grimly continued wiping up more slimy pieces of packaging.

"Well, of course." Sandy looked indignant. "But I can't now! I have to get ready." She glanced at her phone. "Rachel's picking me up in a half hour."

"Sunday night? Isn't tomorrow a school day for her?" As a guidance counselor, Rachel's workday started early.

"Yeah, but it's been going on for a few days and this is the first we could both make it."

"What 'it'?" Alex wondered. "Sea turtles?"

"Mom! The snow protest." Her parents were silent and she glanced from blank expression to blank expression, sighed deeply and spread her arms wide, wiggling her fingers. "The snow protest! The fake snow the city is bringing in for the winter festival! It's wrong! It's a waste of resources! It's ..."

"It's a bunch of teeny, tiny pieces of frozen water, which will melt into the ground and replenish the aquifer," Joe said, examining Mac's snout for any scraps of regurgitated foam. "Are you seriously telling me that a bunch of greenies have nothing else to be concerned about, with everything going on in the world, than the city choosing to water the park with frozen instead of liquid water? For this, you protest?"

"I can't believe you don't take this seriously." Sandy stood in front of the open refrigerator. "Is there anything to eat here?"

"I can't believe you *do*. Take it seriously, I mean," Joe threw over his shoulder.

Alex left the room. Her jaw throbbed. She needed to check the rest of the house. Naughty Sol had disappeared. She found him behind the couch, having the good sense to look sheepish, head on his front paws, lifting one eyebrow at her disapproving glance. She sighed. It was impossible to stay annoyed with him; he was a charmer. Sol now accounted for, Alex decided to just hide in their bedroom with a book until Jonah and Beth had come and gone, taking their dogs with them. She felt guilty about not even wanting to see her own son, but her jaw ached and her head hurt just thinking about it.

Jonah had been a difficult, demanding child from the start. Intelligent and verbal, he was impatient, from toddlerhood, with anyone's inability to see things, and do things, his way. He adapted to his baby sister surprisingly well, at least until she began to be as outspoken, in her own way, as he was. Alex remembered his first day of kindergarten, just after they'd moved to Florida from Texas. It was when she met Gloria Quinn, who taught the other kindergarten class but had a child—her third son, Matt—in the same class as Jonah. Determined to settle into life in their new hometown, Alex volunteered as a class aide. Jonah had no trouble with schoolwork, and in fact made sure the teacher, and his classmates, knew he was done with his work, and bored, frequently. He tried to be helpful by pointing out others' mistakes to them, their classmates, and their teacher. He rolled his eyes at his mother, and in short order included his teacher in his contempt. Despite this, he made friends with a few of the other children. Alex suspected that the ones who befriended him did so in self-defense. She wasn't sure that Jonah actually liked the other children, but they let him boss them around to some extent and he seemed gratified by that. His attitude toward everyone was, at best, disdainful tolerance.

His uncivil tolerance had one glaring exception: Jonah hated Matt Quinn. Every child who Jonah considered his friend believed they were Matt's friend, too, and they were right. Everyone was Matt's friend. Matt didn't read as well as Jonah, but the teacher, maddeningly, seemed to like Matt better. The girls liked Matt because he was "nice," and the boys always wanted to include him. He was not particularly athletic, or funny, or good-looking. He was a sweet-faced child, with green eyes, wavy brown hair and a few freckles. Alex recalled how Jonah would come home from school listing all his annoyances about Matt. Matt mispronounced two spelling words today, easy ones. Matt messed up adding by twos. Matt stole his friends at recess by encouraging everyone to play some sort of improvised cornhole game involving acorns and two paper cups. After a year or so, when this had continued well into first grade, four-year-old Sandy interrupted the diatribe at supper. She knelt up on her chair, one hand on her hip.

Pointing at Jonah with a spoonful of mashed potatoes, she announced, "Jonah hates Matt because everyone likes Matt better. But Jonah's not as nice as Matt. Jonah thinks everyone's dumb."

"Hey," Jonah began. But Sandy would not be interrupted, making a series of statements as if she was a small news reporter.

"Everybody knows Jonah thinks they's dumb." She pointed the mashed potato spoon at her mother. "Jonah thinks Mommy's dumb. Jonah thinks me's dumb." She paused and looked at her dad, head tilted. "I don't know if Jonah thinks Daddy's dumb."

"Yeah, well, you don't know when to use me or I, so you *are* dumb," Jonah retorted, red-faced.

Sandy was impervious to his insults. "That's why nobody likes Jonah so much. Nobody likes it when people thinks they's dumb." She wrapped up her editorial, thrust the heaping spoon of mashed potatoes into her mouth, closed her eyes and sighed with satisfaction. A little gravy dribbled out of one corner of her closed lips, and Alex remembered gently dabbing it and feeling overcome with tenderness and a little awe at her pint-sized truth-teller.

The clatter interrupted her quiet. She heard the door open and lots of barking and voices; Jonah and Beth had arrived in their usual whirlwind, snippets of sentences wafting upstairs—a bottle of something tropical for the parents—they were so very grateful, thank you—the weather was grand, just wonderful—Beth couldn't believe how much they ate, and Jonah complained about having to catch up with work.

Alex waited until they drove out of the driveway before coming down.

Joe was standing desolately in the living room, holding a bottle of rum.

"How did it go?"

"What?" Joe looked from the bottle to Alex. "How did what go?"

"The talk. You were going to talk to Jonah about kenneling the dogs."

Joe sighed. "It didn't happen. Yet. You know how they are—in, out, always a rush."

Alex grimaced and rubbed her lower left jaw. "Thanksgiving break starts in two weeks. I'd rather we not have the dogs."

"I'll call after dinner."

Dinner was plan B, canned soup and a salad, due to Naughty Sol having eaten the roast that was going to be dinner for three nights. They talked about snow protests, the birds that dined outside, and Joe spoke at length regarding his sabbatical project ideas. He wondered if a heuristic research paper on the fishing practices of indigenous peoples of the Eastern Seaboard would be feasible. Alex started a sentence about pursuing art in the wilderness three times, to no avail.

Alex wondered if he would ever give her a gap to clearly discuss her sabbatical ideas. There was a pause, a brief silence. "I was thinking," she began again, "about my year next year."

Joe nodded thoughtfully. "Right. It will be fun to travel up and down the coast, won't it?"

Alex shook her head. "That's not quite where I was going," she said, but Joe wasn't listening; he was stacking his dishes and reaching for hers. Dinner was over. She guessed they would talk about this more later, steeling herself to let Joe know she needed to make decisions about her own sabbatical.

"Are you going to call Jonah?" she asked as they wrapped up the kitchen cleanup.

"Hmm?"

"Joe, let's just get this over with," Alex pleaded, trying to ignore the fact that she was conveniently using first person plural while trying to stay uninvolved. "You know what this weekend was like. I can't face this over the Thanksgiving break."

The phone call went as Alex feared, not as she'd hoped. Worse yet, Joe put the phone on speaker so she couldn't evade participation.

Jonah was angry. You could always tell because he put on "that" voice, the voice Alex had heard since he was about seven, and figured out Mom was not smart about the same things as he, and further that the things she was smart about were not as important, at least in his estimation.

"Dad, I cannot believe you're doing this to us now. I mean, the trip is two weeks out. Couldn't you have brought this up earlier?"

"You were away. And I'm bringing it up now. We can't do this. Your mother can't do this." Alex scowled at him, shaking her head, and Joe made a confused face.

"Mom? What's wrong with Mom?"

"Nothing's wrong, Jonah, I would just like—WE would just like"—Alex looked pointedly at Joe—"to have a vacation, too, and having the dogs here, well, it's not what I'd call a vacation."

"This is highly unfair," Jonah said in his disappointed pedant voice. "I really wish you had been more considerate. I'll do my best to make other arrangements. We can't get a refund on the tickets and—"

His dad rolled his eyes at Alex. "Son, no one's talking about canceling your trip. We just don't want to be stuck with the dogs."

"Stuck!"

Joe continued. "Why don't you ask your sister to stay at your place? Sandy will be off for the week and except for Thanksgiving and whatever she has going socially, she could use some money and—"

Jonah exploded and they heard Beth laugh in the background. "Sandy? Are you nuts?" He switched from his haughty voice to his angry teenager voice. "She's insane! We had her here once. Never again. Never again. She went through every damned cabinet and closet and put sticky notes on everything she disapproved of, with recommendations of better choices for the environment. We're still finding sticky notes and it's been two years."

"Welcome to our world," Alex said.

"There is no way she's dog-sitting." Jonah sounded less certain.

"I'm sure you'll work something out," Joe replied, smiling at Alex.

Alex nodded and rubbed her lower jaw, thinking about what Cody had said about his therapist.

Chapter Four

The Eastern Screech Owl

The screech owl does not screech, but could be described as making a sad whinny or trilling purr. It is a small, monogamous bird, that will attempt camouflage by drawing itself flat and closing its eyes. It sometimes leans sidewise, appearing at a distance like the remaining stump of a broken-off limb on a larger branch.

It was Monday. After three days of four dogs, and relentless, migratory tooth pain, Alex gave in and called Dr. Jan Sameleski. By that point, the paper with her phone number had been rubbed soft and the writing was blurred. Alex almost hung up when the doctor answered the phone herself, having hoped to talk to some administrative person and not have to launch into a ten-minute pre-appointment consult with Dr. Sameleski.

"Um, is this the doctor?"

"Yes, this is Dr. Sameleski. How can I help you?" The voice sounded friendly enough.

"Oh ... I was thinking I would get voicemail or something." Alex examined the hem of her sweater sleeve.

"Well, I'm on a break and could pick up."

Alex started feeling panicky. "I guess I thought I would get a secretary or something. Or voicemail."

"No secretary, just me," Dr. Sameleski said. She added kindly, "It's hard to make this call, isn't it? What can I do for you?"

"My dentist ... a friend of the family, suggested I call you," Alex began.

"And how can I help you?"

"Well, um." Alex swallowed and rubbed her jaw. "I guess I have a lot of stress and everyone seems to think I need to talk to someone." She cringed. That sounded as if she were absolutely loony, the kind of person who couldn't figure out she needed some help and had "everyone" notice she was not okay.

The pleasant voice seemed unruffled by this. "Sure, it sounds as if it's been a stressful time. Just checking that you're feeling safe until we can meet."

"Safe?" Alex wondered what that could possibly mean. Safe from what?

"Any risk of violence toward yourself or someone else? Anyone abusing you?"

Alex took a sharp breath. "No! I mean, well, no. Nothing like that. Just work stress, that sort of stuff."

Dr. Sameleski sounded calm as ever. "Okay, good. You never know. People really suffer with so many troubles, and it's good to have a plan if things are bad." She paused, and it occurred to Alex that this was a second chance in case someone really was in danger but didn't say so at first. *Nicely done*, she thought, and then Dr. Sam continued, "So, let's look at scheduling, shall we?"

The appointment was set, an email was sent to Alex with the link to download paperwork, and then her tooth pain went wild, ricocheting from place to place. The paperwork—over a dozen pages—required more thought than Alex had been prepared to give to this process. No wonder the doctor recommended she do them ahead of time. Alex had thought the remark about sparing her the "dreadful clipboard-in-the-lap routine" was just a nicety. Instead, she had to take questionnaires, and write responses, not just check things off. Who were her most supportive relationships? What were her long-term life dreams? What were her health habits? How much sleep did she get? Pages of questions and an increasingly guilty sense that she was a failure before she'd even started therapy. Why did she have to put down, in writing, that she got so little sleep and not enough exercise, that her diet was so-so and her social circle minuscule? She kept crossing out her answer to the question about how much she enjoyed her work and found it fulfilling. She reprinted the page four times before she gave up trying to make it sound positive but still slightly honest, and finally wrote she didn't enjoy her work anymore and it wasn't fulfilling.

She made the appointment during the midafternoon, flexing some time in her schedule. She kept thinking about just calling to cancel, listing the very good reasons to do so: She needed to help students at this point in the semester, it was nearly Thanksgiving break, and her entire jaw throbbed. She agonized about what to wear, wondering what would look sensible and, well, very sane? She wanted to make a good impression, show this Dr. Sam person that it might be nice to chat a bit but she really didn't need psychotherapy. She settled on her standard uniform: her gray slacks, a hip-length blouse, and a jacket. Glancing in the mirror of the college restroom before she headed off to meet Dr. Sam, Alex sighed. She pulled at the sleeves of the jacket, noticed the hems were a bit dingy, and folded them up. The blouse was worse, so she unfolded the jacket sleeves, tugged at them again, shook her head disapprovingly at herself, and headed off to her appointment.

The office did not look as Alex had expected, but of course, she'd only seen therapists' offices in movies. She briefly considered that perhaps therapists' work was no more like it was the movies than librarians' work was. She certainly had never walked around saying "Shush!" and stamping index cards with the date. Still, it was a surprise to see landscape paintings and even a basket of toys. She sat gingerly at the edge of a loveseat opposite Dr. Sameleski.

Dr. Sam was about her age—mid- to late fifties, she guessed—dressed in black slacks, a beige sweater, and flat shoes, with reading glasses looped on her necklace. Alex noticed she didn't color her hair, either, which made them marked minorities in their age group and won Dr. Sam a bit of preliminary approval.

"So, again, welcome, Alexa. I'm Dr. Sameleski. You can call me that or Dr. Sam if you prefer. How was your drive here? Any trouble finding the place?"

"Thanks, no, everything was fine." Alex reached down into her tote and pulled out the paperwork, clipped and tucked into a folder. "Here's all my paperwork."

"Oh, good." Dr. Sam glanced at it quickly. "Thank you—you actually did all of it." She looked up, smiling. "Not everyone does and I actually do ask these questions for a reason."

There was a short silence.

"So, Alexa, what brings you here?"

Alex wondered why she had filled out all the paperwork if she was going to have to answer what felt like the same question. "It's all in the paperwork," she said, gesturing toward the folder in Dr. Sam's lap, and Dr. Sam just nodded pleasantly, waiting. "Well, Cody—Dr. Quinn—referred me. He's my dentist." *And a kid I've known since he was 9.* But she kept that to herself. "And he says that my dental pain is actually related to stress."

"Is that what you think?"

Alex shifted on the loveseat. "Well, of course I'm stressed. Everyone's stressed. That's just normal." Dr. Sam nodded. "But I guess," Alex acknowledged, "that being so stressed you grind your teeth until you're convinced you need a root canal is not normal."

"Oh, it's more common than you might think."

"Really?" Alex wondered if this was some sort of trick to put her at ease. "It seems kind of crazy. I mean, everyone's stressed," she repeated, and then felt stupid. *That was probably a sign of some sort of mental problem, repeating yourself that way.*

"Well, you're right that everyone is under stress. A certain amount of stress is even healthy; think about exercising. You don't benefit if there isn't some stress. Students don't learn without effort, sustained over time."

Tell me about it.

Dr. Sam continued. "Your mind and body have probably been telling you something—or a few somethings—are too much of a burden for a while, and you've been ignoring the signs. But the body doesn't lie." Dr. Sam sat back a bit. She glanced down at the paperwork, sifting through pages. "So, if it's stress, what sort of things have you tried so far?"

Alex looked back her questioningly.

"To deal with the stress. Usually people have tried some strategies; counseling usually is not plan A." Dr. Sam shrugged. "Most people don't come here first."

"Oh." Alex looked down at her hands. "I try to relax, I guess. You know, read when I'm done with chores. Maybe enjoy nature a bit."

"How do you enjoy nature? Walks? Photography?"

"Well." Alex hesitated. "I mean, I try to take walks. Mostly with the dogs ... and I like to watch the birds outside." She felt slightly ashamed, as if she was failing as a therapy patient. She couldn't for the life of her think of something she did, specifically, for stress except try not to think about things. "I guess I try not to think about things. Or try not to make waves."

Dr. Sam's eyebrow arched as she looked back at Alex. "You have high blood pressure, you say here you don't exercise except for walking dogs, you're not sleeping well. You gave job satisfaction a six out of ten, and you have only two supportive relationships, your husband and your friend Gloria."

"Well, I have other supportive relationships, of course, but those are the main ones. My mom and sister and her family live out of state."

"Of course. I see you have a couple of grown children. How are things with them?"

The next thirty minutes went fairly quickly; Alex was more comfortable talking about her family, her job, the dogs, her husband's upcoming sabbatical, which he might or might not take. She explained about Sandy, who was so bright and ready to save the planet but couldn't land a full-time job, and Jonah and his wife, who were busy making money and procuring an ever-larger menagerie. She described Joe, how intelligent and successful he was, and threw in a few details about her work at the college. Dr. Sam didn't seem to take many notes. She thought there would be a sort of feverish dictation but instead it was like talking to a friendly stranger on the plane. Except then the friendly stranger finally picked up a small notebook, smiled, and said, "Thanks for giving me so much information in this first session, Alex; I appreciate it. I will look over your paperwork and next time we'll focus on the homework."

"Homework?"

Dr. Sam smiled. "Nothing painful, I promise. Two things: Start jotting down ideas about what you would like to have be different in six months. Nothing heroic—but changes you would like to see in your life. Write those ideas in here." She handed Alex the notebook. "And separately, on other paper, each day—well, six times a week—write out, 'I'm afraid that' and fill out the sentence stem, ten times, quickly—no self-censoring—and then walk away. The same sentence starter, each day. Don't worry about repeating yourself. Everyone does. Just do it."

"Okay, ten times? I'm afraid that, and whatever pops up?" Alex frowned. "I'm here about stress. Why am I writing about fear?"

"Think of them as cousins."

"Cousins. So, poking at fear is a way to start coping with stress."

"Exactly." Dr. Sam smiled. "Sort of like going to counseling for what seems like dental pain. And don't feel bad about that. It happens more often than you'd imagine. Sometimes it's headaches, sometimes backaches; people suffer all different ways. If you forget to do the homework because you're busy, let me know. If you decide not to do it, write down why. It's important. Please bring all the homework with you next time."

Alex looked down at her hands and nodded. She briefly pictured Suzanne, sitting in half-lotus on her desk, devouring chocolate and complaining about her back. She wondered if Suzanne ever worried about being crazy, but she doubted it.

"The part about what you want your life to be like, Alexa, that's just as important." There was a pause, then Dr. Sam added, "You realize you hardly told me anything, directly, about yourself?"

Alex shrugged. "Isn't that normal, to tell you about my situation?"

"Absolutely. But don't you think it's interesting that whenever I asked about you, you spoke about someone else? Or tried to, anyway?" Dr. Sam tilted her head. "Any other questions for me?"

Alex looked up, grimacing, and gazed steadily just past Dr. Sam's head. "Not really."

"Like, do I think you're crazy?" Alex jerked her face toward Dr. Sam, who was smiling serenely. "No, I do not think you're crazy. But I know that's what most people who come here are afraid of, that I'll tell them they're crazy or it's all their fault."

"And I'm not? And it's not?"

"Good grief, no. Obviously you're not crazy, and nobody gets to be so powerful in this life to have it be all their fault."

Payment and scheduling were handled, and Alex left, with more paperwork to do.

Homework for therapy.

Chapter Five

November 7

I'm afraid that I don't know what to write.

I'm afraid that this is just a waste of time and money.

I'm afraid that I will look like a fool.

I'm afraid that my job is going to drive me crazy.

I'm afraid that Joe will go off on a sabbatical adventure and leave me stuck with the mess at home.

I'm afraid that I don't see the point of this.

I'm afraid Dr. Sam thinks I'm crazy and is too kind to say so.

I'm afraid that Cody thinks I'm nuts and has already told Gloria so.

I'm afraid that Joe or Sandy will find this and tease me about it.

I'm afraid that

November 9

I'm afraid that this is a waste of time.

I'm afraid that my teeth will never stop hurting.

I'm afraid that I'm going nuts.

I'm afraid that someone will find out I had to see a therapist.

I'm afraid that I'll be stuck with those damned dogs all week for Thanksgiving.

I'm afraid that Joe will cause a fight with Jonah and Beth.

I'm afraid that Joe won't stand up to Jonah.

I'm afraid that this is a bunch of stupid stuff.

I'm afraid that Dr. Sam will see how ridiculous I am.

I'm afraid that

In six months:

I'm supposed to write about what I want life to be like in six months, or what I want to have be different. I want a lot of things to be different. I want to be fifteen pounds lighter. Maybe twenty. I hate my hair but I'm not sure what I can do about that. I wish Sandy had a real job and a nice boyfriend. One that wants to get married and have kids. I wish I didn't have to do the parts of my job that make my teeth hurt.

In six months.

Okay, I think Dr. Sameleski probably wants me to focus on things I could do differently. Not what I want other people to do. Fine. I want to go on sabbatical and do what I want. I want to wake up and feel excited about life again. I don't know if I can do that. Maybe that train left the station. But other people seem to be happy, not just okay. So I'll write as if stuff could happen.

I want to feel excited about life, and do the things I enjoy more. I want to have a year of sabbatical so I can come back charged up and not have my teeth hurt because of stress.

In six months, I want to be thinner and more fit. Able to go for long walks. Who am I kidding? I can barely make it from the parking lot to the library. Walking those damned dogs wears me out, even that crazy little Anastasia. But I still want to be thinner and more fit. Able to go for a hike with a bag that has snacks and my sketchbook. Although maybe if I'm thinner I won't think about snacks all the time. I don't know. But that's what I want, to be starting sabbatical and able to enjoy it.

Chapter Six

"Well, of course, Joe didn't stand his ground and so we're on the hook for the dogs next week," Alex finished.

Dr. Sam raised her eyebrows. They were halfway through the second session and Alex already dreaded the eyebrow raise. "His ground? What about you?"

Alex drew back stiffly. "Joe said he would have a talk with Jonah, and he did, and it went like it always does. I wasn't supposed to even be involved but he put me on speaker and then threw me under the bus. And then Jonah called back a few days later and said they couldn't get a kennel on such short notice, and Joe just wouldn't follow through."

"Maybe you threw Joe under the bus by dumping all this on him." A pause. "Who agreed to take the dogs in the first place? The very first time, I mean."

Alex looked up at a corner of the ceiling. "Me. I mean, they just had the one dog then. Naughty Sol. Solar. So, it wasn't so bad. And then …"

"And then you wouldn't say no."

Alex rubbed her upper right jaw and took a pointed interest in the landscape painting on the wall behind Dr. Sam.

"So, how's the homework? Did you bring it along?"

Alex held out the small notebook. "Here. I tried. Really."

The eyebrows went up. "There's no try; there's just do or don't do."

"Well, I did it. Mostly."

Dr. Sam scanned the pages. She nodded and tapped the margin after a few lines. Looking straight at Alex, she said, "So, you're quite frightened, aren't you? The job, the kids, being judged, me." She paused. "Okay, me, maybe, makes sense. At least at first. Why not be afraid of someone who can have you hospitalized?" Alex's eyes widened. "That was a joke, Alexa. A joke. As we discussed before, almost everyone is afraid their therapist will find them to be crazy. It's perfectly normal. Being so very much afraid of your kids and your job, however, not so much."

"I'm not afraid of my children. Or work."

"Okay, kids first. You're terrified they will be angry at you; you absolutely dread arguments with Sandy and you're intimidated by Jonah. Do you think they won't love you if you say no?"

Alex opened her mouth quickly and then snapped it closed. She made a questioning face, waiting for Dr. Sam to clarify what she meant, but Dr. Sam just sat, silently, looking gently and kindly curious. It felt like minutes passed. Alex sighed. "No. Absolutely not. What kind of child would not love their mother if she said no? I mean, to a reasonable request, why wouldn't a mother say yes, of course, but ..." Alex trailed off. The eyebrows were up. "Well, yes. I am afraid. They're so ... different. Like aliens. Not space aliens, but as if they aren't even the same family as Joe and me. Like the stork brought the wrong packages. I love them, but I do not understand them."

"That sounds sad for you, not understanding the way your children have decided to live."

Alex looked down at her lap, twisting the edge of her cotton sweater. She pulled at a loose thread, tried tucking it back into the weave unsuccessfully. She looked up, off to the side of Dr. Sam's face. "Yes, it's very sad. I feel like I screwed up. Look at Jonah and Beth—four dogs, no kids, jetting all over God's green earth and, well, what kind of person raises a child who doesn't want children of their own?"

"You're assuming them not having children has anything to do with you."

"Well, who else but a mother? Okay, maybe Joe. Or Beth's parents." She considered that. Beth's parents jetted about, and they seemed to see Beth as some sort of attractive accessory. They weren't particularly close. At least, that's the way Beth portrayed it. It occurred to Alex at that moment that maybe Jonah portrayed her in some terrible way—the bookworm-y librarian, hiding in her backyard talking to birds, some sort of Audubon-obsessed crazy woman.

"And you're assuming that people who don't have children necessarily don't *want* to have them."

Alex grimaced. "I guess I was assuming it was a selfish decision and not any sort of, you know, problem. I mean it could be. With fertility. With Jonah's situation. But maybe adopt...something besides dogs."

Dr. Sam nodded. "So, the most accurate thing we can say is, at this time they don't have children and we're not sure what the plan is."

"Fair enough. It sounds kinder, and really it's more accurate, from what I know."

"And your daughter? Cassandra?"

"Yes. Sandy. She's always off protesting something or doing a beach cleanup or bossing us around. She has an MA in environmental psychology—what even is that? And there's some endless dissertation project. I still don't quite understand except that her main subject of conversation is how we'd all be happier if we took better care of the environment. Not that I'm against that, of course." Alex glanced at Dr. Sam to see if she looked disapproving of her criticism of Sandy's passion. Dr. Sam just looked politely curious.

Alex continued, "And of course, she's not married or dating or working full-time. She does a little tutoring and a lot of lecturing of parents. It's like having a teenager with a master's degree, she doesn't do much and she thinks she knows everything."

"She sounds intense."

"Yes, she's very ... intense. A little much sometimes, like a tornado."

"And you're afraid of her, too."

"I'm not afraid of her."

"No?"

"I'm afraid of losing her." The words slipped out, surprising Alex.

"That sounds like a powerful place to stop for today. So here's the homework: Keep doing the sentence stems, but tweak them. Write, 'I'm afraid that my children.' Otherwise, same as last time. Just let it roll. No censoring." Dr. Sam smiled. "And I still don't think you're crazy."

Chapter Seven

November 15

I'm afraid that my children will always boss me around.

I'm afraid that my children will never be kind.

I'm afraid that my children won't be nice unless I do what they want.

I'm afraid that my children will hate me if I stand up to them.

I'm afraid that my children will leave me and I'll be alone when I'm old.

I'm afraid that my children won't leave me and I'll be stuck with them forever.

I'm afraid that my children will never have children. And it will be my fault because I was such a lousy mother.

I'm afraid that my children think I'm weak and stupid.

I'm afraid that my children look down on me.

I'm afraid that my children might be right about me.

November 18

I'm afraid that my children won't have children.

I'm afraid that my children will have meaningless lives. I think they do mostly have meaningless lives. At least Sandy tries.

I'm afraid that my children will have children and keep them away from me to punish me.

I'm afraid that my children think I'm weak.

I'm afraid that my children don't respect me.

I'm afraid that my children disrespect their father.

I'm afraid that my children think we're their doormats.

I'm afraid that my children will find out how disappointed I am in them. How ashamed I am of their behavior.

I'm afraid that my children will just keep dumping on me forever.

November 19

I'm afraid that my children don't respect me.

I'm afraid that my children think I'm stupid.

I'm afraid that my children are angry at me.

I'm afraid that my children will waste their lives on stupid things.

I'm afraid that my children think I'm wasting my life on stupid things.

I'm afraid that my children seem like strangers.

I'm afraid that my children will never know me and I'll just be stupid Mom who does whatever they want. Except for Sandy who thinks I never do anything she wants.

I'm afraid that my children think dogs are a good excuse for grandchildren.

In six months

In six months, I want to be on sabbatical. I want to be doing art again. I want to be able to say, Sandy, shut up. And I want to say, Joe, please listen and don't just talk. I want to tell Gloria to stop bossing me around and talking to me like I'm a slow-witted child.

In six months

In six months, I want to be able to stick up for myself. Just say what I think. Everyone else seems to just pipe up and say whatever they think. I'd like to tell students when they're being impossibly rude and tell Sandy she's an arrogant little blue jay who can't even feed herself, never mind save the world. I want to go back to being ferocious about going after what I want. I remember how upset Dad was about my "useless" majors and how afraid he was that I would just throw my life away. I think he was glad I ended up in the library in a "real job" with benefits and a pension. Like Elsa. And that somehow, I was an art major without becoming completely decadent and drug-addled, as if I would turn into some wacky Warhol wannabe. I wonder what he would think of this sabbatical idea.

In six months

In six months, I want to be as far away from that damned research desk as possible without going all the way to Australia. I don't want to answer questions anymore from people who don't care to listen to the response, and I don't want to have to pretend it's acceptable to be rude to me. I'd like to be able to pull off one of those angry eagle stares. Just sit there with my hands folded on the desk, giving that eagle look, like a hungry, angry osprey and see what that nasty, whiny little Karma character does. As if she'd look up from her phone for more than a moment.

Chapter Eight

The Great Horned Owl

The great horned owl, like other owls, after meals, vomits up a pellet comprising bones, feathers or fur, and various other indigestible parts. It mates for life. It has golden eyes, a distinct call, and can successfully hunt animals much larger than itself. In the United States, it is active from dusk through dark. It is intensely protective of its nest and young.

He slammed his hand on the table so hard the dishes rattled. "And what kind of people would go to the Netherlands for Thanksgiving and NOT visit Leiden?" Joe shook his head incredulously.

Bob laughed and said, "Professor Bonhall, did you think Jonah and Beth were going for a history tour?"

Joe would not be mollified, but he ceded the point. "Well, I mean—who could resist at least tying that in?"

Gloria decided that the main meal was over, stood up and began gathering plates. "I can't believe we're having the same conversation we essentially had at Easter, when they went to the Mediterranean for two weeks and couldn't find time to visit the Holy Land. Alexa, be a dear and get that dish of potatoes, would you? Marlene, would you take the green beans?"

Gloria was a tall woman, broad shouldered and athletic. She wore her white-and-gray hair close-cropped. Her eyebrows, still jet black, were straight, and her nose was narrow. She had a habit of pressing her lips together when she was thinking, and to express disapproval, and in those moments looked very much like an eagle. She was making the eagle face about the irresponsibly vacationing Jonah and Beth now, but her disapproval could turn on any of them in a moment.

Bob and Joe segued from pilgrims to fishing, discussing days they could get together to go fishing, or sit in Bob's garage tying flies, and then the merits of Joe's possible sabbatical researching indigenous fishing practices. Alex and her mother, Marlene, were relegated to the kitchen with Gloria, cleaning up their annual Friday-after-Thanksgiving Day supper.

Gloria was packing leftovers into neatly stacked containers. Without looking up, she suggested, "Alexa, you may go ahead and start scraping the plates, please. I don't like putting them in the dishwasher with food bits on them."

Marlene was already in the sink, washing pots and pans. "Such a lovely dinner, Gloria, thank you! It was a treat to get to spend time with all of you."

"Oh, it's nothing." Gloria waved a serving spoon heaped with stuffing. "Just leftovers, ours and yours."

"Well, family makes everything better," Marlene said pleasantly.

Alex was tying on an apron. "How are things here, Gloria? How are the kids?" She was accustomed to Gloria talking to her in kindergarten teacher mode and wondered, briefly, how Bob managed it. She imagined trying that with Sandy and being talked over, or Jonah lecturing her and stomping out with his tense, disapproving face. Yet all of Gloria's children were close to her, not just Rachel, who had saved nearly enough for a down payment on a small condo while living at home, but all three boys, Cody, Kevin, and Matt.

"Oh, you know—busy, busy. Cody and the twins were here yesterday, and Kevin and Veronica came by with the little ones for dessert, but they were with her family for dinner. We have all the kids tomorrow; Cody's at the clinic and Kevin and Veronica will be Christmas shopping."

"Four at once—that sounds like a houseful."

Gloria brushed it off. "Oh, goodness, no. It's no trouble, except for the screen time rules."

Alex nodded silently, scraping and rinsing dishes. Kevin and Veronica let their children, ages three and five, watch quite a bit of television. They had little screens in the back seat of their SUV so they could each watch a separate video. Cody, burned by technology, allowed the minimum: Family movie time once every week or two was it for nine-year-old Sean and Marta. Gloria was not one to be put off by little challenges in organizing children, or anyone or anything else. She was retired now, but had spent over thirty-five years with five-year-olds and, perhaps more challenging, with five-year-olds' parents.

"How about you, Alexa?"

Alex's jaw pain sprang to life. "Oh, fine, enjoying the break. Although having the dogs is a bit of a bother."

"I'm not sure why you keep watching the dogs. Just say no."

"It's not that easy, Gloria. They spring things on us and I hate to say no. They're young and having fun and—" She glanced at her mother. Marlene gave her a side glance and rolled her eyes. Alex knew her mother thought she should just speak up for herself, not just to Jonah but in general.

"And you are not."

"Not young or not having fun?" Alex turned toward Gloria but she was facing away, stacking containers in the refrigerator.

"Neither, from what I can tell."

"Ouch," Alex replied, trying to sound as if she were joking.

"You need a break," Gloria announced. She turned to face Alex, one hand on her hip. "What you need is a day off. How about Sunday?"

Caught off guard, Alex said, "Huh?" and immediately wanted to kick herself. *Here we go.* The enthusiastic advice that had been welcome years ago, when Alex was new to the area, and then starting graduate school didn't feel as helpful now.

Gloria's lips pursed a bit and her eyebrows drew infinitesimally closer. "A *break*, dear," she repeated, as if Alex could not understand the words. "Let's take a day on Sunday, shall we? Some Christmas shopping, a nice lunch. It will be lovely to catch up without listening to fishing talk. Won't that be nice?"

Alex tried not to think about the degree to which Gloria sometimes resembled an eagle.

"Nice," she echoed.

"It's settled," Gloria said with satisfaction. "Why don't you come by about eleven? Bring Joe and his fishing things; he and Bob can sit around and pretend to work on flies while they chitchat." Gloria always sounded pleased when her plans came together. Alex's pain moved to a different tooth and she reflexively rubbed at her jaw.

Gloria the eagle zeroed in on her. "Alexa, do you have tooth trouble? Maybe you should get into the dentist with that. Dental problems don't magically go away, you know."

Alex felt relieved that Gloria didn't know she'd been in to see Cody about the imaginary root canal issue. She was aware of patient privacy rules but still, one never knew. "It's nothing; I had it checked out. Apparently, I'm still grinding my teeth. An old habit, I guess."

"A mouth guard is just the thing," Gloria advised her. It never occurred to Gloria to ask questions before she gave advice.

"No doubt," replied Alex.

"And now for coffee and pie!" Gloria switched gears. Alex's problem was solved, the men's plans for Sunday were determined for them, and now it was time for leftover pumpkin pie. "Regular or decaffeinated, dear? Marlene? And what about Joe?"

"Decaf, thank you," Marlene said, drying a saucepan and gazing out the window.

"Oh, decaf for both of us, thanks. How's Cody doing with the twins these days? Any word from Jenna?"

Gloria frowned. "Jenna did call them on Thanksgiving, and she was supposed to have them today, but apparently she was doing some sort of video thing at the winter festival."

"It must be hard for Cody and the kids."

"I think Cody's long since gotten over it and the kids seem resigned to their mother being a selfish monster. There's no use having a pity party over it. After all, it would be worse to have her carrying on like this in the home."

Cody's ex-wife was a touchy subject for everyone, perhaps because nearly all the family suspected that they could have been helpful early on, when she first was struggling. But no one had known what to do, and so now she had left the family, having found her purpose as a "social influencer." Gloria had adopted the position that Jenna was just "bad" and therefore they were all better off without her, and she had no patience with any compassion for the pain that led Jenna down this particular rabbit hole.

Jenna had been very close to Gloria. They had been teachers together, and Gloria had, in fact, introduced her to Cody. Gloria thought she'd be perfect with Cody; Jenna was smart, loved children, and was beautiful. Gloria admitted to Alex, only once, that she'd imagined that Jenna's olive-tan skin and dark hair would be a wonderful juxtaposition to Cody's red hair and freckles. Marriage followed in about two years, and then the twins two years after that. The pregnancy had been difficult, and Jenna had been stoic, determined to do whatever was necessary, including three months of bed rest, to protect her babies. Worn down and already very stressed when they were born, she breastfed the twins and the exhaustion contributed to an ever-deepening postpartum depression. Cody had tried to be helpful, Gloria had stepped in, but it was a very difficult time. Jenna became increasingly lethargic, withdrawing and barely able to hold the babies. Her family and her OB/GYN were finally able to convince her to go to counseling and begin taking steps toward recovering.

Once Jenna made up her mind, she was as determined as Gloria, and the same discipline that got her through a challenging pregnancy and breastfeeding twins for six months was poured into the project of healing from depression and exhaustion. Exercise, nutrition, playing with the children, meditation, journaling, counseling—Jenna was determined. She made green smoothies for breakfast and took vigorous walks with the babies in a double stroller twice a day. She did calisthenics in the kitchen and watched inspirational videos on her stationary bicycle. She met with a counselor who encouraged her to make positive changes and let go of toxic beliefs and habits. About three months into her healing, she posted a then-and-now photo post on social media: herself in spit-up stained, misshapen sweats, straggle-haired and smiling sweetly, holding both twins, and a shot of her in her new exercise class, with makeup and more stylish clothes.

Jenna's post was a success; she received many positive comments and encouragement from friends, and friends of friends. Some of them encouraged her to keep sharing her successes and inspire others. So, she did. She started posting every day. She began training harder. She started dressing in workout gear almost all the time, fashionable, sleek workout clothes. No baggy sweats or "mom clothes"—she was streamlined and polished.

Jenna had posted her therapist's suggestion that she not overinvest in others' encouragement as the basis for self-esteem. Jenna fired her therapist because she was holding her back. Plenty of people chimed in with approval for her decision not to be held back by some therapist who didn't want a client to achieve more than the therapist.

Eventually Jenna was not depressed anymore, or so it seemed. She started her own podcast, talking about her experiences overcoming postpartum depression and "interviewing" other people. Mostly, she interviewed her personal trainer, Teddy, who was an amateur videographer.

Then Jenna ran off with Teddy to become a social influencer. It was her destiny, she had explained breathlessly. Marriage to a dentist wouldn't work for her, but she fully intended to be involved with the twins.

That was seven years ago. Since then, Cody had dedicated himself to the twins. He tried to keep technology from poisoning them. Jenna was in and out of their lives on a chaotic basis. Even Gloria barely discussed it.

Alex just said, "Mugs, or cups and saucers, Gloria?"

Chapter Nine

The American Crow

Either hated or loved, the American crow is intelligent, resourceful, social, and cooperative. Young crows will help with nest building and care of the young for several years before establishing their own nests. Crows count, will improvise tools to solve problems, and have a strong memory for both friend and foe.

One of Alex's favorite things to do the Saturday after Thanksgiving was to start decorating for Christmas. The Christmas tree would be decorated on Saturday night, with Joe—and Sandy, if she were home—but Saturday morning she always started getting things out, and this year her mother's flight wasn't until late afternoon, so they had the morning together to enjoy coffee and conversation while they unpacked the holiday season.

Marlene and Alex sat on the floor, sorting through a box of angels, nutcrackers, and elves. Marlene held up a wooden nutcracker painted a chaotic mix of purple, pink, and black. "This one! Didn't Sandy paint this in second grade?"

Alex smiled. "Yes, and she complains every year that I put it out."

"Well, having a sense of humor and proper nostalgia are important," Marlene asserted. "How about we put it somewhere prominent this year?"

"Middle of the mantel?" Alex wondered. "Or next to the crèche?" The nutcracker ended up on the mantel, close to where Sandy's stocking would be hung on Christmas Eve. They debated a few more pieces, and then Alex came to the crèche. The little wood hut was handmade. The floor had small pieces of real slate carefully glued into place. "Ah, beautiful," she sighed. They were both still for a moment. Her father had made it for her and Joe before Jonah was born. She looked over at her mother. "It's hard to believe it's been six years."

Marlene made one of those smiles that looks like trying not to cry. Her eyes were moist. "Yes and no. It seems it can't have been six years already, and it also feels like an eternity." She unwrapped a ceramic shepherd. "It's not easy."

Alex shook her head. "It can't be." She wondered how things actually were for her mother. Marlene rarely complained. She mentioned her husband in conversation. It would be hard to be married over fifty years and not mention someone. "Jimmy loved this recipe," she would say sometimes, if someone complimented a dish, or, if a vacation destination was mentioned, "Oh, Jimmy and I always had fun going there; it was one of our favorite places to just get away for a few days."

Marlene smiled gently and unwrapped another piece for the crèche, this one a sheep. "It's one of those things you can't really know until you go through it, and of course it's different for everyone." She paused. "My friend Jackie—you remember Jackie, right? The accountant from church? She always seemed like she could handle anything, and then when Al passed, she just fell apart. Her kids had to come in and take over everything. She couldn't remember to walk the dogs, much less deal with paperwork and decisions. I would have expected her to organize everything without a hiccup. And Patricia, who everyone thought was as helpless as a kitten, suddenly just managed, which was a good thing, because her kids spun out of control when their father died."

"And you seemed to handle everything well." Alex was hesitant; they hadn't talked about this much before.

Marlene shrugged. "Depends what you mean by everything." She sat a bit straighter and looked right at Alex. "Did you think handling everything meant I was okay?"

Alex felt her stomach begin to turn. She had thought so. She'd been surprised that her mother had managed to make all sorts of decisions and changes in the wake of her husband's passing, and had assumed that, somehow, she was at peace with it. Alex admitted to herself she'd wondered about how happy her parents had really been, because her mother didn't act as upset as they'd believed she would be. She shrugged and sighed. "I'm sorry, Mom. I guess I did. I thought ... I assumed you were okay. I mean, you just went ahead and did what had to be done."

Marlene nodded and went back to carefully unfolding paper from figurines. She placed St. Joseph on the coffee table. "I always suspected so. You and Elsa both seemed to have expected me to disintegrate and when I did what had to be done it didn't occur to anyone that maybe the inside didn't quite match the outside."

"I'm sorry."

Marlene reached over to rub Alex's shoulder. "Oh, baby girl, I don't want you to feel guilty. I want you to know that things aren't always easy, and you can't expect them to be. I didn't *want* to sell the house, or move someplace smaller, or get rid of half our stuff. At least not right away. I slept in your father's shirts for three years." She smiled. "Too much information, right?"

Alex shook her head. "I didn't think it was easy. But I guess I really just didn't … think."

"Well, easily done. It's hard to lose a parent. And a grandparent." Marlene placed Mary next to St. Joseph. She glanced at Alex. "And it's hard to be at the stage you're at. When are you going to do something about this, Alex?"

"Do something about what?"

Marlene looked up from the angel she was unpacking. "Alex, please. I realize Joe's perpetually the absent-minded professor, and Sandy's as self-absorbed as she was in high school, and that harpy you call your best friend—"

"Mom."

"Okay, fine. But it pains me to see you let her talk to you as if you were in kindergarten. Why don't you speak up for yourself? To her? To Joe? To Sandy? Jonah?"

"Mom, I'm fine."

"Alex, honey. Maybe you think you're doing a great job of faking it but you can't fool me. I know what it costs to put on the 'everything's okay' mask." She paused. "Like the outing you're going on tomorrow. You know very well you have no interest—less than no interest—in going to the mall. You'd rather stay here and putter around and enjoy your peace and quiet. You're hoping Joe goes over to play at fly tying with Bob so you can have some time to yourself. You know it. I know it. Just do it."

"Gloria means well."

"I'm sure she does. But you're not Gloria. And you're not Sandy, and you're not Joe. For God's sake, Alex, life is short. Have it." Marlene stretched her arms over her head and rolled her shoulders.

Alex looked at her mother and felt as if she was seeing her for the first time in years. She hadn't noticed how much she had changed in the past few years. Of course, Marlene was seventy-eight. She'd been only seventy-two when she was widowed. She was thinner than she'd been; she'd taken up walking and yoga. "Balance and flexibility are as important as aerobics," she'd told her daughters, but Alex still didn't get any real exercise. Elsa, who had taken up triathlons at fifty after decades of assiduously avoiding the outdoors, didn't want to argue with her mother about the relative value of aspects of fitness. Mostly, Alex realized that her mother looked peaceful; she had the kind of permanent crinkles that smiling gives a person. Alex suspected that she was also often very lonely. "And you?"

"Fair enough. I have a life, Alex. I have a good life. I take some watercolor classes and belong to a book club and a women's Bible study—thank God for those ladies—and I stay fit. Well, for my age, I guess. Of course, I get to enjoy Elsa's family and my grandchildren and great-grandchildren, and I'm here with you in the holidays and you're up with us part of the summer. I have dear friends and we are family for one another, too. And I miss Jim. I'll always miss him." She carefully placed the manger and the baby Jesus figurine by Mary and Joseph. "But I had to learn. I had to learn to speak up for myself, because your father always took care of me. I didn't have to."

"Joe takes care of me," Alex mused.

Marlene shook her head. "It's not quite the same. Joe is wonderful, and I love him, and Jimmy loved him. But Joe doesn't ... he doesn't seem to sense what you need the way Jimmy did for me. If you want to be happy, you'll have to learn to do now what I waited to learn until after I lost your father." She sighed and stroked the figure of Mary. "Don't waste any more time, Alex." She smiled mischievously. "Like Gloria said last night, you're not getting any younger."

"I know!" Alex retorted, and laughed. Then she said, quietly, "Thanks, Mom. Thanks for being here."

"I love you, sweetheart. Be happy, okay?"

"I am," Alex asserted. She watched her mom make that sad smile again and turn her gaze to a cloth-and-plastic elf.

"Is this that Stasi elf that used to spy on the kids?" Marlene asked, holding it up at eye level.

"Mom! Please."

"I don't care. It's creepy. I'm with Jillian on that one." Jillian was Elsa's second grandchild, now eight years old, who, at five, had ignored the admonition to never touch the elf. She had left it in the middle of the playroom floor, face down, limbs splayed, a tragic North Pole crime scene. She was in the middle of outlining the floor around it with yellow driveway chalk when her mother found her, grabbed the elf, scolded Jillian and took away the chalk. Jillian was unruffled by the adult distress, remarking, "She's not my favorite, Mommy."

"Well, Sandy loved it." Alex took the elf from her mother and placed it prominently on an end table, facing Joe's chair. "It can watch Joe first."

"Hmm." Marlene shrugged. "Suit yourself. Maybe the elf should keep an eye on you, make sure you're doing what you should. For yourself, that is."

Alex shook her head, half smiling. "I love you, Mom."

"And I love you, Alexa Companeri Bonhall."

Chapter Ten

Sunday was cool, sunny and dry—a perfect day to sit in the garage with the door open and work on fishing flies, talk when it suited them, and break for a whiskey and a cigar. Joe and Bob were pleased with their end of the bargain.

"Won't this be nice?" Gloria said this as a sort of general announcement to the four of them. Bob was already ensconced in his favorite working chair in the garage, coffee at hand. Joe looked up from pulling his fishing box out of the trunk, grinning.

"It's going to be a great day." He closed the trunk with a thud. "You'll have to go hard at shopping to have more fun than we will."

"Here, here." Bob toasted with his mug.

Alex waved her keys. "Ready, Gloria?"

"Oh, no, Alexa, I'm driving. This is your day! I want you to be totally relaxed!"

Joe wiggled his eyebrows from behind Gloria, so that Alex had to contain her scowl at him. "It's really no stress at all. I prefer driving," she asserted, but it was useless. Gloria was already in her bright red

SUV, rolling down her window and shouting, "Come along! No use wasting time!" over the jangle of holiday music.

Alex got in and buckled up.

"This will cheer you up," Gloria announced, raising the volume on the music. She pressed her lips together in her most self-satisfied smile. Alex opened her mouth to speak, but before she could protest that she didn't need cheering up, Gloria sailed on. "Alexa, dear, you are so very stressed out." Gloria slalomed out of her neighborhood and onto the main highway. She gave a sidelong glance at Alex and added, "You're clenching your teeth. Are you always so tense?" Gloria swerved around another, larger SUV with incredibly dark-tinted windows.

"Not normally," Alex replied, gripping the armrest. Gloria assertively steered through traffic as if the other cars were a flock of sparrows; traffic obligingly scattered. Gloria kept talking, loudly, over the jangle of holiday hits, through the thirty-minute drive.

As they pulled into the mall parking lot, Gloria had segued from her musings on all the fun to be had and was giving one of what Alex and Joe called her "talks." She turned the radio down just a tad. "I know I called this Christmas shopping but I really thought you just needed a day off, a day for yourself," she explained, interrupting herself to imperiously wonder where the good parking spaces were. "So, this is your special day, dear. Let's walk around and just have fun looking at things, and have a nice lunch, and not worry whether or not we get any shopping done for Christmas. It's four weeks away, after all."

Alex nodded and said, "I did hope to get some shopping done. This is really only one of a few days I have to—"

"Four weeks, plenty of time," Gloria said. "And after all, it's just the two of you and your grown children. And those dogs, of course, but it isn't like you have young children to shop for. You can't imagine the aggravation. They're impossible to please these days."

I would love to imagine, Alex thought. Shopping for small children sounded wonderful. But she said, "Well then, shall we?" and stepped out into the parking lot.

The mall was crowded, noisy with people as well as a cacophony of holiday music soundtracks, competing for attention in the promenade as well as from every store front. Gloria scanned the scene. "The Bath Bombshell, that's a good place to start. *Lots* of self-indulgence to be found."

Alex rubbed her lower left jaw and said nothing.

Gloria spent almost thirty minutes in the Bath Bombshell, inspecting merchandise and peppering salespeople with questions. Twenty minutes in, Alex had wandered around the shop five times, trying to avoid making eye contact with Gloria. A sales clerk came up beside Alex, smiling cheerfully. "Welcome to Bath Bombshell! Can I help you find anything?"

Alex smiled back, glancing at the name tag on her vest. "Thanks, no, Aliyah, I'm just looking. I'm with that lady, over there." She nodded toward where Gloria was standing, facing a large display of handmade soaps and interrogating the salesperson.

"Ooh," Aliyah said, and sucked her lips in briefly.

"Were you helping her earlier?"

Aliyah nodded. "But she wanted more information than I had so I had to get the manager." She gave a practiced, bland smile.

"I know. She's pretty intense. I guess you have to be used to all sorts of people to work here, huh?"

Aliyah agreed as she straightened out a few bottles of conditioner. "Yeah, we get all kinds of people. Mostly really nice, though." She pushed some braids behind her shoulder. Her long hair was intricately braided with a few brightly colored streaks woven into the plaits.

"Your hair is beautiful. Do you do it yourself?"

"Thanks." Aliyah reached toward her hair. "No, my aunt does it. She has kind of a side business, you know, doing hair. She's really good at it and a lot of people in the salons, they don't know how to do this."

"It's an art. She must be busy."

"Yes, she is." Aliyah seemed to enjoy having a distraction; she kept straightening up what seemed like already-neat bottles of hair products while she told Alex all about her aunt, who was a social worker in private practice and had partly worked her way through graduate school doing hair for friends, neighbors, and acquaintances. Then some people in the licensed beauty field had badgered the state, pushing to make that illegal, saying you couldn't plait hair unless you were a licensed professional. But that had been worked out, because it wasn't fair.

"Aunt Elbie says, after working inside people's heads all week, it's nice to do something real, with her hands, that you can see made a difference."

"That makes sense," Alex replied. "Aunt Elbie sounds very wise."

"She is."

Gloria waved over at them. "Alexa! Dear! Come over here! This looks perfect for you."

Alex waved and nodded. She turned to Aliyah. "It's been great to talk with you. Thanks for your help today."

"Thanks! Enjoy your day!" Aliyah said, but she looked skeptical, glancing sideways toward where Gloria was waving a box of beauty supplies.

There followed a remarkably long two-hour ordeal, going into four more shops and wandering aimlessly while Gloria inspected the merchandise, badgered salespeople with questions, and occasionally asserted with tremendous confidence what would suit Alex. At the fifth stop, another beauty-focused boutique, Gloria bought two small boxes of goat's milk soaps. "For Veronica. She's impossible. The art department infiltrated her brain and now *everything* has to be creative. Even soap," Gloria complained.

"I was an art major," Alex commented mildly, but Gloria wasn't listening. She announced it was time for a break, and that a very indulgent fancy coffee and a pastry would be what Alex needed to help her relax.

Three espresso shots, sugar, and chocolate stirred into milk, with whipped cream, sounded delicious but not a recipe for relaxation per se. "I was thinking a hot cup of peppermint tea, and maybe a scone," Alex ventured. Gloria looked briefly displeased, but they were eventually able to settle at a small table, just outside the coffee shop in the promenade, with their respective preferences, Gloria's packages and the noisy, bustling mall.

"So, how is Rachel doing these days?" Alex asked casually, hoping to distract Gloria from the mission of forcing her to relax. "For all the time she and Sandy spend together, we hardly see her."

"Oh, she's always on the go." Gloria nodded approvingly. "Good to not sit still! Keep going! Between her job and her activism and Aidan, we hardly see her either."

"Aidan?"

Gloria stirred her peppermint mocha. "Aidan Mahoney. They've been seeing each other for a while."

"Oh? You haven't said a word!"

"Well, you know how young people are, all privacy and hush-hush. I hardly heard a word myself, but she brought him over for Thanksgiving dinner, so I suppose it's serious."

"And? What do you think?"

"Well, he's a teacher," Gloria said, and she pressed her lips into a firm line. Alex wondered if she was thinking about Jenna.

"From her school? That could be a little uncomfortable if things don't pan out."

"Oh, no. The high school. He's a history teacher."

"Another history teacher!" Alexa smiled. "Well, Joe will be glad for the company."

"Well, let's not jump to conclusions." Gloria stirred her drink, looking pleased. She didn't seem to mind the thought of Aidan Mahoney joining the clan.

"But the high school? How did they meet?"

"It was sort of an odd start." She paused. "Bleak, really. You remember that horrible accident last spring, the one on prom night?"

"Oh, Lord, yes. The one where the drunk driver ran the red light and rammed a limo full of teenagers?"

"Yes. Those were all students at the school where Aidan teaches. All the guidance counselors in the district were sent there to help students and faculty the next week, and, well, Rachel met Aidan."

"Oh, that is a rough start." Alex grimaced. She wondered how that would sound in the retelling, decades later. How could you possibly tell the story without sounding ghoulish, about a carload of teens dying on prom night bringing you together? She shook her head and stirred her tea.

"Yes," Gloria agreed. "Aidan was shepherding students to the counselors. He has a way about him. The students tended to go to him and then trusted him when he brought them to see the counselors. A soft handoff, as it were."

"Oh, that's nice. He sounds very kind."

"He is. And the accent doesn't hurt."

"Accent?"

"He's from Ireland. Born there, raised here, mostly, and a naturalized citizen. But the accent comes out, believe me." Gloria lowered one eyebrow. "I suspect sometimes it's intentional, but it does work."

"Well, I'll look forward to meeting him." Alex paused. "It's odd that Sandy hasn't said a thing."

"Hard to imagine Sandy not saying anything. Perhaps Rachel's playing it close to the vest, even with Sandy." Having finished with that topic, Gloria shifted in her chair, putting down her cup and gazing around. "Isn't this lovely?" she observed. "The people all hurrying around, and us just relaxing, having a day of peaceful self-indulgence before you have to go back to work. You poor thing. When *will* you retire?"

The attempt at a dodge had worked only for a few minutes, Alex thought regretfully. "Well, I can't very well retire yet, Gloria. I'm fifty-five and it's too soon. Besides, there's that sabbatical year." She didn't want to discuss her sabbatical and racked her brain for a diversion. "When's Grandpa Quinn coming this year?"

Grandpa Sean Kevin Quinn was Bob's father. He lived in Maine, near Bob's sister and her family, but made an escape to Florida several times a year, the longest trip during the winter. "We're expecting him just after Christmas, probably the twenty-eighth. It will be Christmas number two for the children and a nice change of pace for everyone."

Grandpa Quinn was extremely energetic, full of life, and usually brought out the mischief in children. Little Bobby, for one, did not need the encouragement, and Veronica and Gloria usually tried to bounce Grandpa between houses for sanity's sake over the course of a few weeks.

"That will be fun."

"It will be." Gloria nodded, pressing her lips together. "But about your retirement, I guess it is too soon. Well, you shouldn't get yourself so upset about work. You look stressed."

"Yes, that's what you told me earlier." It was about as snippy as Alex would allow herself to be. "I'm sorry, Gloria, but it's the last day of Thanksgiving break, and I'm not terribly excited about going back for the end of the term."

Gloria was not at all put off. "Well, then, we should make this afternoon count! What would be fun? What do you think, Alexa? You need to shake things up, try something new."

Alex thought to herself that Gloria had worn the same elfin hairstyle and bright red lipstick for the twenty-five years they'd known each other. She did not seem to be the person to give lectures about shaking things up.

"I was thinking a new hairstyle would be nice," Gloria said.

"I think you look fine," Alex replied. "Your hair is sort of short for any big changes. What were you thinking of doing?"

"Not me! You, of course."

"*Of course?*"

"I didn't mean anything by it, dear. You're so touchy. It must be the stress. Well, maybe not a hairstyle. Oh, I know."

Alex cringed.

"A mani-pedi! Just the thing. Let's go." Gloria was up, rustling her package of goat's milk soaps. "A nice, festive mani-pedi."

"Gloria, I'm just not a big manicure fan. I'd rather not do something I'm stuck trying to maintain."

"Oh, we're not doing acrylic nails, dear. Just think of it as a fancy paint job you can take off when you're done. But they do such excellent work. You'll smile every time you see your hands for two weeks!"

Alex wiggled her lower jaw from side to side and listened to it click.
"I'd rather not."

But Gloria was already off, striding through the crowd.

Chapter Eleven

There was what Alex had learned were the usual few moments of pleasantries—how was Thanksgiving? Did Alex enjoy her break? But eventually Dr. Sam settled in diagonally across from Alex, smiled and tilted her head, asking, "So, Alexa, how have things been?" in that other tone, the "We're getting down to business," in a very kind sort of way, tone.

"I don't know. My jaw hurts." She felt Dr. Sam's eyes lock on her hand as she rubbed her jaw. Alex fell silent. As she feared, Dr. Sam was apparently prepared to wait her out. This felt very unfair, this therapist cop-out trick of just sitting there silently, wasting precious and expensive moments. The clock ticked quietly. Dr. Sam sat, unruffled. Alex sighed loudly and wiggled her fingers. "Well, I tried to take a day for myself and this is what happened."

"The manicure is new for you."

Alex curled her fingers into her palms and sighed again. "Yes. It was Gloria's idea. My best friend," she added in response to the unspoken query. "We were Christmas shopping. Or it was supposed to be Christmas shopping."

"Supposed to be?"

"It was an ambush, and apparently at least her husband was in on it. Joe denies knowing anything. For all I know, the kids were in on it too. Poor little Alex needs a 'special day,' and it was a special day of all the wrong kinds." Alex was surprised at the venom in her own voice but Dr. Sam didn't look particularly surprised. She just nodded, so Alex launched into a description of the day—the drive, the crowds, the noise, the shops, the micromanaged tea and scone and the awful manicure experience that gave Alex a headache for the rest of the day.

"So, Gloria decided that you needed a day 'for yourself,' which on the one hand doesn't sound like a bad idea, and on the other hand ..."

"On the other hand, it was not my idea of what a day for myself would look like."

"Fair enough." Dr. Sam raised her eyebrows. "So, Alexa, what would your idea of a day for yourself look like?"

It was quiet for a long time. Alex sat very still and panicked silently, her mind darting about. What to say that wouldn't sound too weird? The secretly crazy librarian, finally cracking—what would that look like to everyone?

"I don't know."

"That's kind of a cop-out. Surely you know what you want to do instead of, oh, being in a crowded mall being bossed around, having to breathe toxic fumes and then have red sparkly nails with"—she squinted—"Christmas wreaths? Am I seeing that right? When you usually have bare nails."

"Well." Alex cleared her throat.

"Where the best part was apparently the chat with Aliyah, the young woman at the shop with the beautiful hair and the interesting aunt."

"Well ..." Alex frowned. "I did enjoy Aliyah! What a nice person. And her aunt sounds fascinating. She's in private practice, maybe you know her. Elbie something. I don't know what. But how many social workers can there be in private practice named Elbie?" Alex stopped, and her shoulders sagged. "Of course, Gloria had to ruin that, calling me over to see some sort of flat iron to deal with my hair. As if my hair was something to be dealt with."

"What keeps you from speaking up? From saying, 'Gloria, I don't want to flat iron my hair.' Or, 'Gloria, I have a sabbatical to plan! I'm too busy to do things that annoy me.'"

"I couldn't possibly mention the sabbatical," Alex blurted out and then sat back, surprised. *I did let it slip but luckily Gloria didn't catch it.*

"Because?"

Alex's thoughts whirled. She imagined Joe and Gloria telling her what would be good for her, and Sandy hectoring her about doing something "meaningful." She imagined Jonah scoffing with that supercilious sideways look, shaking his head with disapproval, as he had since he was a small child. "I don't know. Well, I do know. They'd take it over, all of them, one way or another. Maybe the only way to have a sabbatical is to just sneak off in the dark of night and send a postcard. 'Hello all, it's me. I'm painting and photographing wildlife and hiking. Don't try to find me; I'm hidden away in a cabin in the mountains. See you in six months! Ta-ta!'"

Dr. Sam leaned forward and said quietly, "Alex, I want to be helpful. I can see that you are a good person who is very ..."

"Crazy." Alex was surprised at how thick her voice sounded suddenly.

Dr. Sam shook her head. "Stuck. Feeling trapped. So kind and sensitive to the feelings of others that you've decided not to deal with your own. But the body doesn't lie, Alexa, and pain, fear, and anger will come out physically if you don't deal with them some other way."

"I'm not angry." Alex pulled at her collar, staring off to the side of Dr. Sam's face.

"Interesting piece to quibble over. Maybe you're angry, maybe not. Everyone feels angry sometimes. Aren't you angry about the ambush?"

"Annoyed, maybe, but not angry."

"Same church, different pew. So, what would you do with time for yourself? What would be self-indulgent?"

"I have no idea." Alex looked straight at Dr. Sam and sighed. "That was a cop-out, wasn't it?"

"Well, yes. What did you do for fun when you were a kid? Maybe nine or ten?"

"Oh, I played piano—not very well—and I loved art and being outdoors and hiding under a tree with a good book and a candy bar. Nothing super exciting."

"Well, that all sounds fun."

"It was."

"It is. Or it should be. What parts of that are you still doing? At all?"

"Does putting out birdseed count as being outdoors?"

Dr. Sam grimaced. "Barely. Not quite what I had in mind. Neither does walking your son's dogs on your lunch break."

The conversation went on, exploring Alex's fun activities as a child, how long it had been since she'd enjoyed them, and then the session drew toward its close.

"Homework," Dr. Sam announced. "Keep journaling about feelings—keep working on fear. And start putting down ideas of things to do for fun—little pieces of the kind of things you enjoyed as a kid—and fit a couple of hours of one of those in before I see you next. Jot down some notes about it."

"How am I supposed to find time to do something fun?" It burst out and Alex regretted it; it sounded like whining.

Dr. Sam shrugged and smiled. "The same way you found time for hell day at the mall with Gloria. But we're talking two hours of your choice, not seven hours of hers. Maybe just go to the hobby shop and look around, see what fires your imagination. You never know."

Chapter Twelve

Going to the hobby store on the way home from work wasn't her idea of a good time. Alex started scowling as she navigated the crowded parking lot. Still, there would never be a convenient time to do this—not during the holiday season—so she had reluctantly let Joe know she'd be late, that she had "homework" at the hobby shop. Joe had cheerfully asked her to pick up some specific kind of thread for him and said he'd see her when she got home. "Have fun!"

Have fun, she thought, absent-mindedly rubbing her upper left jaw. She grabbed a basket, just in case. Her instructions were to just walk through the store looking at hobby and art supplies: No commitment, no "heroics," Dr. Sam said. This was not the time to commit to something hard or expensive; just look and think about ways to have fun. *Still, you never know*, Alex thought. Maybe something would appeal.

About a third of the way through the store she came upon the inks, stamps, and related projects. She recalled the fun she'd had with Sandy, years ago, making their own wrapping paper. They'd stamped Christmas images and colored them in, listening to music. They had started at the table but ended up stretched out on the floor, surrounded by art materials, laughing and talking. She thought about how much fun they used to have, giggling and doing creative things. Even during high school, Sandy had been able to spend time with her mom without grumbling or wanting to spend money. At some point in graduate school, Sandy had started to slip away from her.

Alex sighed and wandered off, finding herself in the drawing department. Colored pencils, loose stock and in tins. She recalled how promising new art supplies felt when she was a kid, how she could imagine the beautiful pictures she would make. She picked up a pencil, eyeing it; the core was centered perfectly, a good sign. She replaced it and picked up a package of high-end colored pencils with brilliant, waxy cores, and then put it back. She made her way through paints, woodcraft, to different threads and yarns. She found Joe's thread, wandered the fabric department, and found herself back by the stamping supplies.

Gift tags and thank you notes, she thought suddenly. She wasn't exactly in the market to make her own wrapping paper, but she suddenly pictured using paper and ribbon, stamps and colored pencils to create gift tags, listening to quiet holiday music. It sounded peaceful. Her chest felt quietly warm. That sounded good—so good, in fact, that she imagined Dr. Sam being surprised at her finding something so easily after her foot-dragging. Feeling a sudden burst of enthusiasm, Alex picked up a black stamp pad, then her eyes rested on a stamp of a cardinal on a pine branch. "Perfect," she murmured. She made her way back to the paper, and then to ribbons, excited to find a perfect spool of a soft red plaid.

On the way to the circuitous checkout process, she went past the baking department, where a glowingly ebullient woman with wild white curls, wearing an elf hat, bounced up and down on the balls of her feet and waved green flyers. She locked into eye contact with Alex. "Thanks for coming to Andy's Hobby Haven!" she chirped. "I hope you found what you were looking for!" Before Alex could say she hadn't been looking for anything, actually, the elf continued. "We're having a gingerbread house class on Saturday morning! Only ten dollars for supplies! Space is limited." She thrust out a flyer and leaned forward, whispering conspiratorially, "Last year they gave out hot cocoa, too. With marshmallows." The elf smiled delightedly. Alex found herself smiling back. "I hope you'll come," the elf said.

"I might," Alex said, taking the flyer and tucking it into her back pocket. "I just might." She walked on, hoping the elf wouldn't follow her.

Back at home, Joe asked about the hobby store visit, interested, and Alex found herself feeling a mix of embarrassment and excitement, something she couldn't quite explain to herself. The gift tag and note card idea had seemed so exciting and full of promise at Andy's Hobby Haven, but now she felt a little foolish. She wondered if Joe would think it sounded juvenile.

"It's kind of silly," she finished, after explaining what she'd bought.

"Not at all!" Joe asserted. "I think it sounds great. Maybe start tonight! I'm up for a quiet evening with music." They were putting a quick supper together, and Sandy wandered in.

"What's great?" she asked idly.

Alex glanced over. "Doing some crafts this evening, listening to music."

"What crafts?"

"Fishing flies for me, some art for mom."

"Oh." Sandy wasn't interested in their hobbies today. She watched her mother head toward the sliding glass door to feed the birds. "Mom! Seriously. You overdo it."

Alex stepped outside. "Hello, everyone!" she called softly, and placed sunflower seeds out in the usual places. Stepping back in, she replied, "I'm not overdoing it, Sandy."

"Feeding the wildlife just breeds dependency."

Joe interrupted the process. "Sandy, how about putting out forks and knives? And getting everyone water?"

Sandy was not deterred. She kept mumbling about dependency and learned helplessness while setting the table.

After grace, dinner conversation rambled. Joe was grading papers, and complained about the number of students who failed to follow instructions. Alex was tired of students' panicky demands that she, and every other librarian, pull a magical solution for a neglected semester out of a hat. Sandy was picking up more tutoring hours as finals approached.

At a lull in the conversation, Alex tried to sound casual. "Gloria mentioned Rachel's been seeing someone, Sandy. Have you heard anything?"

Sandy rolled her eyes. "Oh, yes. Aidan."

"What's he like?"

Sandy shrugged. "He's nice. Smart. *Dad* would like him." She examined a forkful of arugula. "Is this organic? He teaches history at the high school."

"Sounds like a good guy," Joe offered.

"Oh, yeah, he's nice. Sometimes he comes with us, sometimes not. Lots of papers to grade, you know."

"No doubt." Alex wondered why the reticence; it wasn't like Sandy not to have a strong opinion on everything. She suspected either Sandy disliked Aidan or resented him horning in on her friendship with Rachel.

"The art thing, what's up with that?" Sandy asked, as if she had suddenly recalled the earlier conversation.

"Nothing's 'up' with it." Alex felt defensive, bracing herself for criticism. "I've always enjoyed being creative and I'm doing a little dabbling." She shrugged, trying to look nonchalant. "You know, former art major, wanting to get a bit into it again."

"Trying to shake things up a bit," Joe said cheerfully.

I'm tired of being told to shake things up. Alex kicked Joe softly under the table. He looked offended.

"Shaking things up! That sounds great," Sandy began.

"It's more like, just a little creativity to balance things out," Alex interrupted.

"Oh, I think shaking things up is just what you need, Mom. You're in a rut. You just go to work and come home. You wear the same clothes you've been wearing since, what? I was in high school? And you never do anything. I mean, at least Dad has fishing." Joe looked offended again. Sandy plowed on. "Even if fishing isn't exactly a good activity."

"What's not good about fishing?"

"And now it's my clothes? What's wrong with my clothes?" Alex frowned. She caught Joe's glance and he shrugged a bit. "What's that for?" she asked him.

"Well, Alex, honey," Joe began, but Sandy talked over them both.

Sandy, having moved into lecture mode, ignored both parents' questions. "I mean, it's great that you're ready to start caring about something. Get off the hamster wheel and into the world! There's so much good to be done."

Alex's entire jaw throbbed. "Sandy, I take … issue with your assertion that I need to 'start' caring about something. I'm not sure what it is you think I've been doing with you all these years."

"Oh, Mom," sighed Sandy. "You're too sensitive. I know that. I meant, outside the family." She looked from her mother to her father and back, apparently nonplussed by the sudden coolness in the room. There was a strained silence and then she carried on, chirpily. "I know! It will be great! We'll have fun. Mom, there's a beach cleanup Saturday morning. Come with Rachel and me. We'll be looking for sea turtle and bird nests and picking up junk."

Alex shifted and felt a rustling in her back pocket. "I can't make it Saturday." She smiled. "I have a class that morning."

Joe seized on that. "A class? What class? Where?"

"A class at the hobby shop," Alex said casually. "Just a little Saturday morning, one-time thing. Something Christmasy." She didn't want to go into details, but the gate was open, the damage was done. Her fantasy of sneaking off with a vague excuse of Christmas shopping and coming home with the class over and done melted.

"I think that's great," Joe affirmed, nodding with satisfaction. "I've been encouraging you to do that. Just a little surprised you're picking the hobby shop. I thought maybe you'd finally sign up for something at the village art center. You know, unpack your old art supplies, have a little fun." When Alex didn't immediately respond, he went on. "You used to really enjoy art. I think it would be good for you." He rose from the table to go to the living room and rummage through the basket they used as a magazine rack. "Isn't there a catalogue from the art center in here? Ah, here it is." He started leafing through it. "I'm sure there's something here you'd enjoy." He sat down at the table, waving the catalogue.

"I'm sure there is." She felt as if her insides were on fire. *Used to enjoy art? I was an art major. I practically lived for art*, she fumed.

"I might want to sign up for something, too," Sandy said. "Maybe one of those painting in nature classes? Plan air?"

"Plein air," Alex said. "Painting outdoors at the scene, yes, they have those, weather permitting."

"That would be fun," Sandy continued.

"I'm sure you girls would have fun," Joe added. His job done, he set down the catalogue, leaned back, and sipped his coffee with a satisfied air.

Alex rubbed her lower jaw. She glanced down at her lap and then at her sleeves, wondering who else had been noticing the state of her wardrobe.

Chapter Thirteen

November 29

I'm afraid to make a fool of myself at gingerbread house class.

I'm afraid that the gift tags will look pathetic.

I'm afraid that Sandy will always boss me around.

I'm afraid she'll be in charge of me when I'm old and take away all my choices.

I'm afraid she'll never grow up.

I'm afraid I'm a failure as a parent.

December 1

Things I did for fun when I was a kid

Drawing

Painting

Playing piano

Reading

Being outdoors

This is a waste of time; where am I supposed to do art or even read without being on duty?

December 2

I'm tired of writing the same sentences over and over. I'm afraid, okay? I'm afraid of everything and no therapist is going to fix that. It's embarrassing and awful. I didn't used to be afraid, I used to be intrepid. And now I feel like I'm going to vomit when my son's phone number shows up in caller ID. What kind of mother is that? I'm afraid this is a waste of time and money, just frittering away pretending that suddenly I will be brave. Like I used to be.

In six months

In six months, I want to be different in an on-purpose way. What if it isn't a waste of time and money? What if I really can go ahead and do what I like sometimes? If I close my eyes, I can remember what it felt like to hike through nature, the way the breeze feels on my face and that it's so beautiful it makes you cry sometimes if you really stop to drink it all in. That's what I want. I want to sit on a porch and drink coffee and then do some art and then go for a long walk and eat without worrying about where the salad greens came from.

In six months

In six months, I want my mom to smile when she hears what I'm doing and not have that sad look. I know what that is; she thinks I'm throwing the years away and that by the time I'm her age I'll be bitter or just so shut down that I even forgot how to be bitter. Maybe so. Maybe that's the real choice. It makes it easier to choose, at least in my head.

Chapter Fourteen

Over the next three days, Alex changed her mind about the gingerbread house class five times. She decided to go, then panicked at visions of herself covered with frosting with a post-earthquake excuse for a gingerbread house, and decided against it. Then the insolent student who thought followers on social media were the same as peer reviews came back to the research desk and Alex's jaw throbbed. Twenty minutes into a second attempt to help Karma understand the basics of research, Alex suddenly pictured the cheerful elf, her eyes gleaming at the idea of hot cocoa and gingerbread, and decided she absolutely needed to build a gingerbread house on Saturday morning.

Then she'd come home, tired and achy, facing chores and Sandy's hectoring, and it felt as if one more thing was just too much. She slipped out to the back deck with a cup of tea to take in the evening. The sun had set, the few clouds in the west had just tinges of color. The stars were popping out, visible despite the suburban streetlights. Alex sighed and let the warmth of the cup seep into her achy hands.

Alex had not always been so wavering. At one time, she'd been full of curiosity and gifted with youthful certitude. She'd headed off with a scholarship to take on two majors. Her father had his doubts. He worried about the wild people she'd be with in art classes and thought it best to just focus on a "real" major, but her mother had said, "Darling, she has to do what's right for her, not for you." James Alexander Companeri had shaken his head. "Elsa was more practical. She majored in business and look at her; she has a very good job at that bank." Alex had cringed and Marlene, who didn't miss much, waved her hand at her husband. "That would kill Alexa. Like a bird in a cage. The same way tramping around outside with ticks and mosquitoes would upset Elsa. You worry too much, Jimmy."

Alex had gone off to study art and wildlife biology. While her hair grew longer and her hiking shorts shorter, her grades were excellent and she stayed off drugs, so Jim was relieved, and Marlene asserted regularly that she was not at all surprised. Then Alex brought Joe home for Thanksgiving.

Alex had overheard a piece of the conversation her parents had in the kitchen. "A history professor?" Jim had whispered to Marlene, through gritted teeth, while they were alone in the kitchen. They were finishing making dinner while Joe was in the living room, explaining Thanksgiving to Elsa's preschoolers. "Two of them with three majors between them, and no employability."

"You worry too much," Marlene had said. "Jimmy, you always take such good care of me. And we have to trust that Alexa will find the person who can be almost as good to her as you are to me."

"Almost?" Alex recalled her father's skeptical tone.

"There's no one like you," Marlene said firmly. Alex remembered her father nodding to himself as he carried in the turkey.

Alex's past certitude about school, and her dreams, and Joe, didn't seem to extend into her own choices now. Instead, the equivocation over a gingerbread house class kept repeating, and on Saturday morning she found herself in the kitchen, tallying up very good reasons not to go. The laundry, the bills, the grocery shopping, all waiting for her all week. And the bathroom needed cleaning. If she just skipped this class, she could knock those chores out by lunchtime.

Joe ambled through with his coffee mug in hand. "Just go, honey. Go. All this will still be here when you get back." He shrugged. "Or maybe I'll take care of it."

Andy's Hobby Haven was even busier on Saturday morning. Alex had the flyer in hand, and the same elf was at the door. She recognized Alex and bounced on the balls of her feet, waving. "Oh, good! You came for the class! I'm sure you're going to have a great time! The classroom is in the back, to the left, next to the basket department. Have fun!"

"Thanks." Alex made her way through throngs of people, most of whom looked as if they were having a good time. A relentlessly cheery holiday soundtrack played overhead, and employees with green vests and red Santa hats attempted to restock shelves around the crowds.

The classroom was set up with an open U of tables, and the instructor's table at the open end with a stack of supplies and an intimidatingly beautiful gingerbread house on it. The instructor greeted Alex and invited her to have a seat. She sat adjacent to a table with the only two students there so far, both women.

"Hello." Her nearest neighbor smiled. "I'm Annetta!"

"Alex," Alex said. "Hello!"

Annetta's neighbor leaned forward. "I'm Karen. Nice to meet you!"

"Hi, Karen," Alex replied. "Are you two regulars here?"

"I am," Karen said. "But she's a newbie." She elbowed Annetta playfully. "I had to do some arm-twisting on this one."

Alex nodded. "I had second and third thoughts myself." She glanced at the head table. "And seeing the finished product … I'm ready to leave now."

"Oh, pooh," Annetta replied. "There's nothing to be intimidated about. This is going to be fun." She lowered her voice. "And I heard there's cocoa."

"Did the elf tell you that?"

"What elf?" Karen asked.

"Oh, you know. The elf," Alex began, but then a few more people came in, including two mother-and-child pairs.

The instructor came in, wearing the store polo shirt and a Santa hat. She introduced herself. "I'm Jonette. Welcome! We're going to have a lot of fun this morning." She looked around at the group, hands on hips. "Some housekeeping! The restrooms are down the hall, that way," she said pointing, "and there will be hot cocoa coming in, service to be at the table there in the front." She gestured to a small table in a front corner of the class. Jonette scanned them with a slightly disapproving look. "Parents, you will have to be responsible for your children. This is an adult class, and the cocoa is served hot."

"No one said anything about it being for adults only," said the younger of the mothers, puffing up a bit and rubbing her child's shoulder.

"No, it's not adults only, but the craft is complicated, so it does require adult supervision. So does the cocoa." She began handing out cardboard cartons. "Each carton contains all you need to assemble and decorate your own gingerbread house! Please remove the top and turn it upside down, placing it in front of you on the table. Then place the doily which is the top item in the box on the upside-down lid. This will be the platform for your gingerbread house."

So far, so good, Alex thought. *No disasters yet. Box top upside-down, doily centered. Check.*

Jonette held up a jar and a plastic spatula. "Here is your frosting! It will be the mortar to hold your house together as well as the snow to decorate the roof. It does dry fairly quickly, so keep it covered when not in use."

Annetta raised her hand timidly. "If we're using it to put everything together, when would it not be in use?" She looked around sheepishly. "Sorry, probably a dumb question."

"Oh, no, there are no dumb questions," Jonette responded. Alex wondered, briefly, if Jonette would retract that remark before too long. "Just rest the cap on it between jobs," Jonette continued. "So, if you put two walls together and are holding them for a few moments to let them firm up, have the cap over the frosting."

"Oh, okay, thanks," Annetta said.

Jonette continued the effort to be cheerful, helpful, and firm. She was one of those no-nonsense types. Probably another retired kindergarten teacher, Alex guessed: perfect for reining in a group of novices attempting to stick pre-cut gingerbread together with frosting. The five-year-old ended up with gumdrops stuck in her hair. Alex accidentally used the roof pieces for two of the walls, leaving her with pieces with windows for the roof. "Oh, no, your roof is ruined," Karen said sympathetically.

"Skylights!" Alex suggested, and this was greeted with hilarity by her classmates. Annetta decided she would use walls for the roof on purpose because she loved skylights. Donna, across the room, and her eight-year-old daughter Amanda, decided to try to saw a skylight into their already properly placed roof. The lady next to them looked alarmed when Donna pulled a complicated pocket knife out of her purse and said something vague about weapons in the store. Jonette rubbed her temples and attempted to regain control of the class. Soon there were four cottages with skylights, two with a dangerous weight of candies stuck on top, and four that, at least in the basic elements, still had a vague resemblance to the model at the front of the class.

Alex, Annetta, and Karen chatted for a while after class, sipping cocoa, and agreed they really must take another class together. The next one, in January, would be some sort of centerpiece decoration. "See you in January!" they called to Jonette, who smiled wanly as she scraped a layer of hardened frosting embedded with candies off one of the chairs.

The elf, on seeing Alex, bounced up and down and waved. "So glad you came! It looks beautiful! Hope you had fun!"

"I did." Alex smiled and held her creation just a little higher. On the way to the car, ten separate people stopped her to admire her gingerbread house. An older gentleman told her there were holes in the roof. His wife rolled her eyes and explained to her husband that the holes in the roof were skylights. "They were on purpose," the woman asserted as they walked away. "Anyone can see that! How creative!" Alex laughed as she carefully set the box on the floor of the car.

Back at home, the gingerbread house passed Joe's inspection. "It looks great, hon. But there are holes in the roof."

"Those are skylights," Alex said firmly. She decided not to mention that it had happened by accident, and that she'd pretty much caused chaos with the skylight idea.

"Will we be allowed it eat it?"

"Not yet, but, yes, of course." Alex frowned. "I'm not sure I want to eat something that's been sitting out. I mean, what about ants?"

"Ants don't eat much," Joe said.

Sandy looked up from her phone. "But some ants' saliva has chemicals that are irritants."

"I'm sure," her dad agreed cheerfully. "Irritants are everywhere." He winked at Alex. "How was the beach cleanup?"

"Great so far! We're meeting up tomorrow to do some more. How about it, Mom?"

Alex was carefully cutting card stock for gift tags. She pretended not to have heard. "Hmm?"

"The beach! Mom, the beach cleanup. We're going back out tomorrow, so you still have a chance."

"I didn't realize I had missed my chance." Alex carefully rounded the corners of a cardstock rectangle to soften it.

Sandy rolled her eyes. "Mom, come on. You're not doing anything." She failed to notice her mom's astonished face. "It'll be fun. Please come."

"For an hour or two, that's it," said Alex, and frowned when Joe kicked her under the table.

Alex changed her mind about the beach cleanup a number of times. Recalling the gingerbread house class felt good; thinking about going to the beach with Sandy and Rachel did not. She envisioned a vast expanse of beach, the murmur of soft surf and the cry of seabirds muffled by Sandy's hectoring, lecturing, and pointing imperiously at microscopic scraps of paper while a horde of huddled parents and well-intended teenagers gleaned trash with rubber gloves. Her jaw hurt every time she thought about it. *If I go just once, she'll leave me alone,* she thought, despite knowing that Sandy was not one to leave anything alone. But she hadn't wanted to go the gingerbread house class, and it had turned out okay. And it would be nice to spend time with Rachel, too.

Sandy and Rachel had met when they were three, the year the Bonhalls moved to Sunflower Beach for Joe's new teaching position and Alex dove into volunteering in Jonah's class. The girls locked into an instantaneous friendship, as small children often do, and were soon inseparable. Clothes and toys were shared indiscriminately, and both sets of parents sometimes found "new" items in the laundry and toy shelves. "Is this Rachel's?" Alex would ask, holding up a bright purple sweatshirt with a glittery unicorn. "Uh-huh," Sandy would answer, not even looking up. "She has my red one." At some point, they became obsessed with the idea that they were really twins. Cody and Kevin were old enough to just smile and shrug, and Matt was cheerfully accepting, but Jonah could not let it alone.

"You're ridiculous," he announced. "You can't be twins. Twins have to come out of the same mommy. That's how it works."

"We're twins," Rachel asserted, and Sandy finished, "Real twins. Really, really twins."

"You can't be." Jonah, at six, was furious at their violation of the rules of nature. He pointed imperiously at Rachel. "You have a mommy and a daddy." He turned on his sister. "And you have *my* mommy and daddy." He folded his arms. "Different mommies and daddies. You can't be twins."

"We were twins in heaven," Sandy told him confidently.

"Before we were even *born*," Rachel explained.

"That doesn't make sense," Jonah replied, but he sounded uncertain.

The adults looked at each other and shrugged. Who could argue with that? Who knew?

The twinship continued. Kevin heard the expression "soul sisters," and suggested it a few years later. They were soul sisters, but they were not just sisters, the girls insisted.

"Soul twins." Matt closed the subject, and so it was. Sandy and Rachel were the Soul Twins. They went through undergraduate school together, majoring in psychology, volunteering for the same graduate students' experiments and laughingly telling how they'd faked their responses to various questionnaires. Alex wondered about that; how often did miscreant, mischievous undergrads, required to participate in a research project as part of a course, skew what was presumed to be scientific data? On the other hand, Rachel and Sandy had had a tenuous relationship with hard science all their lives, beginning with their biology-defying twinship. They were usually inseparable, in agreement on almost everything, and able to burst into laughter that made no sense, and had no apparent context, to anyone within hearing.

Being with Sandy and Rachel always meant feeling a bit like an extra, just tagging along. While the beach cleanup was not as militant as she'd feared, it was hard on her back. Besides that, she had to put up with Sandy and Rachel's mindless pattering about what they observed. As far as Alex could determine, they were gung-ho for helping nature but not so big on understanding it.

It was a beautiful Sunday morning, with a cool breeze off the water and soft waves in the low tide. A typical Florida winter day in the fifties, but a few stalwart tourists were already lying out in the sun, determined to bring a tan, or a burn, back north. No locals would be at the beach in a swimsuit in this weather; they were all wearing sweatshirts. It was almost eleven in the morning, and the shadows of the houses still stretched onto the sand.

Sandy and Rachel kept pulling a bit ahead of Alex, picking up trash, complaining about people's piggishness and commenting on wildlife.

"It's not a seagull. It's a plover, for crying out loud." Alex finally burst after what seemed to be the twentieth misidentification of a bird in five minutes.

Rachel took no offense. "Cool, a plover. I like how they run." She looked up the dunes and pointed. "What's that?"

"A tern."

"And that?"

"A skimmer."

"I thought they were all seagulls."

Alex found it incredible that someone who had grown up near the beach didn't know a skimmer from a plover. She said, "Well, they're all coastal birds and it's easy enough to think of them as a family, isn't it?"

"It's great that your mom knows so much about birds! I didn't know that." She glanced at Alex. "I mean, Aunt Alex, I know you're all into feeding birds and everything, but I didn't know it was your thing."

"I wouldn't call it my thing," Alex began, but Sandy interrupted.

"Ugh, she's obsessed with them. Don't get her started. Let's go up toward the sea oats and look for trash there."

Don't get her started? Alex's jaw twinged. She waited to see if Rachel had more to say, but the friends hurried ahead, complaining about how many beer cans they'd found in the area they'd cleaned yesterday.

"Mom, keep up," Sandy tossed back.

Don't get me *started*, Alex thought, stooping to pick up a plastic cup. She threw the cup, hard, into her trash bag.

Chapter Fifteen

"How's the experiment in doing things going?"

"I am really enjoying some arts and crafts. It sounds stupid, but it's fun and relaxing to just make gift tags and a few note cards."

Dr. Sam tilted her head. "What part sounds stupid to you?"

"Well, not stupid. But, you know, kind of a waste of time. Or just maybe kind of old-fashioned."

"What makes this a waste of time?"

Alex shrugged and looked past Dr. Sam's head at the painting behind her. "Well, you know. I'm not accomplishing anything."

Dr. Sam folded her arms. "I thought you were making gift tags and note cards. Are you planning to use them?"

"Well, yes. Of course. I know. It's not a waste of time, then, per se, but it's so ... old-fashioned."

"And what's the problem with that? Have you noticed any particularly pleasant 'new-fashioned' stuff lately?" Dr. Sam asked, making finger quotes. "Maybe something I don't know about?"

"It's not a problem." Alex sat up a little straighter and looked straight at Dr. Sam. "I enjoy it."

Dr. Sam nodded. "Good. That's part of the point, isn't it? To create something beautiful, to enjoy doing it, and share that with other people?"

Somehow, when Dr. Sam described it, her gift tag making sounded … significant. Meaningful, even. "And I let Sandy talk me into going along on a beach cleanup, which was more fun than it might sound." Alex paused. "It was especially nice to see and hear the birds, and the water, and experience the light on a winter morning at the beach."

"Beautiful." Dr. Sam paused and looked at her curiously. "How often do you let yourself just go enjoy the beach?"

Alex shrugged. "Oh, once in a while." Dr. Sam's eyebrows went up. "Well, not for a long time. Maybe not since last spring, after the spring break when kids left town."

"What is it that keeps you from doing things you enjoy, or trying things that you might enjoy?"

"Oh, you know how it is. Work, family." Alex massaged her left jaw. She caught Dr. Sam's head tilt. *Oh, no,* she thought, reflexively steeling herself.

"Work is 37.5 hours a week for you. Your kids are grown. Your commute is short. And from what you've described, your husband and you are close and yet he finds time for his interests."

Just one big interest, Alex thought.

Dr. Sam went on. "And I wonder if you've noticed how you always end up rubbing your jaw when you're saying what you think I expect you to say. You know, like, 'work and family.'"

"It's not that," Alex protested. "I have a condition. Bruxism. I grind my teeth and this time of year, it's so bad that it feels like I need a root canal. Except the root canal pain floats around. That's why I came in the first place."

"I know, you came in for the stress underlying the bruxism. I want to understand, Alexa, really. I hear you. I also think that you might ultimately have less stress and less pain if you would not work so hard to hold back your words." A pause. "So, tell me what you really think about what I just said. Not what you think I want to hear from you."

Alex was silent for a long time. Dr. Sam just sat there, quietly waiting. Alex opened her mouth and her jaw made a weird popping sound. She tried to ignore the pop and the slowly building tension in her chest. "It feels massively unfair, like you're one more person telling me this is all my fault, that I'm the bad one, the ridiculous one, the one who should change."

"I'm sorry that is what you got out of that, Alexa, because that was not my intention. Having the power to make a situation different is not the same as holding responsibility. That's like blaming the fire-fighters when they show up to put out a fire. In your case, you get some responsibility. You are kindhearted and generous, and reluctant to step on other people's toes. These are good qualities, and they are sometimes biting you in the butt—well, maybe hitting you in the jaw, in your particular case—because you erroneously expect others to consistently behave in kind."

"And they don't."

"No, I imagine they very often do not." Dr. Sam paused. "Your look ahead, your writing about 'in six months,' it looks like you're coming into some useful information. Being outdoors, being in nature, time to do art." Dr. Sam waved the notebook. "What pieces of this can you really start doing already? And what parts can you start sowing seeds for?"

"Well, I sort of am already. And I was looking at art catalogues ..." Alex's voice trailed off.

"I said sowing seeds, not browsing the seed catalogues. Sign up for an art course. Look at places to go and start gathering real information. Talk about it to someone so you have a partner in crime, so to speak. Stop thinking about thinking about it." Dr. Sam shrugged. "Or don't and be resentful at everyone you love."

Alex wiped her eyes. "You're making it sound easy. But it's not so easy."

Dr. Sam nodded kindly. "It's not easy. You're right. But it's really, really important. You know no one is going to walk up to the front door and say, 'Ta-da! Here's your late-middle-age life, just as you've always dreamed.' It's going to take work."

The conversation continued. Dr. Sam suggested Alex continue her journal, do things she enjoys, and consider letting one or two truly trustworthy people serve as a kind of accountability partner as she experimented in doing those things.

Alex said she would try. Dr. Sam raised an eyebrow.

"Trying sounds like a prepared excuse."

"Okay." Alex sighed. "I will. I'll keep doing what I've been doing, and I'll try to figure out an accountability partner or two."

"I look forward to hearing how it goes."

Chapter Sixteen

My late-middle-aged life.

Well, that sounds un-promising, which is probably not even a word. Okay, well, fair enough. If I live to be ninety, then middle-middle age would have been 45, which seems like a long time ago sometimes. Fine. Well, my late-middle-aged life. What did I imagine? I don't know if I even imagined anything but maybe I sort of expected stuff. I expected grandchildren and that they would be nearby, and I could be hands-on and be involved. I think I sort of expected that Joe and I would do more together, like hiking or camping or just going to the state parks. Not just fishing, fishing, and more fishing. Nothing against his fishing. I just haven't figured out how to get better at doing what I want. I think I sort of imagined that I would have more time to do what I like doing, sort of that pre-retirement ramping up of hobbies so they can be avocations. How come other people manage this and I don't?

My late-middle-aged life

I'm supposed to have an accountability partner and I keep putting off asking Joe. He's the logical choice but I know what he'll do. He'll confuse accountability partner with coach and planner-in-chief and the next thing I know he'll have swept us off on some plan that he thinks is just perfect. And no one will remember to ask me what I think.

Maybe I can just be my own accountability partner in the journal. Like make a list of tasks and see if I can follow through on them, checking them off. I don't see why that can't work. On the other hand, I've written down "clean out the closets" every month for the past five years, at least, since Elsa gave me that book on tidying up. Ha, at this point it's more like Swedish death cleaning. But that's not really funny.

Chapter Seventeen

The Osprey

The osprey is a coastal bird of prey, with dark brown upper plumage, a white underside, and dramatic black and white markings on its face and head. It can appear very stern. Its vision is impressive, and it often locates its prey underwater from far above the surface.

Letting Joe know about the homework should have been easy; she'd let him know about Dr. Sam before the first phone call and, except for a circumspect "How was your appointment?" he had been very unintrusive. She'd shared some generalities, the need to do some thinking, perhaps some journaling, and Joe had neither probed nor, as she feared, given further instructions. Still, Alex found herself putting off the conversation. She told herself that there hadn't been time, but, of course, there had been. When she sat down with herself and her journal, she realized she was afraid: afraid that having an accountability partner meant there was no turning back, although what that meant she didn't quite understand, even when she wrote it down. She was supposed to be going toward what she wanted, so being discouraged from turning back should have been something appealing.

She also was afraid that Joe would get so excited about it that he would overrun her with suggestions, barreling through with good ideas that were not her ideas, like taking an art class at the local art center with Sandy. She thought, gratefully, that at least Sandy, after an initial flare of interest, had seemingly forgotten the idea. There was no counting on that, though; Sandy could, at any time, burst into the kitchen waving the course catalogue and announcing they had to, absolutely had to, sign up for some particular course and, well, could they loan her the fee for the class? And the supplies? Just thinking about having more of other people's plans imposed on her made her jaw hurt. *Maybe later*, she told herself firmly. After supper, when they were relaxing in the living room—that would be a nice, quiet time to talk with Joe.

Two days went by while Alex kept putting off a simple conversation. The morning chats over coffee seemed the wrong time, while they each previewed the day ahead and discussed the schedule for the weekend. Two days of dinner prep, with Sandy in and out, felt too risky; she'd started to speak and then, when interrupted, had gratefully ceded the floor. Once, Sandy had asked what she'd been saying before Sandy interrupted, and she'd deflected to, "Oh, nothing important, just blathering about the day."

She felt increasingly embarrassed at her own timidity, which seemed to make it harder, not easier, to speak up. By dinner preparation time on the third day, she was angry enough at herself to be aggressive in chopping vegetables for salad. Bits of yellow pepper bounced off the cutting board in every direction. She caught herself, looked up at the ceiling, and took a deep breath. And another.

"So ... Dr. Sam suggested I need accountability partners," she said, a little too casually. "Tomato on your salad?"

"Yes, to tomato. Accountability for what?" Joe was tending steaks under the broiler. He turned, looking concerned. "Is there some sort of ... problem?"

"Problem?" Alex's voice climbed a bit. It felt accusatory.

"You know. Problem, like, some sort of, well." Joe hesitated. "Like an addiction? I mean, I don't think you're addicted to anything. But usually an accountability partner means there's a problem."

Alex chopped at a green pepper as if it were a mortal enemy. "No, no problem. It's for my homework. Which is to do things I enjoy or try things I might enjoy."

"Ah. Like the gift tags?" Joe opened the dish cabinet. "Will Sandy be here for supper?"

"Her group has a meeting. Something about debriefing on the outcome of the artificial snow protest." Alex sprinkled some cheese on the salads. "Yes, the gift tags were part of that."

"And the beach cleanup?"

Alex frowned. "It didn't start that way but there were definitely some good moments in there."

"What about a class at the art center? Given that any thought? I think it would be good for you."

Alex nodded, put the salads on the table and went out to the deck to put out some sunflower seeds. "Hello, little friends," she said. She thought about being told what was good for her and rubbed her jaw. Going back in, she went into the kitchen to make up plates with Joe.

"What else is on the agenda with that counselor?" Joe asked.

"Not sure. I guess it's a series of little experiments." Alex paused. "What do you think?"

"I think it's great. I think it's time for you to have more fun doing what you like to do."

Alex thought miserably that if she knew how to manage to do what she wanted to do, she'd feel less lost. She shrugged. "I do a lot of what I like to do. I guess it's time to ramp it up and be more ... definite about it."

Joe looked up quizzically. "I don't see you doing a lot of what you like to do." He speared a morsel of steak and examined it with satisfaction. "It seems you mostly work. And then come here and work. Or just sort of drift."

"Drift." Alex put down her fork and placed her hands on the table as if it were a piano. "I'm not drifting."

"Oh, honey. Don't get annoyed. You know what I mean."

"No, no, I don't. Drifting? You think everything that gets done around here is just 'drifting'?"

"I'm sorry. You know I don't mean that. I mean, you have a bunch of interests and it seems that what you would like to do always ends up last. Never a priority. You never say no. Look at that outing with Gloria the other weekend; was that your idea of a good time? No, but you just went along with it, like with Jonah's dogs, and Sandy."

Alex took a deep breath, silently telling herself to slow down. "Right, I know. I put everyone's everything first." She wondered, briefly, if Joe would recognize himself in that 'everyone.'

"And I'm glad you're finally taking some time to think about what you'd like to do." Joe nodded, apparently to himself, and Alex was surprised at the twinge of resentment she felt.

"Yes, I am." Alex stabbed a bite of steak. She didn't want this particular topic to continue because she was close to losing patience. "Now, about your sabbatical ..."

Joe was expansive about his plans, debating how a road trip could be broken down to maximize the time spent during the good weather up north. They were clearing dishes when the phone rang. Alex looked at the number and her heart sank.

"It's Gloria."

"Go ahead and answer it. I'll finish the cleanup."

Gloria was full of news. "How are you? Oh, it's been such a week already! I can't believe how much is going on, so much good news to tell!"

"Wonderful."

"Matt and Tim sold their condo and bought a house, and it's zoned so they can have their office on one side."

"Is that the split plan they were looking at, the one just a couple of miles from you?"

"Yes, it's a lovely neighborhood and very close."

"That's great; I know they wanted the extra space and that will save them on overhead."

Gloria charged onward. "Cody is really enjoying his new position at the dental clinic nearby. That's the one you go to, right? Maybe you'll see him there sometime." Alex silently gave thanks for Cody's discretion. "Oh, and his twins are in the Christmas pageant at church. So are Kevin and Veronica's little ones. We're having such fun!"

"We?"

"Well, I'm the director this year," Gloria explained. "Didn't I mention that last weekend? Last year's director's kids were finally all either too big or too busy and they needed someone to step in. So of course, I made myself available."

Of course you did, Alex thought, and then felt guilty. The children's Christmas pageant was part of the Christmas Eve Mass every year and much enjoyed by the congregation, partly because the children were adorable and partly because the pageant replaced the homily.

"It's been so much fun to be involved in that again—haven't been part of this since Rachel was an angel back in third grade. You remember, right?"

"Yes, Sandy was a shepherd. She mostly bossed around the littler kids who were sheep."

Gloria laughed. "Well, both girls grew up to be bossy angels, didn't they?"

Bossy angels, Alex mused. Interesting. "I guess you could say so."

"What have you been up to?" Gloria asked. "Rachel mentioned you were on the beach cleanup."

"Yes, I was. It was nice. Mostly." Alex paused. "And I've made some time for crafts."

"Such as?"

"Well, it sounds kind of funny and old-fashioned, but I'm having a lot of fun making handmade gift tags for Christmas."

"How nice for you. That sounds relaxing."

"It is. I guess it's time for me to make more time for things I enjoy." Alex wondered how a word like "nice" could sound so offensive. *Why does everything I do get reduced to "nice"?* She wondered what it would be like to just throw "nice" at people. Oh, director of the pageant? How nice for you. A sabbatical to go fishing? How nice for you. Your daughter has a smart, handsome boyfriend with a charming accent? How nice for you. She took a deep breath and tried to focus on Gloria, who was explaining things in her clear, clipped way.

"Well, of course. I mean, you're not retired but you don't have a houseful of kids. It's important to branch out. We women put ourselves on the back burner and then forget to take ourselves off it."

Alex couldn't imagine Gloria ever being on the back burner. She pictured Gloria in front of a stove with every burner going full blast, pointing and giving strident instructions in all directions. Gloria had always been in charge, managing everyone like she ran her kindergarten classes. Alex shook her head, remembering how Gloria had encouraged her to get involved at the school, and then go finish her education. *For all her bossiness, she's been such a good friend.*

"Well, it's kind of a little project for me," Alex admitted. "Just pushing myself a bit. Joe is going to be my accountability partner." She immediately slapped her forehead.

As she expected, Gloria swooped. "Accountability partner! Of course. I'll be your best advocate, honey, you know that. I think it's a great idea. Otherwise, you'll keep wasting your time cleaning up after Sandy and walking those pampered dogs for the rest of your life." Gloria had an ability to speak as if taking a breath were a waste of time. "Jonah and Beth are fully capable of running their household. It's your turn, Alexa."

The conversation was sliding sideways. Gloria was right, of course – ever ready to defend her and then direct her. "Enough about me," Alex said, more loudly than she intended. She caught Joe looking at her, questioning, and shook her head at him. "Tell me more about the Christmas pageant."

An even worse turn, because Gloria was never one to miss an opportunity. "Of course! The pageant. Perfect. You need to do more fun things and I could use the help. You have no idea what it's like to run a pageant with four of your grandchildren in it."

Alex winced and took a deep breath. "The idea is not for me to just do things other people think are fun," she ventured, but Gloria kept talking.

"Not to mention all those other kids! And the parents. They haven't gotten any better over the years, but I can handle them."

I'm sure you can, Alex thought, and rubbed her jaw.

Eventually she got off the phone, feeling dazed, and sat in the living room across from Joe.

"That sounded arduous," he said.

"That's the word. At least one of the words." Alex paused. "And apparently, I'm now the assistant director for the church Christmas pageant."

Chapter Eighteen

December 5

I'm not even sure what the point of this is. I'm so angry with myself I can't think straight. I can't believe I let Gloria know about anything I'm doing for myself.

I'm angry.

I'm angry at Dr. Sam for calling me out about my jaw pain.

I'm angry at myself for not saying no to Jonah and Beth.

I'm angry at Gloria for rubbing it in about her four grandchildren when I have four grand-dogs and she knows it hurts me.

I'm angry at myself because of course Gloria's happy about the kids. Who wouldn't be? I'm mean and petty.

I'm angry at myself because Gloria has always encouraged me. I'm just not sure she'd encourage me now.

December 6

Christmas pageant rehearsal after work tomorrow. Not sure what that has to do with trying things I like to do or might like to do.

I want to stay home and make gift tags.

I want to sit and watch the birds come and go.

Maybe I can buy a birdfeeder for Matt and Tim as a housewarming gift. I wish Matt and Tim were my kids. I envy Gloria those two. Being around them feels peaceful and easy, no judgments, no harshness. Why do people have to be so mean? So difficult to be around? Okay, so "I want," I want to have nice children, the kind you can be proud of and laugh with and not constantly hedge what to say.

I want Joe to listen to me. Really listen, and not get excited and take over.

December 8

I want to quit my job.

I want to win the lottery and move away. Maybe not tell anyone where I'm going. Okay, of course Joe can come. And we'll tell the kids, but it will be far enough away that they won't be able to dump dogs and bills on us.

I want to have time to do things I enjoy. And yeah, I know, I bet Dr. Sam will ask why I don't have any time to do things I enjoy? And the answer is, I don't know, there's just always something. That's all.

In six months

In six months, I will be on sabbatical. And I will be doing art and learning more about birds and not doing so many things I don't like doing. I'm going to do this. I promise myself. Can I be my own accountability partner? Maybe. But that probably won't count for Dr. Sam. I'm supposed to be doing things already. I'm going to go ahead and start looking at classes and at places to go. That idea of a cabin in the woods, that still sounds awfully good. And quiet. Maybe some water nearby; that makes for good painting and good birding.

Chapter Nineteen

The church hall was full of activity, and Gloria stood, hands on her hips, in the middle of it all, tall and clear-voiced. A few parents were wrestling with the props—a makeshift stable that was barely three-dimensional, a cardboard star covered with foil to be hung from a fishing pole during the pageant at Christmas Eve Mass. A man and a woman were arguing heatedly regarding the respective virtues of the type of fishing line for the job. Two younger moms were fussing with their children's costumes and taking pictures of their little lambs. One of the little lambs kept clobbering the other two with a shepherd's crook.

One of the younger moms was Veronica, Gloria's daughter-in-law and mother of two of the lambs. The violent lamb was one of hers and Veronica was not amused. The other mother was even less amused.

"Bobby! Put the shepherd's crook down and come stand by your sister and Jamie."

Alex stepped next to Veronica. "The usual chaos in the flock?" she joked.

Veronica rolled her eyes. "Oh, yeah, you know how Bobby can be. I just want to get some good pictures! How hard should that be? Alicia—is Jamie okay?"

Alicia was Jamie's mom. She was rubbing his head with the look of a woman trying hard to appear calm. "He's got a bump. From being hit in the head."

"Oh, sorry." Veronica looked abashed. "Bobby! Come over here and apologize to Jamie this instant."

"Baa! Baa! Sorry!" Bobby said. "I'm a sorry sheep!"

Alex sidled away. Gloria caught sight of her. "Alexa! You're here! Excellent!" Gloria scanned the melee around her. "I need the Magi and the kids who are carrying the camel. Can you round them up and bring them to that corner in the back? They need to practice processing."

The camel kids were always the oldest—one for the head, one for the hump, both inside a large, heavy costume that had been old and musty twenty-five years ago. Alex suspected they were the ones outside and stuck her head out the door. "Are you two walking the camel this year?"

The younger one said, "Yup. Does she want us in there?" She, no doubt, was Gloria.

"Yes, we have to practice processing."

Alex went to look for the Magi. She spotted two of them easily: Sean, Cody's son, and Jamie's older brother, Max. They were in costume, dragging robes on the floor. Sean kept tipping his turban off center, and Max's crown was down to the bridge of his nose.

"Hi, Sean. I see you're a Magi this year."

"Yup. So is Max. And Marta." Marta, his twin, was nowhere to be seen.

"Nice," Alex said. "Hi, Max. Where's Marta?"

Sean rolled his eyes. "In the supply closet."

"The supply closet?"

"Yeah." Sean squinted as his turban slipped forward over one eye.

"Why is she in there?" Alex scanned the parish center; the supply closet door was shut.

"She's upset." Sean took his turban off and studied it. "She's hiding from Grandma."

"She doesn't want to be in a possession," Max offered.

"Ah." Alex nodded. "A procession." She could imagine that—neither Marta nor Sean was particularly outgoing. "Does Grandma know?"

"Yes. No. Marta tried to say something but Grandma didn't listen." Sean pulled the turban on low, like a ski cap, and peered around the room.

Alex sighed. "Okay. You guys wait here. I'll go fetch Marta."

Alex went to the supply closet, tapped at the door, and stepped in. Marta was sitting on the floor, drowning in brocade, holding her cardboard crown. She looked up bleakly, tears on her cheeks. "Aunt Alex."

"Hey, little one. What's going on?"

Marta snuffled and said, "I don't want to be in a possession."

Squatting beside Marta, Alex corrected her without thinking. "Procession, uh-huh. I can see that. So why are you a Magi?"

"Grandma decided."

It figures, Alex thought. "Did you tell her you don't want to be a Magi?" she asked, rubbing Marta's back. The flocked velvet left loose threads on Alex's hand; she wondered if this costume were even older than the camel.

Marta gave her a sidelong look. "It doesn't matter. Grandma *decided*."

"I see." That sounded about right to Alex. "What did you want to be?"

"A shepherd. Or an angel. Someone who didn't have to be in a possession." A pause. "I don't like walking in front of everyone through the whole church."

Alex nodded. "I wouldn't either."

They sat quietly. Marta played with the tassel of her brocade robe, twisting her face for a while before speaking very quietly. "I wouldn't mind being part of the camel, maybe, but I'm too short. The bigger kids get to be the camel. No one stares at them." She paused. "Well, everyone stares, but they can't tell because they're inside the camel. So it doesn't bother them." She looked into Alex's face, and finished, "But it bothers me."

"Maybe we can explain to Grandma," Alex suggested, with a little more cheer than she felt. Her jaw throbbed. Marta sucked in her lips and looked away. "Maybe I can explain," Alex corrected herself. "I'm sure Grandma just thought being a Magi was special, and you'd enjoy it."

Marta shrugged. Alex, rising, reached out her hand. Marta took it and stood with her. "Tell you what," Alex said, with more confidence than she felt. "Why don't you go meet with Sean, Max, and the camel, and I'll go talk to Grandma."

They stepped out of the supply closet. It was too late. Gloria had cornered the Magi procession members and waved her arms broadly upon seeing Marta. "There you are! Where have you been? We have to rehearse. Marta, you're the tallest, so I want you in the very front of the procession, then Sean, and then Max, and then the camel. Here you go, right here," she said, as the reluctant Marta was almost lifted into position.

"Gloria, a word with you," Alex said quietly. Gloria glanced over but was busily straightening out Sean's cloak. "Gloria, a word." Alex beckoned, stepping away from the children. Gloria sighed and followed.

"What is it?" she asked irritably. "I really could use a hand here, Alexa. I asked you to help me, not visit with the children." Gloria's eyes scanned the entire room even while they spoke, on the lookout for any hint of disorder.

Alex swallowed hard and spoke quietly, mindful of the children nearby. "Gloria, Marta doesn't want to be one of the Magi. She wants a ... less showy role. A shepherd, maybe. Don't we have a shepherd who would enjoy being a Magi? Maybe a tall, extroverted shepherd?"

Gloria's lips pressed together, and her eyebrows gathered. She looked more like an eagle than ever. "Oh, honestly. Marta wants to be a Magi," she said, turning. "Don't you, Marta?"

Marta looked from Alex to Gloria and back. Alex shook her head gently and smiled encouragingly. Marta shook her head back.

"No, Grandma. I want to be a shepherd. I don't like *processions.*"

Gloria threw up her hands in annoyance. "Oh, honestly. A big fuss about nothing. It's an honor to be one of the Magi! For heaven's sake." She scoured the noisy room and began flapping her arms broadly. "Jolie! Jolie! Come here." A shepherd, about twelve, came over hesitantly, looking uneasy. Gloria put her hands on her hips. "Jolie, I need for you to be a Magi. Marta wants to be a shepherd. She doesn't want to be a Magi. Swap costumes, okay? And since you're taller than Sean and Max, you can be first in the procession."

"Really?" smiled Jolie, looking relieved. "I had to be a shepherd three years in a row already. Thanks, Marta." She was completely sincere, oblivious to the family drama that had unfolded. "Are you sure you don't mind?"

"No, thank you!" said Marta and glanced anxiously at her grandmother. Gloria, however, had moved on to putting the camel in order. Marta beamed at Alex.

Alex made the barest nod, and then turned her attention to the sheep, where yet another fight had broken out. This time, Jamie had the shepherd's crook.

The next day was the actual "rehearsal," the first day being a messy process of assigning roles, readjusting them, and trying to keep parents from, in Gloria's words, interfering with the process. Alex suspected that, based on the number of pointed remarks about keeping the process "orderly," her intervention on Marta's behalf was not appreciated.

Marta, on the other hand, was happily holding her shepherd's crook, smiling and looking downward, and occasionally having to jerk the crook away from the grasping hooves of her cousin Bobby. Bobby was not likely to be promoted to shepherd next year, as he took too much pleasure in smacking the other sheep.

Alex busied herself with small details: the drooping, loose fringe on the camel's costume, the inevitably tilted halos on the angels. She was using duct tape to mend a bent wing when Cody appeared at her side.

"Need some help?"

"Yes, thanks—an extra pair of hands would be great. I can't hold this in place and cut the tape at the same time."

"Thanks for helping Marta yesterday."

Alex looked up and raised her eyebrows.

"She told me what happened. About wanting to change roles."

"Yes, poor little thing. Did she tell you she was hiding in the supply closet?"

Cody nodded. "Didn't surprise me. Neither of the kids has a thing for being the center of attention. Thank God."

"Amen to that," Alex agreed, and then flushed. It sounded like a put-down of their mom, and it hadn't been intended that way. "Sorry, Cody."

"No offense. I know what you mean. I'm not a big 'steal the show' guy myself."

"Me neither," Alex replied.

Marta rushed up, hugged her dad, and grinned at Alex. "Hi, Aunt Alex!"

Alex beamed back. "How are you, Marta? Keeping your cousins in line over there?"

"Oh, yes! I like being a shepherd. Even though Bobby is a really bad sheep."

"I'm sure you make an excellent shepherd. I think you'd make a great angel, too."

Marta tilted her head. "I bet if I was an angel, Grandma would make me be the one who does all the talking. So, I think I'll just be a shepherd."

"Sounds like a plan," her father said, catching Alex's glance as they shared a smile.

Chapter Twenty

"So, how are things going, Alexa? What's been different since we met?" Dr. Sam smiled encouragingly.

Different? Alex frowned. "Well, apparently I am the assistant director of the church's Christmas pageant. The one they do during the service on Christmas Eve."

"Oh? That sounds interesting."

"I guess so, but it wasn't quite my idea. Gloria kind of pushed me into it."

"The shopping and manicure Gloria?"

"Yes."

"She sounds ... persuasive."

"Ha! Persuasive like some sort of raptor. She's like an eagle, overseeing everything, scowling, and then she starts flapping her arms and making that face and—"

"Eagle?"

Alex sighed and looked off to the side, studying Dr. Sam's diplomas on the wall. "Well, there's this thing that I do ... with birds."

"And?"

"And I kind of describe people as birds. In my head, I mean. No one really knows I do this. Well, Joe does. But no one else. It's not just how they look; it's how they behave."

"Interesting. And Gloria's an eagle?"

"Oh, yes. Actually, in her case, she's sort of like that blue puppet from the kid's show. But a real eagle would work. Maybe an osprey? She makes that face." Alex knit her brows, leaned forward and pressed her lips together. "And you know you're in for it. She always seems to be scanning the scene."

"Ah. Any other birds?"

"Ha! Just about everyone's a bird. I look up so much about birds that my phone's newsfeed sent me notification that a university is advertising for an ornithologist. Apparently, I'm a bit of a bird freak."

"That sounds quite interesting, actually. How do you decide? Which bird for which person, I mean."

"Mostly by behavior, over time. You'd be surprised how complex birds are. It's fascinating."

"Any examples of people–bird pairings you'd care to share?"

"Okay ... well, Joe is an owl, of course. He's smart and a little unusual, and he either has a lot to say or not much at all. And even his throwaways are interesting and useful. Like owl puke."

Dr. Sam's eyebrows shot up.

Alex grimaced. "Owls vomit up pellets that have the skeletal pieces and other indigestible parts from their meals. They can be dried, sanitized, and used for science lessons. You dig out the little bones and figure out what they've been eating." She paused. "Kids love it. At least some kids."

"Oh, I see. That makes sense."

"And Sandy—Cassandra, our daughter—she's a blue jay. Bossy, but she sticks with her own. Lots to say and she broadcasts it in every direction. She's always looking for danger and wanting to get a group on the problem, like how blue jays will mob a bird of prey to drive it away, for example."

"So, is this just entertainment? Or does this help you somehow?"

Alex frowned. "I guess it helps me ... have more to learn. And it's a kind of shorthand for me, in my head. 'Oh, another blue jay,' and then I can relax and have a sense of what to expect."

"And what about you?"

"I used to think I was a sparrow, but I changed my mind." Dr. Sam nodded, and Alex continued. "Because apparently sparrows tend to do very well around people. They're very adaptive. And I, clearly, am not doing very well around people. And adapting is not my strong suit. So, the sparrow idea went." She paused. "I thought about crows; they stick with their family group and help out over generations. Last year's chicks grow up and help their parents with the latest hatchlings. But crows are right out there when they're not happy about something. I mean, you never have to wonder. That's not me." Alex paused and looked straight at Dr. Sam. "I can't really decide. Maybe I'm more of a burrowing owl."

Dr. Sam smiled quizzically. "So, you think of yourself as a bird that lives in the ground, mostly stays on the ground—one that *could* fly, but somehow usually does not?"

Alex shrugged. "I suppose that's about right, isn't it?"

Dr. Sam looked up and off to one side, a look that Alex had learned to recognize as the "thinking hard face" and had come to dread. It usually ended with words that were spoken very gently but were challenging, sometimes terrifyingly so. The silence stretched. Then Dr. Sam looked straight at Alex, smiling. "So, let's play with this, your knowledge of birds and how they're a kind of shorthand for you in figuring out the lay of the land. Let's say you were a blue jay, like Sandy. How would that change things? What would I notice was different if you came in and were a blue jay instead of a burrowing owl?"

Alex's eyes darted about and then settled on her hands, which she had started to wring. "I suppose I'd speak up for myself, right off. No bashfulness about it, maybe a bit brazen. I'd still take care of my flock, so to speak, but I wouldn't be pushed around." She paused and started to smile.

"What's funny?"

"Oh, just thinking. Blue jay parents, when the fledglings are mostly grown, will sometimes push them to be independent by refusing to feed them. I mean, the fledglings can fly and are eating just fine, and they see the parent, who is hardly bigger than they are, and do the helpless baby bird routine."

"That sounds like fun to see."

"Oh, that's not the funny part. The funny part is when the parent decides not to feed them. They hop around, facing away from the fledgling, and give a little tail feather wiggle. So I was, well, picturing doing that to Sandy. Hopping around and wiggling my"—Alex looked down at her lower half—"tail feathers, so to speak." She rolled her eyes. "What a picture!"

Dr. Sam laughed. "What would she do? Sandy? If you just said, 'Oh, Sandy! For goodness' sake,' and did a little hop and wiggled your butt?"

"It would be like this." Still seated, Alex leaned forward, wiggled her bottom, and flapped her bent arms like wings. She laughed. "Oh, I guess Sandy would be struck speechless, at least for a few seconds, for the first time ever."

"It sounds as if it could be worth it." Dr. Sam tilted her head. "And Joe? What would be different in your interactions with him, if you were a blue jay instead of a burrowing owl?"

Alex took a deep breath. "I'd speak up. I'd squawk, so to speak, if he tried to take over every conversation."

"So, I'm Joe. You be you, as a blue jay, and start talking about your sabbatical."

Alex stared past Dr. Sam's head at the landscape painting. "Joe, I've been thinking about my sabbatical."

"That sounded kind of burrowed. As in, from deep in one, Alexa."

Alex sighed. "I hate role play."

"Just humor me. I think it might help."

"Ok." She took a deep breath and looked straight at Dr. Sam. "Joe, I've been thinking a lot about the sabbatical I have this coming school year."

"Yes," said Dr. Sam, lowering her voice and tucking her chin back. "I have, too! Won't it be fun to go up and down the seaboard, learning about fishing?"

"Yes. No. Wait." Alex caught herself. "No, Joe, I meant my sabbatical, not yours. I don't want to learn about fishing."

"Yes, it will be fun, and I'm sure you'll find lots of time to sketch or whatever," Dr. Sam continued in her fake Joe voice. "Imagine the historical sites! The beautiful terrain! Learning more about how the terrain and conditions informed the fishing habits of indigenous peoples."

My gosh, she's good, Alex thought. *Does she know Joe?* she wondered, racking her brain for Joe having mentioned seeing a therapist. She was sure he hadn't mentioned it, but there was that remark about all his coworkers having one.

Dr. Sam was still talking. "And of course, at some point, Bob and Gloria will join us for a while." She winked at Alex.

"Oh, no," Alex interrupted. "No, that's it. That's where I draw the line."

"Where? When I described your passion for art as sketching, or when your imaginary sabbatical was turning into one more vacation stuck with Gloria?" Dr. Sam asked, in her own voice.

"The whole thing. The sketching. As if my art degree was an experience in doodling. We met at an art opening, after all. And babysitting Gloria and cleaning up after everyone ... the whole thing." Alex paused. "Have you met Joe? Because you nailed him."

Dr. Sam smiled and shrugged. "Thanks, but no, except for your stories, no Joe. But I think I've met people like Joe." She waited a breath. "Well? How was being a blue jay? Care to keep practicing?"

"I didn't do so well. I sort of froze up." Alex sighed and pulled at her sleeves. "I guess I need practice."

"So, let's go." Dr. Sam paused. "Now I'm Sandy. Mom, you never do anything." Dr. Sam's voice changed pitch again, this time higher and just slightly whiny. "I mean, you just putter around. You need to find meaning! Purpose! Why don't you come with me and Rachel to the sea turtle meeting on Tuesday night? It's not like you're going to be doing anything."

Alex frowned. "Well, Sandy, thanks for insulting me."

"Huh?" Dr. Sam tried a vacuous stare, but her reading glasses fell from the edge of her forehead onto the bridge of her nose, landing askew. Dr. Sam just poked them back up and kept trying to look blank.

"You know you just insulted me, saying I never do anything here. Maybe you should stick around and help out, then you'd notice what actually happens."

"I don't mean chores and everything. I mean, you know, stuff that matters."

"You seem to think food and clean clothes matter. How do you think they get here?"

Dr. Sam rolled her eyes and made an exaggerated sigh. "Ugh, Mom. You're so oversensitive."

Alex stepped out of role play to lean forward and say, "Okay, well, have you met *her*? Because this is creepily accurate."

Dr. Sam shook her head, smiling, and went on, in her slightly singsong Sandy voice. "I mean, Mom, seriously. You just sit around, reading old books and listening to old music. The world is falling apart and you're reading Jane Astin."

"Austen, for crying out loud, Jane Austen," Alex said tersely, feeling her temper rise. "Maybe you're not one to judge having a meaningful life, Sandy, not until you're a real grownup and independent."

"Mom! You know I try. I mean, tutoring doesn't pay much."

"I hear you. So, apply for some full-time jobs."

Dr. Sam leaned back and folded her arms, grinning. "Nice! Too bad you waited to really get annoyed until Jane Austen was slighted. I'd like to see you get there when you're the one being insulted."

Alex smiled shyly and looked down. "Yeah, I'm kind of a book nerd, I guess. But it did feel good."

"Did it feel better than flying from fence post to fence post and otherwise sticking close to the ground, or going for invisible and underground?"

"Yes. Yes, it did." She looked up at Dr. Sam. "I hear homework coming."

"Well, since you're on a roll with this, maybe add to the journaling and fun things for yourself a little active work at being a blue jay, or something, besides your very comfortable, safe burrowing owl."

"I can try." Alex shook her head and added, "No, I will. I will do those things."

"Well done."

It didn't occur to Alex until much later to be a bit surprised at how much Dr. Sam knew about burrowing owls.

Chapter Twenty-One

Mourning Doves

These small, mostly gray birds are adaptable, and may mate for life. They defend their territory but are otherwise unaggressive. Their soft, sad sounding call, as if "woo-wooing" to their mate, is easily identified.

Final grades were in, and the quiet week and a half before Christmas was finally here. Alex and Joe had little to do but savor the days and get through the looming Christmas pageant.

Saturday morning Joe and Bob were going fishing with Matt and Tim. Bob didn't work Saturdays anymore; Kevin, his and Gloria's second son, was slowly taking over the optometry practice. Bob had told Alex and Joe that easing into fewer days' work was part of his preparation for retirement. He thought he'd gradually lighten his load, letting Kevin learn about the practice, maybe hire another optometrist, and

Bob could just fill in here and there. Meanwhile, Gloria had ideas about retirement as well as the proper use of free time, and Bob generally looked pleasant and placid as she described her expectations to anyone with them when the topic arose. Bob had been transitioning for five years.

Gloria had plans, mostly for Bob. He was, she asserted, going to finally put the garage in order. He would start exercising and minding his blood sugar. She had ideas about him taking over part of childcare and joining her in doing science lessons for the kids. "And not baking soda volcanoes," she'd say grimly. "We expect more!" Alex wondered what Bob actually thought of all Gloria's ideas. She suspected there was a clear connection between Gloria's elaborate plans for him and his snail's pace approach toward retirement.

Matt and Tim needed the break from organizing their new home and office, so they were joining Joe and Bob for fishing.

Bob, Matt, and Tim all arrived to pick up Joe, before sunrise.

Alex had coffee ready. "How are you guys? Looking forward to the day?" She tilted a cheek toward them, and each one gave her a quick hug and kiss on the cheek before taking the proffered mug.

"Thanks, Aunt Alex," Matt said, curling his hands around his steaming mug. "This is awesome. We haven't found the coffeemaker just yet; it's been instant coffee all week."

Tim shrugged. "But we'll dig it out eventually. Thanks, this is perfect. It's going to be a great day." Tim shook his hair out of his eyes. He had had the same floppy, longish bangs since college, and with his pale hair and eyes, at first glance he still looked more like a teenaged surfer than an accountant.

Bob sat down with a sigh. "Coffee! Thanks, Alex, just how I like it."

Alex shook her head. "Too much cream and sugar. You know what Gloria would say."

Bob shrugged. "It's my sugar, not hers."

Alex turned to Matt and Tim. "How's the move been going? Are you loving the house? The neighborhood?"

Matt grinned. "It's been so easy to separate the one end, the bedroom, bath, and spare room, into office space for the accounting practice." He took a sip of coffee. "The screen room being there meant the separate entry way was simple. It's a nice, screened-in foyer for the business."

"And the neighbors are great," Tim volunteered. "We've met all the adjoining neighbors, and the people on the other side of each of them." He tapped his belly, flat under a loose sweatshirt. "The food's been great, too."

"Are they bringing casseroles and stuff?" Alex asked.

Matt shook his head. "No, this neighborhood is even more old-fashioned. We've had a get-to-know-you meal with each of them in the past two weeks."

"We're going to reciprocate with a thank-you cookout during the latter part of the holidays, probably when Grandpa Quinn's visiting. He'll love it." Tim smiled. "There are a couple of older ladies who will probably have their eye on him."

Bob grunted. "Good luck with that." His father was notoriously a confirmed single since his wife had passed, much to the dismay of the ladies of his acquaintance. Bob sighed. "I've been looking forward to this for a month. Alex, you've got to get Joe to stop working so hard."

Alex shrugged. "You know how it is—the end of semester crunch. The students go a little crazy, try to catch up on late work, and then final grades are due. No getting around it." She sighed. "But at least it's over for this term."

"Is he still talking sabbatical?"

Alex laughed. "Nothing but!"

"Nothing but what?" Joe came in, adjusting his fishing vest. "Aah, coffee. The beverage of the gods."

Alex handed him a steaming mug. "Nothing but sabbatical. Bob was asking."

"You know," Joe replied, "I'm looking forward to picking your guys' brains on this today. I've been thinking about a sabbatical that involves fishing."

Tim laughed. "Well, Joe, say no more! It sounds perfect!"

Matt threw an arm around Alex's shoulders. "What about you, Aunt Alex? You ready for a sabbatical fishing expedition?"

"I don't know about that one," Alex began, and Tim interrupted.

"Alex needs her own break." He smiled brightly. "You work too hard. I bet you'd like your own sabbatical." He paused and added, "Don't you have one coming up?"

"Library getting to you?" Bob asked. "It seems like it would suit you great—all that quiet."

"I wish," Alex said. "It's mostly helping students."

Matt gave her shoulders a gentle squeeze. "Dad, have you even been in a college library in forty years? Anything but quiet. Seriously, Aunt Alex, you need a break." He looked over at Tim, who chimed in.

"Maybe you need a birding trip, Alex." Tim closed his eyes and took a gentle sniff of his coffee. He opened his eyes and added, smiling, "Some birds would do you good. A little reading, a little hiking."

"And art," Matt added. "Aunt Alex, you used to do a lot of drawing with us when we were kids. Remember how you used to draw animals' outlines so we could color them in? Like a custom-made coloring book."

Alex turned to gaze up at him. "Yes, but I'm surprised you remember."

Matt feigned offense. "Surprised! I'm stunned. I always wanted to make those perfect, like a stained-glass window or something. Of course," he added, "art was not my forte."

"Art and birds," she murmured.

"Seriously, Alex, you know what you need," Tim said. "Just do it."

Alex smiled at Tim while giving Matt a side hug. "You're probably right," she said, and added silently, *Doves. Definitely doves.*

"Well, those fish won't wait," Joe said, getting up. "Is lunch ready?"

"Already in the cooler, waiting for you boys," Alex said. "All set to go."

Joe gave her a quick kiss. "You're the best, sweetheart."

The back door swung open and Jonah came in, looking around at all of them. "Dad, Mom. What's going on?"

"Good morning," Alex said, frowning a little, and rubbed her jaw.

"Good morning." Jonah's greeting was flat. "Seriously, what's up?" Jonah scanned the group and didn't bother to hide his mouth tightening at Matt.

"Fishing day," Joe answered. "Bob and I are long overdue, and Matt and Tim needed a break from unpacking."

"G'morning." Matt smiled.

Tim raised his mug cheerfully. "Good morning! How are the pups?"

"Fine, thanks," Jonah answered, then added, "In the car, actually. I needed a favor today. Beth and I have to take care of some things." His voice faded. Neither of his parents was smiling. They weren't frowning, of course, but they had the same look of politely feigned interest they used when he talked too much about his work in software design.

Alex felt a surge of panic. Her mind reeled and she remembered Dr. Sam telling her to be a blue jay, but she couldn't sort out how to begin. Her inner blue jay seemed to have vanished.

Joe was nonchalant. "Well, I'm going fishing. Your mom's not available, and your sister is sleeping. She was out late at some sort of meeting last night. Something to do with sea turtles. Or plastic soda containers. Or maybe keg cups, I forget. So, it looks like you and Beth are taking the dogs on an outing." Joe drained his cup. "And since you're blocking Bob's truck, and we have to get going before the day is too far along, we'll see you soon."

Jonah blinked and looked over at his mom, who was rubbing her jaw. He scowled at Matt, whose arm was draped over his mom's shoulders. Alex knew he'd found Matt's comfort with her, and everyone else, annoying since they were in kindergarten. Matt acted like everyone was a dear friend and, worse yet, seemed oblivious to Jonah's dislike.

"Mom? Can't you help us out?"

Alex sighed and looked at Jonah. Just before she spoke, she felt a gentle touch, just a brush, really, like a bird's wing on the back of her shoulder. "No, Jonah, I have plans for the day. Maybe another time." She felt Matt's thumb gently pat the back of her shoulder and she stood a bit straighter.

"Fine. Really, fine." Jonah shifted in his jacket. "Have fun fishing, guys. See you, Mom." He kissed the air next to his mom's cheek. He left quickly and the door shut just a little too hard. Alex gave Matt a pat on his back in thanks.

Joe shrugged at the door. "Let's give them a minute to text whoever they're going to try to dump the pack on next and then skedaddle." He gave Alex a fake stern look. "No caving. They may come back after we're gone."

Alex smiled and said, "I've got this. You boys go have fun. I'm going to have a day." She paused. "Maybe I'll do like I used to do for those preachy people who came around and duck under the windows where they can't look in and see me."

"Or you could just say no," Joe said, and Alex wondered how he forgot so easily that he didn't usually say no, either.

Matt grinned and stage-whispered, "And we won't tell Mom you're home alone."

Tim laughed. "Amen to that!"

Bob hoisted himself out of the chair. "Got plans for the day, Alex?"

"Oh, I have plenty to do," she replied. "Some projects, you know."

The projects would wait until after she sat with a second cup of coffee, watching her birds. She saw the fishermen off, thinking about Matt and Tim. Sometimes she felt just a little envious of Gloria and Bob. They'd taken it better than she'd expected, that Christmas break of sophomore year when Matt came home and brought Tim with him. He had dated girls, but none seriously. He hadn't said anything specific about Tim. He just said he'd like to bring a friend home for vacation. Tim was a sophomore, too, he explained, a fellow accounting major, and they'd met in philosophy class. That's what Gloria had shared one day over coffee between Thanksgiving and Christmas. It was at Christmas Eve Mass that year that Alex had learned that the friend was Tim and that Matt and Tim were not just friends. Alex smiled, thinking of that Christmas Eve Mass, sitting with the Quinns, as always, and meeting Tim for the first time. He had shaken Joe's hand and hugged Alex as if it were the most natural thing in the world—and so it had been.

She had watched Gloria carefully, but saw not a trace of upset. Alex shook her head, remembering. *I still can't believe it. She took it so well, almost as if she'd known all along and besides that, as if it just wasn't a big deal. And Gloria has been so strict about the rules for everyone else.* Alex chuckled. At the Christmas-evening supper and gathering for the four parents, Gloria had waved her arms, exclaiming in amazement that Kevin had the temerity to be annoyed that Veronica had to stay in the guest room while Tim bunked down with Matt, that it wasn't fair. "Fair?" Gloria had nearly shouted, almost knocking over a bottle of wine. "Fair? I asked him if he wanted Tim and Veronica to share the guest room. That put an end to that nonsense." Alex took a sip of coffee and smiled. *Gloria. She can make me absolutely crazy with her rigidity and then she turns around and is so flexible. And it's hilarious how matter-of-fact she is, acting as if she can't imagine why we were all surprised at how she accepted Matt and Tim while she's harping on Cody that he has to have an annulment before he can even begin dating.*

Alex finished her coffee and headed toward the garage, where an old storage tub of art supplies was buried under cardboard boxes, to take inventory and see what was still usable.

Chapter Twenty-Two

December 15

Anger. Supposed to write about anger.

I'm angry that Jonah and Beth just stopped by with four dogs like I have nothing better to do than dog-sit on a whim for them.

I'm angry that they don't appreciate anything I do for them.

I'm angry that they are so entitled and selfish.

I'm angry that everyone else seems to think it's just fine to go off and do whatever they want.

I'm angry that I never really do whatever I want.

Why don't I just do something I want?

December 16

I'm angry that everyone thinks they're an expert on what I should do.

I'm angry that Joe says, "Do whatever you want," as if I was supposed to know what that even is. Well, I know. But they're not going to like it much.

I'm angry that I don't feel sure that I even know what I want to do.

I'm angry that I have this stupid homework.

I'm angry that no one listens to me.

I'm angry at myself for not sticking up for myself. Dr. Sam's right. I have to be more of a blue jay.

I think I would be too dangerous because I would be a very angry blue jay.

In six months

In six months, I'll be able to stick up for myself without feeling like I'm going to throw up. I'll say things like, no, I don't want to go to sea turtle nest meetings, and no, I don't want to work on the Christmas pageant or walk your dogs. In six months, I will have lost fifteen pounds and have clean closets and new art supplies. I just did the math and I guess I have to start losing weight now because I don't see me doing this quickly. Not during Christmas break.

In six months

In six months, I will be on sabbatical. Just about, anyhow. I'll be able to walk five miles without any problem. Except for a lot of hills, but generally speaking. The closets will be organized so it won't be an avalanche every time I have to get out towels. In six months, I will be doing some art every week, even if it's just a couple of hours on the weekend. Every week.

Chapter Twenty-Three

The Brown Thrasher

The brown thrasher is a beautiful bird with a striking reddish-brown upper side. The males can be very aggressive in defense of the young, attacking people or other animals without reservation. At other times, they can be hard to spot, remaining in dense shrubbery, in pairs or solitary.

Monday morning, Alex was up early, having her coffee and watching the birds. Joe wouldn't be up for a while, and the art class she was trying—a "paint it and take it" still life class at the local art center—didn't begin until nine thirty. It was kind of a lark, really, just something she'd seen in the local paper and signed up for on Saturday while Joe was fishing with Bob, Matt, and Tim. She thought it would be a good day to break her rustiness with art supplies by doing something structured. The class was a three-hour session, and she imagined stopping for a coffee on the way home, maybe even sneaking a book along, and really stretching the break.

The phone rang. Gloria, at 7:30 a.m.

"Hello?" Alex almost always answered as if she didn't know who was calling. It was partly habit and partly a resentful gesture. Requiring them to identify themselves was a step toward making them work a little, seeing as how they were intruding. It seemed the least they could do.

"Alexa? It's me." Gloria was her usually brisk self. "How is vacation? Are you busy?"

Alex felt a sigh coming on. "Yes, Gloria, I'm busy. Christmas is practically here." She was annoyed when people asked if she was busy, as if they doubted she could possibly have anything to do. What did Gloria think she did all day? Christmas break had begun only just yesterday evening; she didn't count that first weekend as part of the break, because weekends happened every week.

"Ah, well. I was calling to see if you were free to come over and visit for a while. All four kids are here and we're making cookies. I thought you might enjoy it."

"What time would that be?"

"Well, I'm making up the dough this morning but I'd rather not sugar them up until after lunch."

The classic school teacher's trick; send them home bouncing instead of putting up with it all day herself. *Smart*, thought Alex. "So … what? Three-ish?"

"Yes," Gloria said. "Just bring yourself! Oh—Rachel mentioned she and Sandy might join us. Won't that be fun? Three generations of us baking cookies! It's like a Norman Rockwell painting!"

"Sounds lovely," Alex said. "See you then!" She hung up and wondered why she had said she'd go.

First came the art class, which started out uncomfortably for Alex; she was embarrassed by her long absence from using art supplies. She was anxious she'd completely forgotten how to handle paints and brushes. She entered hesitantly, holding the canvas panel in one hand and her tote of supplies in the other.

"Good morning!" the instructor said, waving from across the room where she was helping another student get settled. An elderly woman wearing cropped pants, a T-shirt, and an impossibly splattered apron covering her from shoulder to knees, she waved her arms toward the tables, set up in a large U shape, and added, "Sit anywhere! I'll be over in a moment." Alex edged toward a table at the rear of the room. The instructor came over, grinning. "Catholic, hey? Everyone's Catholic the first time they come to a class." At Alex's confused expression, she clarified. "You know—try to sit toward the back! That's what we do!"

Alex laughed. "Yes, that's my tendency—hide near the back."

"Well, not here," the instructor informed her. "Oh, I'm Liz. I'm one of the painting instructors here at the center. Welcome. And you are ...?"

"Alex. Alex Bonhall. This is my first time here. I've been on the mailing list, but, well. You know ..."

Liz nodded. "Yes, I know. I didn't start painting until I was sixty-five! Can you imagine? A new hobby in retirement, I told myself, and here I am! Fifteen years later and I'm teaching. It's a riot!" Liz squinted over Alex's shoulder. "Another student! Sorry, Alex, let me go meet this person."

"Of course," Alex said. *Eighty*, she thought. *Eighty years old?* Liz was, well, wrinkled, but she was so lively, so happy, that it occurred to Alex she could be just about any age, any age old enough to have a lot of wrinkles. Sixty-five when she began painting. Alex wondered if maybe there was hope for her after all. Maybe she could recover her old skills and learn some new ones.

In a few minutes the class was filling up, twelve students in all, spaced around the classroom. A man around Joe's age sat next to Alex in the last empty seat. "I'm Bill," he said, waving a handful of paintbrushes in greeting.

"I'm Alex." She paused. "This is my first time here and I'm a little intimidated."

"I hear you. But Liz is fantastic. You'll see." Bill expertly set up his materials. "Everyone loves her."

Bill was right. Liz was relaxed and cheerful and there were no experts in the class. Alex's painting came out far better than she'd expected, and she imagined herself signing up for more classes in the new year. Her coffee break was a treat, and she stopped at home to drop off her painting before going to bake cookies.

Joe, relaxing at home, was skeptical about the baking. "Are you sure you're up for this? I thought you needed a break."

Alex felt mildly annoyed, because she knew he was right; she should have just said no to cookie baking. "I do. But this is just some Christmas cookie decorating. Mostly damage control. I guess all four kids will be in on it."

Joe grimaced. "You mean Sean and Marta will be decorating the cookies. The other two will make a mess. At best."

"Well, they're much younger." Joe looked straight at her with unblinking eyes. "Yes, I know. Sean and Marta were entirely different at those ages, but then ..."

"Then, everyone's not Cody," Joe finished. "Let's face it. He got a raw deal and turned it into something incredible."

Gloria's kitchen was warm, and in true Gloria fashion, she had a cookie-decorating factory set up. The table was covered with a drop cloth, plastic dishes were set out with various chocolate chips and small candies, and shakers of different colored sugars were arranged down the center of the table. She had a large bowl of icing covered, ready for her to slather on each cookie so the children could decorate it before the icing hardened, and trays set up with pre-baked cookies ready to be decorated and put back on the trays to finish drying. The four children already had oversized T-shirts over their clothes as smocks and were jumping around listening to Christmas music and singing along.

"It smells wonderful." Alex smiled. "How is everything?"

Gloria scanned the kitchen and stretched to see what the children were up to in the family room. "All well here. They're already bouncy and they've barely started sneaking sugar. As if I don't know what they're doing."

"Oh, you know how it is. Sneaking a little extra chocolate chip or cinnamon hot is part of the fun."

"As long as you can keep Bobby from sucking on cinnamon hots and then sticking them on cookies."

"Please don't tell me," Alex groaned.

"Oh, only a couple of them, at Halloween. But sucking on them turns them pinkish instead of red, so it's easy to tell which one's he's gotten to." Gloria was unruffled by the prospect of recycled cinnamon candies.

"Ah. Look for the pink ones." *Avoid eating any cookies with anything pink or with cinnamon hots*, she thought, *just in case.*

Cookie decorating began. There was a lot of yelling and giggling and an unusual breakout of purple Christmas trees and orange snowmen. Sandy and Rachel arrived a little later and joined right in, as if they were still kids.

Gloria managed the process, and Alex tried not to be fixated on the cinnamon hots. Gloria somehow was able to have a conversation, of sorts.

"So how is your first day of vacation?"

"Very nice," Alex said. "I went to an art class this morning." She immediately regretted saying so, because Gloria was quick to leap.

"Art class? How nice! What did you do? Where did you go?"

"Oh, it was just a little 'paint it and take it' class at the beach center. A one-time thing."

"Well, isn't that fun! What brought that on? I didn't know you were *that* interested in art."

"Oh, I am," Alex replied, a little miffed. "Was." She paused. "I was an art major, Gloria. Didn't I ever mention that? Art and biology? I've taken art classes before. I just haven't for a while."

Gloria was unoffended. "Of course, I knew that, I just spoke without thinking. Temporarily must have forgotten. It's been a while since you've mentioned it or really done anything with your education. Well, how nice that you took a little time for yourself. Good for you."

Alex rubbed her lower jaw, trying to contain her impatience at the repeated verdict of "nice." "We were painting a still life with sunflowers."

Sandy glanced up. "Cool, Mom. That sounds fun."

"It was." Alex looked up, a bit surprised at Sandy's simple approval.

"So, doing some new things," Gloria mused. "Bobby! Take the cinnamon hot out of your mouth. No, not into the dish. Here—give it to me. Rachel, would you help Bobby wash his hands? He's a bit sticky. Why, Marta, what a lovely angel."

"Thanks, Grandma."

Alex said, "Well, it's good to try new things from time to time."

"Ha! Mom, you almost never do anything new."

"Sandy, that's hardly fair," Alex argued. "I just did that beach cleanup with you and Rachel."

"What do you do at a beach cleanup?" Marta asked.

"Dummy, you clean up a beach," Sean replied.

"Don't call each other dummy," Gloria commented absent-mindedly. She was pulling frosting out of three-year-old Gina's hair.

"I know that," Marta said. "I meant how. Like, do you get to drive one of those sweeper machines? Or is it picking stuff up with your hands? That's what I meant." She scowled at Sean.

"It's fun," Rachel told her. "We have gloves, and big bags, and we go out in teams. During nesting season, we look for sea turtle nests so they can be marked for safety. But that doesn't start until spring."

"Picking up garbage sounds yucky," Bobby remarked. He was covering a snowman with chocolate chips to make it entirely dark brown. "My snowman looks like poop," he announced.

"Gross," said Sean approvingly.

"Well, we have gloves, but yeah, sometimes it's gross. People leave garbage and it's dangerous for the animals." Rachel frowned disapprovingly. She seemed to have more disapproval for garbage than a poopy snowman.

"And for people," Sandy added. "It's lots of fun. My mom went last time, and we saw a lot of different kinds of birds. My mom is kind of an expert on birds."

Marta and Sean seemed to perk up at this. "We love birds! We have a birdfeeder in our yard. And there's a cardinal family that is around most of the time," Sean said.

"Maybe we can go on the beach cleanup," Marta said. "Aunt Sandy, could we go?"

"Um, that's up to your dad," Sandy replied. "We can ask him."

Rachel rolled her eyes. "I've asked them about going on a beach cleanup for two years and now all of a sudden they're interested."

Sandy shrugged. "Birds must have been the selling point."

Meanwhile, Gloria had most of the frosting tugged out of Gina's hair. "Nothing like a new hair color," Alex joked. "Maybe green is her color!"

Gloria's eyebrows drew together and Alex felt a pang in her upper jaw.

"Well, Gina, that should be it. Your mother will have to give you a good shampoo this evening." Gina was smiling happily.

"Can I do more cookies now?"

Gloria frowned. "I think you're just about done. Oh, okay—one more. A tree? Or an angel?"

"Tree!"

"Bobby—Bobby. Put down the yellow sugar. There's no room on the snowman. The sugar won't stick to the chocolate chips." Gloria sighed and turned her focus back to Alex.

"It's not yellow sugar. It's pee," Bobby mumbled. Sean laughed.

"Stop encouraging him," Rachel scolded.

"Well, while you're shaking things up, how about a new hair color? Your gray has been showing up more, maybe it's time to give yourself a little refresh." Gloria turned her assessing gaze on Alex.

"I really don't think so," Alex said, drawing back a little. She put her hand to her hair. *I'm a blue jay*, she thought. *A blue jay.* "I think my hair's fine. I haven't colored it in ages and I hardly see a reason to start again now."

"Oh, Mom, it would be fun. Don't be so serious," Sandy interjected.

"I'm not being so serious. I just don't see why I should color my hair." She frowned. "Do you remember what it was like to grow it out? It took forever."

"Red. A nice, perky red. Just something to brighten up that mousy brown." Gloria kept talking as if the rest of them were merely background noise.

"Mousy brown?"

"Red sounds fun," Rachel commented. "It would really go. You have such nice skin. And just a few freckles."

They're age spots, you idiot, thought Alex, and rubbed her face. She pictured herself hopping in a semi-circle, flapping her elbows and wiggling her behind, but somehow, she felt as if she were frozen in place.

"Red would definitely do it," Gloria pronounced.

"Beet juice, Mom," Sandy suggested. "A nice beet juice rinse. It would be temporary and liven things up."

"I don't need livening up."

Marta appeared suddenly at Alex's side. She looked up, whispering, "I don't think you look like a mouse. Unless looking like a mouse is good."

"Thanks, Marta." Alex gave her a quick hug.

"Marta, don't whisper around other people. It's rude. Beet juice. How fascinating. Gina, stop eating the chocolate chips."

Cody came in, surveying the scene. Marta and Sean nearly tackled him. "Daddy! Hi, Daddy!"

He put an arm around each and rustled their hair. "How are you guys? Having fun?" He grinned at Gloria. "Mom, you're amazing. How many cinnamon hots did Bobby recycle?"

Gloria frowned. "I think only one or two. But we'll want to check the cookies before eating."

"Gross!" Marta laughed.

"Super gross!" Sean shrieked.

"Gross!" Gina shouted, throwing her arms up like a referee, inadvertently tossing the contents of a jar of purple sugar. Gloria sighed.

"I think we're done here," she announced. "Kids, go wash up. Rachel, Sandy, please help me clean up." Gloria put her hands on her hips. "Girls, just dump all the bowls out onto the drop cloth and we'll just throw the whole mess away. I don't think anything's safe to store." She lifted the bowl of chocolate chips. "Yes, there are three pink cinnamon candies in with the chocolate chips. Out they all go."

Marta was hanging on Cody's arm. "Daddy, Aunt Rachel and Aunt Sandy are going to clean the beach. Can we go?"

"Ah, not sure. I need info. Remember?"

The twins frowned and then said, almost in unison, "Who, what, where, when, why, and how."

"And?"

"Us, with Aunt Rachel and Aunt Sandy. And Aunt Alex." Alex turned in surprise.

"What?"

"We're going to clean up garbage at the beach. And learn about birds from Aunt Alex."

"Where?"

"The beach."

"Which beach?"

The twins looked at Sandy, who smiled and answered, "Little Fish beach, Saturday morning, 8:00 a.m. to noon. We can drive over together." She paused and added, looking at Cody, "Well, unless you can join us, too. Then we can meet up there. There's not room in Mom's car for everyone."

"I'd love to," said Cody.

Chapter Twenty-Four

"A lexa, your hair looks ... different."

To Alex's surprise, Dr. Sam skipped the usual, gentle ramp up of, "So how have things been?" or, "What's been better?" and jumped right into the hair. It must look even worse than she'd thought.

"You could say so." Alex grimaced. "Not quite what I'd wanted."

"What did you want?"

"Nothing, actually. Nothing. This wasn't really my idea, per se."

"So, whose idea was it? If it wasn't your idea to color your hair ... red? Maybe eggplant, I guess we'd call it."

"Well, I guess it was my idea. No, really, it wasn't. Gloria suggested I needed a change and then Sandy suggested beet juice because it's natural and temporary and then, well, this. My hair is a purplish reddish brown and so are half our bath towels." Alex sighed. "I do look like an eggplant. I'm shaped like one and now I'm the same color."

Dr. Sam glanced down at Alex's journaling. "Lots of anger the last week or so. Good. But you're missing some important people here. Or at least one person."

"What do you mean, missing?"

Dr. Sam leaned forward a bit. "Alexa, you're mad at this one, mad at that one. For example, 'I'm angry at Sandy for bullying me about my hair.'"

"Well, I am."

"Fine, you have a bossy daughter who still thinks she knows everything. And you let her push you around. Whose fault is that?"

"So, it's my fault?"

Dr. Sam sighed. "I'm afraid you're going to be angry at me, and that's part of the gig. This is my job. Alexa, you're not having your own life and you're giving other people permission to use you up. Then you blame them. Things keep "happening" to you—to you, personally—and you duck behind that it wasn't your idea. You're like Rapunzel, waiting for someone to come along and give you permission to be free." Dr. Sam paused. "Well, except for the hair color, but otherwise ..."

"Ouch."

Dr. Sam shrugged. "I know. We all have those ouches. The question is, does this one fit?"

Alex was silent for a long time. She was hoping Dr. Sam would break the silence but she knew already that Dr. Sam's capacity for sitting comfortably inside of tension was impressive. Alex studied the landscape behind Dr. Sam's head and the lamp on the side table. Finally, Alex looked down at her hands, clenching and unclenching her fists. "I know I don't stick up for myself."

"Mm-hmm."

"It's like the dogs. Walking the dogs at lunch. It was a short-term thing, supposedly, and then it just kept on ... keeping on. I didn't plan on walking the dogs during lunch. And I am angry at Jonah and Beth for being so selfish. Doesn't it even occur to them that I don't want to do this?"

"No, I'm sure it doesn't." Alex looked up in surprise. Dr. Sam continued without hesitation. "People who speak up for themselves and ask for, even demand, what they want, assume everyone else will do the same thing. If you don't speak up, they assume there's no problem. Stop expecting them to be like you."

"I didn't raise selfish children."

"You've been busy training selfish adults, then."

Alex felt like the session was swirling out of control. She wasn't feeling quite comfortable.

"This is uncomfortable for you, isn't it? It's okay, Alexa. Just say so." It seemed like Dr. Sam could see through her. Alex shrugged and looked at the floor between them.

"Well, I feel like you're saying it's my fault."

"Let's separate 'fault' and 'having some responsibility,' okay? You have a responsibility to decide what is, and is not, okay. Do you want to spend your lunch breaks for the next semester walking Jonah and Beth's dogs?"

"No."

"Then say so. It's a perfect time." Dr. Sam pretended to poke at a phone and hold it up to her ear. "Hello, Jonah? It's Mom. Honey, I'd thought I'd give you a heads-up so you and Beth can make arrangements. I won't be able to help out with the dogs at lunch time next semester. Mm-hmm. Mm-hmm. Yes, I'm sure it is hard to find reliable help. Especially with four of them. That's why I thought I'd better let you know as soon as possible." She winked at Alex and flapped her elbows like wings, wiggling in her seat.

Alex flushed. "You make it sound very easy."

"It's simple, not easy."

"But he's going to make a fuss! He's going to argue. He's going to ask questions."

"Questions that you are under no obligation to answer except to repeat you won't be able to do it." Dr. Sam wiggled a pen. "Write down the basic script if you're anxious about doing this. It helps."

"Well, he won't let it rest. And when he does, he'll sulk about it and make remarks."

"Then confront him on that." Dr. Sam sat up even straighter and faced off to the side. "Jonah, it's almost Easter, and you've been acting a bit ... short with me since the Christmas season. What's going on?"

"And he'll say, 'Nothing,' and act all innocent."

Dr. Sam made an attempt at a semi-sulking and disingenuously innocent face. "So? Innocent sounds better than sulky. Besides, all that is his problem. Not yours." Dr. Sam did the eyebrow thing. "What is it you're afraid of, Alexa?"

"Afraid?"

"Fear and anger are partners. Haven't you ever seen a trapped, frightened animal? They're almost always aggressive. They act angry because they're terrified. You seem to feel angry, but I suspect you're also terrified. What's the bad thing that happens if you say no? No, I won't give up my lunch to walk your dogs. No, I won't tolerate an adult living under my roof with less responsibility than the average twelve-year-old; grow up or move out. No, I don't want you to take six months to travel the Eastern Seaboard pretending to study fishing with your friend while I get stuck at home with Sandy, Gloria, and the dogs."

Dr. Sam had been reading the journals and listening more than Alex had suspected. She sighed. "I know I'm afraid. I'm afraid they'll be angry at me."

"People who love each other sometimes are annoyed with one another. Frustrated, irritated, disappointed, angry, flat-out raging. So what? What's the bad thing that happens if they're angry?"

"I don't know. No one really gets angry at me. I never like loudness. Fussing. I like peace."

"This isn't peace, it's a demilitarized zone. You're angry, whether or not they know it. The question is, what are you going to do with this anger, Alexa?"

"Do? What? Start acting like a jerk? Maybe be bossy like Gloria and Sandy?"

Dr. Sam grinned. "That's a false choice, and you know it. Don't hide behind dualistic thinking, Alexa. Anger is fuel. Think about it. It's energy. We use energy for good, or for bad. You can use gasoline to drive someplace wonderful, or you can make Molotov cocktails. Which I strongly recommend against, by the way." She paused. "So, use the energy of your anger to make positive changes. It's how all positive change happens in the world. Someone sees something that should be different, is energized, and does something constructive."

"What would be constructive? I'm just trying to be nice."

"I know. Think bigger, Alexa."

Alex didn't know what that was supposed to mean. More ambitious? She wondered if Dr. Sam was telling her to aim high or some other motivational claptrap.

Once again Dr. Sam seemed to read her mind, or at least her facial expressions, with eerie accuracy. "I don't mean turning into some sort of hyper-motivated overachiever, Alexa. But is it really nice to let Jonah and Beth believe that it's okay to treat their parents with such disregard? To see other people as not deserving of the same consideration as them? What kind of parents will they grow up to be? What kind of friends or employees must they already be? Isn't it odd that they have no friends to rely on? That it's just parents, his parents, all the time?"

"I hadn't thought of that. That they don't really seem to have close friends. Well, she does, but not them as a couple."

"Maybe there's a reason for that."

"Well, I guess most people wouldn't put up with being treated that way. Sometimes I'm surprised they found each other."

"And is it really nice to let Sandy pretend she's a teenager, doing some part-time tutoring and being a perpetual volunteer, never becoming self-reliant, constantly working on, what? Her dissertation? Who is it nice for, Alexa? Them? Or you?" There was a pause. "Who are you if you're not on active duty with the kids?"

Alex looked away. "This is just what I do."

"Being loving, generous, and kind are important. And that is what you do. And sometimes kindness means letting go of their little hands and letting them stumble and figure it out. You know this."

"I don't know what to do."

Dr. Sam smiled and reached for her planner. "Well, you're going to have four weeks to think about it. I take time off during the holidays, and you do, too. Please use this time to think about what you want your life to be shaped like. New homework. Two things."

Alex let slip a groan and Dr. Sam laughed. "I heard that. Okay, here goes: journaling, freeform, whatever comes to mind, fifteen minutes each morning. Early, before you really start your day. No editing or self-censoring. And start saying no. And if you balk, write about that."

"No?"

"As in, no, I don't like the beet juice dye and I'm washing my hair ten times to get it out. With vinegar or beer or whatever it takes. Look it up; there must be a safe way to undo this. No, I don't want to be assistant director of the Christmas pageant next year. Take me off the list. No, I won't be walking dogs on my lunch break." Dr. Sam smiled. "Besides, you're going to be busy trying to sort out a sabbatical."

"Sorting out? As in, planning my project," Alex paused. "My sabbatical."

Dr. Sam's eyebrows wiggled.

Alex smiled sheepishly. "I wonder what Joe will say when he finally gets it through his head that my sabbatical isn't his."

"Oh, I forgot," Dr. Sam teased. "Only Joe can have fun! What is this, Alexa? He goes fishing up and down I-95 and you get an outing to the hobby store?"

"Well, if you put it that way, it does sound unfair. But it's not his fault. It's me."

"Nice work. See you in a month."

Chapter Twenty-Five

It was a beautiful Saturday morning, a bit breezy for a beach cleanup, but perhaps all the better. Junk would blow around freely and be easier to spot, Alex thought. She drove in circles, looking for a parking spot in the municipal lot.

"Mom! Right there. No, there." Sandy was anxious. "Look, Rachel is here already, and Cody and the kids are there. We're late."

"We're not late, we're parking. And 'there' doesn't help me know where to look." Alex glanced over. "And who's that other person? The man next to Rachel?"

Sandy scowled. "Oh. Aidan's here. Great." She started twisting her seat belt.

"I've heard good things. It will be nice to meet him." Alex glanced over. "Very good-looking. At least from here." She slowed down, scanning for a parking spot. "Are they serious, do you think?"

"Ugh, Mom." Sandy adjusted her sunglasses. "Try not to be nosy."

"Don't 'ugh' me." Alex frowned, and then backed carefully into one of the few remaining spots. "I'm looking forward to this morning. See if you can restrain yourself from nagging me."

"Nagging?" Sandy sounded offended. But her mother was already out of the car, waving.

Sean and Marta were hopping around. "Yay! Aunt Alex! Sandy! What do we do?"

Rachel rolled her eyes. "They've been driving us crazy. What took so long?"

"Sorry, yes, we're a little late. It's 8:02, Rachel. And you know we were driving around here finding a spot." Alex looked at the group. "Cody! Good to see you!"

"Aunt Alex!" Cody gave her a hug. "And this is Aidan. Aidan, this is Alex Bonhall. We call her aunt because, well, our families have known each other forever."

"Nice to meet you." Aidan smiled. He had just a slight western Irish accent, barely noticeable, wavy dark hair and blue eyes.

"And you as well." Alex smiled back. She wondered if Gloria was going to have yet another beautiful child-in-law. Jenna hadn't quite worked out, of course, but Veronica was pretty, and Tim was angelic. Aidan, with his Irish good looks, would certainly wrap up the family portrait nicely.

Sandy shrugged at Rachel as they fell in as line leaders. "Can we just get going?"

Rachel looked over her shoulder. "Come on, everyone, the group's gathering over there. We can't be late."

Cody fell in with Alex. "The hair color's fun."

She looked up at him, rolling her eyes. "You know it was your mom and Sandy's idea."

"It figures."

"Beet juice."

"Ah."

"Beet juice," Aidan repeated. "Interesting."

"That was my idea," Sandy tossed back. "It's natural! No toxins! No animal testing!"

Cody smirked and quickly recovered to a neutral face. The twins latched onto testing.

"Did you know animals take tests?" Marta asked.

"No ... Which tests?" their dad asked.

"Haha! Rabbits take multiplication tests!" Sean said, a little loudly. Rachel shot him a look of disapproval but his dad laughed.

"Eeew, gross." Marta acted as if she hadn't set up the joke. This was one of their favorite general routines: One set up some joke, the other took the bait and finished it, and the first acted as if the whole outcome caught them by surprise. They were giggling and hanging on one another as they approached the cluster of volunteers.

Cody tried to shush them. "Guys, please. Let's get ready to listen to instructions." The group of volunteers was gathered and a man in late middle age with a very thin ponytail, clipboard in hand, was giving directions, while a woman about the same age with a silver crew cut handed out plastic gloves and large garbage bags.

"What is it with bosses and clipboards?" Alex whispered to Cody, who shook his head.

Clipboard man scanned the group sternly. When it was appropriately quiet, he smiled broadly. "Okay, everyone! Welcome to Beach Cleanup Day! This is our last cleanup until after New Year's, so let's make it count. I will need everyone to sign in, with your email or phone number, and I will need parent signatures for any minors present. You're signing your understanding that the Beach Sanctuary Safety Club is not responsible for any injuries you incur as a volunteer and that if you break any laws or local ordinances during the cleanup, you are on your own."

"Breaking laws?" Alex asked quietly.

"Mom, shh." Sandy nudged her side.

"How can you break laws picking up junk? I don't remember this from last time."

"Mom. *Stop.*"

"Just wondering."

The clipboard holder clipped his lips together firmly and scanned the group. *Another osprey*, Alex thought. *Look at those eyebrows! Perfect.* The osprey cleared his throat. "Are there any questions?" he asked, staring at Alex. She reached up to rub her jaw and thought otherwise.

"Yes, I have a question." The osprey just barely nodded, so she continued. "What laws might I accidentally break? I mean, just being on the beach picking up trash?"

"Okay, thank you. A good question." The osprey scanned the group, frowning. "For those of you who are new to the Beach Sanctuary Safety Club"—the osprey let his eyes range over Alex, Cody, the twins, Aidan, and a few other people—"it's possible to accidentally stray into the sea oats, which are a protected species, or onto private property that abuts the beach. So just stay out of the dunes with grass growing on them, and you should be fine."

"Thanks," Alex replied, and Sandy nudged her again. Alex elbowed her back. Sandy had the temerity to look surprised.

The cleanup began, with most people wandering off with a partner or two. Rachel and Aidan headed off, with Sandy trailing them. Cody started out with Alex and the twins.

It was a glorious morning: bright sunshine, soft clouds, and the gentle waters of the Gulf of America lapping quietly at the white sand. The shorebirds were busy—swooping and calling gulls, scampering plovers. Pelicans, like pterodactyls, passed over the water and then dove, suddenly, with surprising elegance. The twins were preoccupied with small seashells, finding still-living coquinas and helping them back into the water, and pointing out the birds.

Alex was enjoying Sean and Marta. They were picking up some trash, so it was still, barely, participation in the beach cleanup. It didn't seem, to Alex, that the success of the cleanup should rest on the shoulders of children and their honorary aunt, so she felt no pressure to bully the children into ignoring the beach and its residents.

"What is that one? The one running?" Sean pointed.

"It's a plover." Alex stopped and reached into her bag. She'd brought her bird handbook along, just in case. "I marked the pages with the birds I expected we might see this morning. The plovers start here."

Sean took the book, and he and Marta studied the pages. "Maybe it's a Wilson's plover? Here for the winter?"

"Sounds like a good bet!" Alex said. "Very nice work!"

Cody continued on. He had nearly caught up with Sandy, who had continued ahead after Rachel and Aidan had stopped. Rachel was standing, hands on hips, scowling back at Alex, Marta, and Sean.

Alex watched as Cody came alongside Sandy and they began talking. At least, Sandy was talking, based on the fact that her arms were waving around, which made her trash bag billow behind her like a pirate's sail. Cody was nodding, his hand up to shield his eyes from the bright sun as he looked down at Sandy. Alex wondered if he'd remembered to wear sunscreen.

Rachel beckoned to Alex and the children. "Sean! Marta! Stop dillydallying."

"Ah, come on," Aidan protested. "They're just kids! They're having fun. Let them be."

"We're not dillydallying," Marta explained. "We're identifying the type of plover."

"It's not a bird walk," Rachel said shortly, and marched along, going closer to the dunes to gather some empty cans and crumpled food wrappers.

"Have you got a bird book there?" Aidan asked.

"Yes! Aunt Alex brought it!" Marta waved the book.

"Oh, come on," Rachel snapped, grabbing Aidan's hand and pulling him away. "Let's go." She stomped, as best she could, through the dry sand.

The twins and Alex stood watching Rachel angrily kicking up sand behind her as she went.

"Rachel's cranky," Marta observed.

"She's jealous," Sean added.

"Oh?" said Alex.

"She likes having Sandy all to herself. And she likes having Aidan to herself. And she has to share Sandy with our dad." Sean paused. "I don't think she wants to share Aidan with us."

Interesting, sharing Sandy with Cody. Alex wondered what she had been missing.

"Rachel likes having everything all to herself," Marta remarked and then said quickly, "Sorry."

"Sorry for what?" Alex asked her.

"That was probably mean."

"I guess it depends. Are you trying to make Rachel look bad, so I won't like her?"

"No!"

"Is it true?"

"Yes."

"So, it's true but not a happy truth. Sometimes it's good to be careful with things we don't have to say. But it's okay. Rachel and Sandy have been best friends since before kindergarten, so they're kind of used to doing everything together."

"But Rachel's the one who brought her boyfriend and now she's acting mad because Sandy's spending time with our dad." Marta paused. "Maybe she feels left out."

"It feels bad to be left out," said Sean.

"I don't mind it as much as Rachel does. She hates being left out," Marta said. "I'd rather be left alone than bossed around."

"Maybe Aidan likes being bossed around," Sean commented.

"He doesn't let Rachel boss him. She tries to act bossy, and he just smiles and does what he wants," Marta said. "Like when she told him he had to stay and watch football on Thanksgiving and he was like, 'No, I've got my own football to watch at home, thank you,' and then went home. Only he didn't mean football, he meant soccer. But he calls it football."

"Dummy. That's what they call soccer where he came from." Sean picked up a crumpled paper plate and thrust it into his bag.

Alex almost spoke, then thought better of it. She gazed up at the dunes. "Oh, look, kids," she said. "Let's see if we can identify what kind of bird that is—the one on the fence behind the dune."

"Will Rachel and Sandy get mad?" Sean asked.

"About?"

"About us looking at pictures of birds."

"They're already mad. At least Rachel is," Marta opined. She was standing still, looking at one of the shore bird pages.

"We're picking up trash and picking up bird sightings at the same time. What's wrong with that?" Alex wondered.

"Nothing," Marta said. "And I think that's a snowy egret. We see those at the park a lot. And in the front yard." She frowned. "They eat lizards, I think. And other stuff." She closed the book and handed it back to Alex. "Could you hold this again? That way I can pick up some garbage, too."

The trash pickup was a success. At 11:45 they were all gathered around the osprey again, who signed them all out, thanked them for coming, and reminded them all that for a $25 donation to the Beach Sanctuary Safety Club they could have a commemorative T-shirt. Only adult sizes L and XL were left. That made it simple for Cody to say no. The group headed back to the parking lot.

"That was fun," Aidan said. "Thanks for asking me along."

"It was good," Cody agreed. "This was my first time out."

"Maybe you'll come out again sometime. Tourist season always means a mess on the beach," Sandy said casually, looking off to the side as if studying the palm trees.

Rachel looked disapproving, and it occurred to Alex how much Rachel could resemble her mother. "Did everyone have fun today?" Rachel asked, putting on her best guidance counselor voice. "Marta? Sean?"

"Yes!" the children replied and then burst into comments about the birds. "We saw plovers! And an osprey! Two kinds of seagulls, an egret, and some storks."

"Which did you like best?" Cody asked.

"The plovers," Marta said firmly. "They're small, and they run so fast and dare to go right up to the waves! I like them."

"I like the osprey. They're awesome hunters," Sean said. "Plus, they have those great eyebrows. Kind of like the clipboard man. And Grandma."

Alex counted to ten, trying to control her laughter, and then counted to ten again. She avoided making eye contact with anyone.

"That's not very nice," Rachel scolded.

"But he didn't say it to be mean," Marta argued. "And it's true. It's not a happy truth, so he just has to be careful about when he says it. And try not to be mean about it."

"What's mean about looking like an osprey?" Sean was genuinely puzzled. "I think they're awesome!"

"Yes, they are," said Cody, tousling his son's hair.

They parted ways, with hugs all around. Back in the car, Alex waited until they were on the road to comment casually, "So, did you enjoy the beach cleanup? I thought it went well."

Sandy was sitting with her arms folded, staring out the side window. "Yeah. I guess."

"Well, I had fun."

Sandy slapped her folded arms against her chest. "Yeah, well, you and the kids just played. Forget beach cleanup, it was the Audubon Society convention."

Alex frowned. "That's not fair, Sandy. We picked up trash and yes, we had fun. They're kids, for crying out loud. Better for them to have fun and want to do it again than be miserable."

Sandy grunted.

Alex tried to cheer Sandy up. "Well, Aidan seems nice."

"Hmph."

Ah, it was Aidan. "You don't like him? I mean, I hardly spoke with him, but he seemed pleasant enough." Alex tried to sound casual, as if she couldn't care less whether Sandy had an opinion.

Sandy shifted in her seat and started twisting a long strand of hair. "No, he's good. The whole day was good, okay? All good. It was just a weird morning. That's all."

Alex glanced at Sandy. "Good weird? Bad weird?"

Sandy shrugged and said, "Good. I guess. Mom, I'm tired. I don't feel like talking about it, okay? It was just a beach cleanup." She sank down into her seat and reminded Alex, suddenly, of her middle school years. Sandy was almost never at a loss for words, but when she was, it meant something was brewing. *Great. More storms on the horizon.*

Chapter Twenty-Six

*S*andy's upset about something that happened at beach cleanup. Of course, so was Rachel. Stir in a male or two and they revert back to middle school, except in middle school you could parse it all out pretty easily and they were on the same team.

The beach cleanup was fun. My God, Marta and Sean are wonderful—real kids, just free and silly and unspoiled. God bless Cody and, well, Gloria. They're such joys. I wish—well, I wish I could have grandchildren like that but at least I can be Aunt Alex, the crazy fun aunt.

In six months

In six months, I'll be free. It feels so wonderful to be on break, I wonder how sabbatical will feel. Will it feel even worse the weeks before going back, like the last few days of break? And those stupid emails that start before we're even back, rah-rah for the new term. Does anyone actually feel that way? Even Dr. Greene can't be that excited about it. Oh my *gosh. This is what I do. I'm ruining my own fun before it even starts by imagining how miserable it will be when it's over. I talk myself out of doing things I enjoy. Oh, crap, I can't wait to see Dr. Sam's face when she reads this next year.*

Chapter Twenty-Seven

"Remember, we need to be there at 3:00 p.m. The service starts at four, and the pageant happens right after the gospel." Gloria had given the instructions at least twice a day for the past two weeks, and this time Alex rubbed her forehead instead of her jaw before replying,

"Yes, Gloria, I know. Be there by three, and then help the kids get back to their seats with the parents during the homily." Alex had been disappointed to learn there was going to be a homily after all, and hoped the pastor wasn't going to talk too long.

"I was just reminding you." Gloria sounded annoyed. "It's always more complicated than people think. You can't imagine how difficult the parents can be! They're constantly underfoot."

"I know." Alex took a deep breath. "We're on for the usual Christmas Day evening coffee and dessert tomorrow, of course? Our place?"

"Coffee and dessert, yes. We're looking forward to it! We'll be there about six."

"Perfect. See you later. At three."

Alex put the phone down and sighed. Joe looked up from his book. "Gloria being Gloria?"

"As always. No wonder Bob's always looking for an excuse to go fishing." She frowned. "That's not why you go fishing, is it? To get away from me?"

"Good Lord, no. Are you putting yourself in the same category as that relentless drill sergeant? No. Anytime you want to come along fishing, you let me know. Just bring a book. Which I guess you always do, everywhere."

Alex smiled gratefully. "I wouldn't want you to be trying to get away." She paused. "I guess that's why the sabbatical talk has me a little discombobulated. It sounds like a good way to get away. For a long time."

"Oh, honey. No. That's not it. I'd love for you to come along and do your own sabbatical. We could have an adventure. No students, no dogs, no bossy best friends."

"I thought you were working on Bob to go."

"Bob's plan B. You're plan A."

"Ha, I get it. A for Alex."

"A for always first for me," Joe corrected. Then he laughed. "But Bob and I *are* going fishing Thursday. Boxing Day."

"That sounds great." Alex headed toward her chair. "I'll be having a cozy day, especially if I can keep Sandy off my back."

"What's that supposed to mean?" Sandy blurted from behind them, in the kitchen.

"When did you get here?" Joe asked.

"I just walked in and heard Mom being snarky."

"I wasn't being snarky." Alex, stopping short of her chair, turned back toward Sandy and crossed her arms.

"Off your back? What's that?" Sandy was making her "hurt" face, channeling her inner indignant six-year-old self.

"Oh, Sandy. For crying out loud. You know very well that you can't bear to see me doing anything I might want to do without butting in, criticizing, or telling me what I should be doing instead. You couldn't even let me enjoy the beach cleanup with the kids without swooping in to criticize us for not picking up as much trash as you did."

"Well, it was a beach cleanup. I mean, Mom." Sandy's voice was climbing.

"And we helped clean a beach. That's what I mean, Sandy. You're being critical. I wish you would just lighten up and not act as if I need a boss."

Joe raised his eyebrows and lowered his gaze to his book. Alex caught that; he was lying low, keeping an eye on everything and holding back to see what might happen.

"I'm just trying to be helpful. I mean, you seem so bored." Sandy shrugged. "You know, you just sit or putter around. You never do anything."

"I'm not bored." Alex paused. "What is it you mean when you say I 'seem bored'? What exactly is it you see as so painfully boring?"

"Just sitting there, reading. I mean, really? What are you reading? Some old book? Have you even looked at the book I loaned you? The one about the effects of laundry detergent phosphates on old-growth forests in the Northwest?"

"No, I haven't started that one. Yet." Alex lifted her book. "This is a collection of short stories by Swedish authors. Translated into English, of course." She held the book out and gazed at it approvingly. "Very good, to tell you the truth. Maybe you should have a look at it. When I'm done, that is."

Sandy appeared nonplussed. "Well. I don't know. Maybe." She turned away, opening the refrigerator. "Is there anything to eat here?"

Alex pulled her lips in, took a deep breath, and counted to ten. She realized she'd been doing a lot of counting these days. "Sandy, we always have food. If we ever get so desperate that we don't have food, I will be sure to let you know so you can make other plans."

"Ugh, Mom. You're being so ... I don't know what."

"Tired, Sandy," Alex offered. "I'm tired of the criticism. What do you think that sounds like? Is there anything to eat? What the hell do you think your dad and I do with our money, go out to dine at the finest restaurants and leave you with gruel? The answer is, there's always food and other adults magically make it happen, and you come flying in, chattering like an adolescent blue jay, and act as if the fruits of our work may or may not be good enough for you. Well, if you don't like what's here, go buy your own. You're an adult. Act like one." Alex sat down, pointedly picked up her book, opened it, and held it nearly to her nose.

Sandy stared at her mom, who was assiduously not looking at her, and her dad, who met her gaze placidly. There was a long pause, and then Sandy, apparently realizing that her father was not going to rescue her with some joking remark, muttered, "Sorry. I didn't mean anything by it," and turned back to the refrigerator. "Mom, there's some leftover pizza here. Okay if I eat that?"

"Sure, honey," Alex answered, keeping her voice as lilting as possible, under the circumstances. She wiggled her eyebrows at Joe, who nodded almost imperceptibly before returning to his own book. They had an hour or so before they needed to leave for church.

They arrived right on time. The camel cast members, out of costume, were sitting near the church door on one of the benches in the prayer garden. "Hey, Mrs. B!" shouted the front half. "Want a brownie?" The back end of the camel laughed uproariously and elbowed the front end. "They're awesome!"

"Thanks, guys, I think we'll pass," Alex said. "We'll see you inside in a few minutes. You know how Mrs. Quinn likes things to be on time."

"Sure you don't want a brooooooownieeee?" the front half reaffirmed, waving one around. Alex waved over her shoulder and she and Joe hurried in.

"That can't end well," Joe commented. Alex just shook her head.

The large entry room of the church was crowded already, as family members of the choir as well as all the children in the pageant wanted to be there in plenty of time. The pageant participants were in the largest meeting room, in costume, except for the camel. Gloria came toward Alex, arms waving. "Finally! You're here!"

"It's three. You said to be here at three."

"Well, yes, but as you can see, it's a bit chaotic. Can you get these parents out of here? They all think it's picture time. And I need to find the camel."

Alex decided not to mention the current state of the camel.

Shooing out parents was hard, but reminding them the whole cast was going to line up for pictures in front of the church before being escorted back to their families helped, except for Veronica, Gloria's photographer daughter-in-law, who felt that her combination of semiprofessional and familial status gave her an exemption. "I'm helping," she explained. "I'm in charge of getting a lot of photographs for the parish scrapbook and as giveaways for the families involved."

"Oh," said Alex. "Fine. I'm going camel hunting."

Veronica said, "Huh?" but did not look up from adjusting the camera, and then went purposefully toward the sheep. "Bobby! Gina! Smile, sweethearts!"

The pageant went off with barely an error. Bobby did kick both other sheep, and his cousin Marta obligingly tapped him with the shepherd's crook, the first time on the behind and the second on the back of his head. He baa-ed at her, and the nearest angel gave him a stern look. The main angel forgot some of her words, and had to have another angel stage-whisper them to her.

The procession did not fare as well as the main set. Jolie, tall and dignified, carried off her role with aplomb. Sean and Max did as they were supposed to as well, but they were smaller. Sean's turban kept sliding down over his eyes, and Max stumbled a few times when his robes tangled around his ankles. Worst of all, and not unexpectedly, the camel had a bit of a problem, confirming Alex's suspicion that the brownies were laced with marijuana. The front end could not walk straight, and the back end found this hilarious; it kept laughing. It had enough sense left to know it ought not be laughing and tried to stifle it. The result was a camel that stumbled up the aisle behind the Magi, with its back half making odd, snorting sounds.

From their pew along the center aisle, Joe nudged Alex. "The camel is high," he whispered, under the choir singing "We Three Kings."

"I believe so." Alex sighed. "I guess it's obvious."

"Let's just hope Gloria doesn't figure it out."

Gloria didn't seem to have figured it out. Having expertise in small children and experience only with her own, and Alex and Joe's, teenagers, it apparently never occurred to her that her camel could be using drugs. She shrugged the camel actors' behavior off to "predictable adolescent irresponsibility." She gave the camel players a brief lecture before they left church after Mass, scolding them on the importance of being serious. Alex admired their ability to contain themselves, looking down and off to the sides, their faces red with muzzled laughter, which Gloria approvingly described later as proper embarrassment.

Alex and Joe sidled away, closer to the exit, and waited for Gloria, Bob, and their extended family to gather so they could all wish each other a merry Christmas Eve before heading home. Marta and Sean were very enthusiastic about the pageant.

"I liked being a shepherd," Marta announced. "Except I had a naughty sheep." She made an exaggerated fake frown at Bobby.

"Marta hit me," Bobby complained, to no one in particular.

"I tapped you. After you kicked Gina and Joey."

Sean pushed his turban back on his forehead. "Being a wise man was nice. But I really want to be a camel when I'm old enough. That looks like fun."

"I'm sure it does," answered Alex.

"They were laughing a lot, so it must have been fun," Sean continued.

"Yes, I talked to them about that," Gloria announced. "Did you see how they behaved when I talked to them just now? Such nice boys! A little silly but they knew enough to be embarrassed."

"Yes, I noticed they seemed a bit sheepish," Joe said helpfully.

"They were camels, not sheep," Bobby replied.

"Bobby, darling, sheepish means embarrassed," Veronica said, stroking his head. It seemed to Alex that Veronica looked a little pale, something she hadn't noticed in the chaos before Mass. Kevin, as always, looked unflappable; he resembled his father physically but was more like Gloria in his carriage and no-nonsense demeanor. Alex wondered how he and Veronica managed. She was always willing to try to explain things to the kids, squatting down to be at their level and "meet them where they are," although occasionally that meant Bobby taking a swing at her with one of his toys.

Tonight, Christmas Eve, there was no calming them down, and both Bobby and Gina were soon running around their parents in circles. Eventually, some sort of family portrait was achieved, with different adults cycling out to do the photography. Father Anthony came over and offered to take one with someone's camera so they could all be in it, and they agreed. Everyone knew that the picture would be crooked, and at least two people on the right side would be blocked by part of Father's thumb. He never could get the hang of taking pictures with a phone.

Chapter Twenty-Eight

December 24

Anger at myself. Feeling like no matter what I do, it's at least partly wrong.

Torn about confronting Sandy—she looked so stunned, poor thing. Like a deer in the headlights. Actually at a loss for words.

Glad Joe didn't rescue her or jump in with over-explaining so I didn't end up looking like an idiot who can't speak for myself.

Anger at me for not telling Gloria to stop bossing me around. Just let me know what to do and stop dictating.

What would happen if I just spoke up more? Like with Sandy?

I survived the pageant. Now get through Christmas. Don't stir the pot.

December 25

Christmas was lovely—very peaceful.

Happy to have the pageant over with.

Happy to have time with friends and family this season.

Happy Joe and Bob are going fishing tomorrow and that I'll have a day for quiet relaxation.

December 26

The boys just left to go fishing. Thank you, Lord! It's so quiet and peaceful. Just a few hours of respite and quiet.

Grateful Christmas Day was peaceful and that no one misbehaved. Grateful for the break from work.

Looking forward to Mom's visit, hoping we have some time to just soak up each other's company. Feeling guilty about not understanding what life has been like for her since Dad died. I guess I just thought she was doing fine because she acted fine.

I wonder if everyone is doing the same thing to me. Thinking I'm fine because I don't say anything.

Chapter Twenty-Nine

Boxing Day dawned clear, cool, and calm: a perfect day for some wintery fishing. Joe was out the door early, and Alex had his sandwiches and snacks packed. They had a quick cup of coffee together before she saw him off.

It was a day of long moments and quick hours, the texture of day that allowed the mind to stretch, wander, and rest. Alex spent the first hour or so in quiet wandering, going from room to room, slowly savoring the Christmas tree, gazing out a window, letting her eyes linger on shelves of books and old photos of Jonah, Sandy, Joe, and herself. She looked for a long time at an old, old photo of Joe and her, when she was expecting Jonah. She hardly recognized herself. It wasn't the longer hair or the fact that, even pregnant, younger Alex was twenty pounds lighter; she realized with a start that she had looked hopeful and happy, as if she expected the very next moment to be a great surprise, and the next to be an adventure. She tried to remember feeling that way. She could almost hear Dr. Sam suggesting she let her mind wander through memories to find some that felt similar, to tap into the themes and situations that set her up for that emotion.

She made a mug of hot chocolate and considered this question of hopefulness, of happy anticipation. She couldn't remember the last time she felt that way about her job, or dealing with Jonah and Beth, or even Sandy. The best mood she usually mustered was one of quiet contentment or just relief. It occurred to her suddenly that there ought to be something besides feeling "bad" and "glad I'm not feeling overtly bad." She stood at the sliding doors, watching the morning. The day was bright, and it would be in the high sixties soon. She slid the glass open and felt the breeze, heard the tinkle of ornaments catching the air currents as they passed through the house.

There ought to be something, she thought, *something besides just getting through day by day*. The question of the sabbatical, *her* sabbatical, lingered. Was the answer there, figuring out the year and carrying it out? What would happen by taking that step away from all the routine to figure out who she was, now, and what had happened to that art and biology major with the wide, far-seeing eyes?

She sat on the floor, cross-legged, sipping her cocoa and eating a purple-sugar-crusted snowman cookie, thinking. She stayed there for a long time, before standing up stiffly. She went purposefully to the spare room-turned-office and dug out a fresh notebook, went back to the floor with a cup of coffee, and began to write. Except for breaks to stretch and grab another snack, she was there until midafternoon. She realized with a start that Joe could be home any moment. She felt a twinge of annoyance followed by guilt; on the one hand, she looked forward to his coming home, and on the other, she didn't feel ready to interrupt her day or share what she was experiencing.

She tucked the notebook into her bedside table drawer and wandered again through the house. She opened their bedroom closet and stood there, staring at her clothes. It occurred to her that she didn't particularly like most of her clothes and, touching a few pieces, she could not recall ever really liking them. It felt as if some other person had gone off and bought things that might suit a stereotypical middle-aged lady librarian from an old movie, just modernizing them a tad, and that she, like a good cast member, had simply put on what the wardrobe people supplied. She wondered if she should talk to Dr. Sam about this, about this burgeoning realization that so much seemed to be "not me" while it was, after all, all hers. She pictured the eyebrows going up and the birdlike head tilt, the question being turned back onto her until Dr. Sam somehow came up with a synopsis that made more sense than all the words Alex had poured out. She'd said as much, once, and Dr. Sam shrugged and said, "I'm just saying it back to you in a slightly different way—nothing new. Things sound different when someone else says them aloud, don't they?"

Alex wondered, suddenly, if it would sound different to say her thoughts aloud. "I don't even like most of these things," she said, quietly, and felt ridiculous. Alex pulled a blue, black, and white shirt off the rack and held it up. The collar was limp and she realized with horror that the armpits were yellowed and that she'd been wearing this regularly, usually without a jacket or sweater. "This is a mess," she murmured. She reminded herself no one was home, took a deep breath and said, with more assurance, "I don't like most of these things! I can't believe I've been wearing this stuff." She sighed. "So why do you? Why do I?"

The back door slammed. Alex replaced the shirt, quietly shut the closet door, and called, "Hello!" as she headed toward the kitchen. It was nearly four o'clock. Joe was back, bubbling with energy.

"What a day! The fishing was great. No keepers, of course, but we kept the herons and pelicans happy. How was your day?"

"Lovely. Lots of time for reading and thinking. Much needed. Hot cocoa?"

"Ah, make mine coffee."

"This late?"

"I won't make it until supper otherwise."

Joe smiled at Alex and said, "I still can't believe you didn't tell Gloria what was going on with the camel on Christmas Eve."

Alex smiled back, shaking her head. "Can you imagine? 'Gloria, the camel has been eating special brownies to deal with stage fright, and has a bad case of the giggles.' No, that wouldn't fly."

"I can't believe she just blamed it on teenage silliness. She's raised four kids. Surely she can tell stoned from plain silly."

Alex shrugged. "Maybe Gloria doesn't like the facts as well as she likes to think she does. After all, what are we supposed to do with a laughing camel's behind five minutes before the Christmas Vigil Mass? Call the police? Make do with half a camel? At least the front end wasn't giggling." She paused and looked off to one side, exaggeratedly thoughtful. "Perhaps ask the assistant director's husband to step in and be a camel's behind to help out the team?"

Joe grunted. "Point made. Better to have said nothing."

"I talked to the kids. And to the camel's parents. Discretely, in private. The kids are fifteen and I don't think their parents had any idea."

Joe looked at her sideways. "The shaggy-haired kids? I've seen the parents. They knew. Trust me."

Alex shrugged. "They didn't exactly seem surprised but I hope they appreciate that I was trying to be tactful."

"I'm sure."

The phone rang. Alex rolled her eyes. "Gloria already! Bob can't have been home more than five minutes." She picked up the phone. "Gloria! Hello!"

There was silence on Alex's end. She turned to stare at Joe, who sat up and put his mug down. Alex turned pale and ran her free hand through her hair repeatedly. Joe gestured and mouthed, "What?" but she only shook her head. Finally, Alex said, "Gloria, I'm sorry. We're on our way." She paused to listen. "See you in a few minutes, as soon as we can get there."

"What? Sorry?" Joe leaned forward.

Alex put the phone down and sucked in her lips before speaking. "Bob was in an accident. He's in an ambulance on the way to the hospital. Gloria's following after. I told her we'd meet her at the ER."

Gloria was alone in the ER when they arrived. She looked smaller than usual, pale and disheveled. She rushed over to them. "Bob's going through all sorts of imaging. They're not sure what happened, but it looks like"—she made a choking sound—"it looks like he had some sort of heart attack and that caused the accident."

"Oh my gosh." Alex hugged Gloria and Joe hugged them both. "Was anyone else hurt?"

Gloria shook her head. "It was a one-car accident. He just careened off the road. The car is a mess. I can't believe they got him out in one piece. Well, sort of one piece."

"Sort of?"

"He's all beat up. The airbags deployed, he's black and blue every-where. He has some broken bones and they're checking for internal injuries." Her voice cracked. "They're going to get back to me once they have more information."

"Are any of the kids coming? Do we need to call anyone?"

"Matt and Tim are on the way. Kevin will come after work. Rachel's coming any minute. Cody—oh, gosh. I forgot."

"Forgot?"

"He's got the evening shift. I'm supposed to watch the twins. I can't, I just can't." Gloria looked, impossibly, even more panicked.

Alex held her hand. "I'll take the twins. Just call Cody and tell him to bring the kids over to our house instead of yours. What time should I be there? I want to stay with you as long as I can."

"He works from six to nine thirty, so he drops them off by five thirty." Gloria texted Cody. "Done. Thank you."

Alex glanced at her watch. "Okay, I'll head out in about ten minutes. Joe, can you stay here and catch a ride home later, maybe with Matt and Tim?"

"Absolutely. I'll stay here as long as Gloria needs me."

Gloria smiled bleakly. "Thank you."

A young woman stepped out from the exam rooms and scanned the three of them. "Mrs. Quinn?" Gloria nodded. "I'm Dr. Absel. We've gotten some preliminary reports back on Robert. Can I continue speaking in front of ...?"

"Our best friends. Yes, please, doctor."

"Robert appears to have had a significant cardiac infarction, which led to the accident."

"His heart? A heart attack?" Gloria reached a hand toward Alex. Gloria stood, and Alex and Joe stood with her, each taking one of Gloria's arms. Gloria pressed her lips together and shook her head firmly. "A heart attack," she repeated. "The widow-maker?"

She's thinking of Grandpa Quinn and his close call, Alex thought, holding Gloria's hand.

The doctor shook her head. "Not quite that type. And, well, fortunately, Robert has survived. The cardiologist will, of course, give you a full report on the damage and what follow-up will be necessary." She paused, looking at all three of them. "In the accident, Robert suffered considerable bruising to his upper body and face. No broken bones in the rib cage, shoulders, arms, or face."

"Oh, thank God," Gloria breathed.

"But he has multiple fractures in his pelvis and both legs, and some significant swelling in the lower abdomen. We need to get the swelling down to avoid organ damage and get the bones repaired. He's being moved to intensive care." The doctor looked down at her clipboard. "The surgeon will be along shortly, after he's seen the imaging."

"Can I see him?"

The doctor frowned. "He's sedated right now."

"I don't care." Gloria drew her eyebrows together and pinched her lips.

The disapproving eagle look even works on exhausted ER residents, Alex thought, because the doctor pulled her chin back and mumbled, "Of course. This way, please." She then called down the hall to one of the nurses, "Edmundo! Can you accompany Mrs. Quinn to her husband?" She turned back to them. "I'm afraid the rest of you must wait here."

Alex squeezed Gloria's hand as she stood up. "Gloria, Joe's going to stay in the ER and meet the kids. Just text when you have info. I'm going home to meet Cody and the twins."

Gloria's temporary show of strength was fading. She smiled a little and said, "Thank you." Alex hugged her, hugged Joe, and whispered, "Thank you!" to him. Then she headed for home.

Cody and the twins were in the driveway when she arrived. "Cody! Marta! Sean! Sorry I'm late." Alex stretched out her arms and they all stepped in for a group hug. "Your dad will be okay." She smiled down at the twins. "Grandpa will be okay." She nodded toward the house. "Let's go in. It's chilly. Cody, you have to rush, right?"

"Yeah. Mom filled me in a little. I guess she's waiting to hear from the surgeon."

"Does Grandpa have to have an operation?" Marta looked concerned.

Alex glanced at Cody, who said, "Yes, Grandpa has some broken bones and it will take a surgeon to set them all right so he can heal properly."

"Oh, okay," Sean said. "I had a broken bone once. When I fell out of the tree."

"Technically, you fell out of the tree onto the porch roof and rolled off," Cody clarified. "But, yes, you did have a broken bone. Grandpa has a lot of them."

"I remember the tree and roof incident," Alex remarked, shepherding the kids in. She looked up at Cody. "The kids can stay as long as needed. I'm guessing you'll want to stop by to see your folks before you head home. If it makes sense for them to sleep here, that's fine. I have extra toothbrushes and plenty of space."

"Thanks, Aunt Alex. I'll let you know what's going on. Usually, it's pickup at Mom and Dad's and straight to bed on these late nights." He sighed. "But I don't want Mom alone at the hospital."

"It's really no problem," Alex said. "I'm on vacation."

"Are we sleeping here?" Sean asked.

"We'll see," Alex answered. "Daddy will decide later and let us know. Bye, Cody."

"Bye, Daddy!" the twins shouted and then they came the rest of the way in, shedding their jackets. "Aunt Alex, what's wrong with Grandpa, really? Why does Daddy need to go to the hospital, too?"

"To see Grandma, silly," Marta said matter-of-factly. "She's going to be worried. So, Daddy has to go cheer her up."

"We could go cheer her up."

"Hmm," Alex said. "Hospitals can be kind of boring if you don't work there." She paused. "Grandpa was in a car accident, and he got some bruises and some broken bones. So, he needs lots of care and an operation to fix things up."

"We can't help with an operation. We'd have to wait," Marta added. "Plus, they all have televisions. Daddy gets upset when we watch a lot of television." She paused to think. "It's better to be here."

Alex nodded. "How about if we go to the kitchen and figure out some supper? Did you kids eat yet?"

"No!"

The three of them were up to their eyebrows in flour and cheese, making homemade mini-pizzas, when Joe called with an update. Bob would be in surgery for a couple of hours, and he, Matt, and Tim were going to stay with Gloria, who was alternating between her in-charge self and near panic. "Cody said, yes, keep the kids there. He's going to take a late shift with his mom after he's done at work. He'll be by in the morning for the kids. I'll catch a ride home later from Matt and Tim after surgery."

Alex turned to the kids after she'd put down the phone. "It looks like you're sleeping here, kids. After pizza we'll figure out sleeping arrangements. We do have a guest room with a big bed." She paused, considering. "You know what sounds kind of fun? Sleeping by Christmas tree light. How about if we set up the air mattress in the living room so you can sleep near our Christmas tree? Do you think that would be okay?"

"Oh, yes!" Marta said and Sean echoed. "Yes!"

"Uh, oh," Marta said. "We don't have toothbrushes here. Or paja-
mas."

"We don't need toothbrushes," Sean offered.

Marta grimaced. "Ew, gross. You're stinky without a toothbrush."

"So are you."

"I have brand new toothbrushes—one for each of you. Now, pa-
jamas are a bit of a problem. How about using some of Sandy's old
T-shirts?"

"A GIRL T-shirt?" Sean protested.

"Well, most of Sandy's T-shirts are actually men's shirts, for anyone
to wear. I'll make sure I pick you out one of those," Alex assured him.

"I hope it has cool stuff on it. Like maybe sea turtles or sharks."

"She definitely has T-shirts with turtles and sharks."

Sean relented. "Yeah, okay."

"Good. It's decided. But before bedtime we'll have some stories. I
have some really good Christmas ghost stories."

"Cool!" Sean pronounced. He was layering pepperoni and slices of
cheese on a very small crust. "This pizza is going to be perfect!"

Chapter Thirty

The holiday plans included grandparents visiting from out of town, and the next day, Grandpa Quinn arrived, a day early on account of the accident. Joe picked him up at the airport, updating him on the latest about Bob. It seemed there was new information hourly. Grandpa had peppered Joe with questions. He wanted to drop his things off at Gloria's and head straight to the hospital to see his son. Joe suggested they give Gloria a call first, but Grandpa Quinn would have none of it. It was useless to argue with him.

Joe let Alex know they were on the way to hospital, and she called Gloria. "Gloria?"

Gloria's voice was quieter and flatter than usual. "Alexa, dear. I'm glad you called."

"Of course. Partly this is a heads-up; Joe's on the way with Grandpa Quinn."

"Thanks. It will be good to see him." Gloria sighed. "I guess I need to actually pay attention to how he got past all this, the heart attack and everything. Of course, he was much younger, but on the other hand, for younger men these big heart attacks are more often deadly. That's what the doctor said. As if that was supposed to make me feel better, that Bob has to recover from all this in his 60s instead of his 40s. And Quinn didn't have a car crash with his heart attack."

"I think Bob will be glad that Quinn's here. I mean, they're very close."

"Yes, and I'm glad, too. It just feels like a lot. Well, Quinn will spend a little time at Kevin's and then off to stay with Matt and Tim. You know how those three are. Thick as thieves."

Alex tried to sound cheerful. "And they'll have some fun. I bet some of the boys' neighbors will enjoy meeting Quinn."

"You mean the widowed ladies? They're already looking forward to it. Ha, they don't know what they're in for." For a moment, Gloria sounded like herself. "They're not ready for eighty-six going on twenty-six, half Tasmanian devil and half Irish setter."

Alex laughed. "You're right, of course. But has anyone ever been ready for Quinn besides Molly?"

They shifted the topic to Bob. Gloria said the medical team was a little more positive; things seemed be improving. Alex asked if anything needed doing around the house, laundry or grocery shopping. Gloria didn't think so, and then she said, "Well, here comes Grandpa Quinn. We'll talk later, dear."

"Bye, Gloria."

Joe came home thirty minutes later and walked in shaking his head. "Grandpa Quinn's at the hospital. If they didn't have their hands full already with Gloria, they'll be just about overdone with Grandpa."

Alex nodded thoughtfully. "I think we all have our hands full. Poor Gloria. Poor Quinn—imagine, seeing your son this way."

Joe was quiet.

The next few days were a blur.

Alex did her best to fill Gloria's shoes with the twins, who were good sports and in fact seemed to settle easily into the quiet rhythm of life at the Bonhall house. On December 29th, Alex's mother, Marlene, arrived for her New Year's week visit and pitched in, relishing Marta and Sean as if they were her own great-grandchildren. Sandy was underemployed; no students were interested in using the Christmas break to catch up. Even the activists were inactive during the break. It would have been a perfect time to focus on the endless dissertation process, but the twins' presence was an excuse for Sandy to completely immerse herself in childhood again. Alex had to admit that having Sandy, with her boundless energy, rustle the children off for beach walks and argue with them over the rules during endless board games was a welcome backup. Marlene taught them how to make art out of found objects, collage and frottage, and provided general moral support for everyone. By the end of the week, Cody and the twins were joining them for dinner unless Cody was working late.

That was welcome, too, because a strange pall had fallen over Joe since Bob's injury. His appetite was off; he was preoccupied and rest-less. Alex's attempts at conversation fell flat. He seemed to rally a bit for the sake of Cody and the twins, and, of course, Sandy was usually able to poke him into at least a short flare of annoyance.

Five days after the accident it was New Year's Eve. That morning, Alex and Marlene had driven to a nearby park for a long, leisurely walk and the privacy to chat without intrusion. They walked for a while, Marlene catching Alex up on life in their hometown, Elsa's wing of the family, and the goings-on in her circle of friends. After a quiet stretch, Marlene cleared her throat. "So, what's been going on for you, honey? Have you thought more about the sabbatical?"

Alex wondered how it was her mother could cut right through all the niceties sometimes, and at other times allow things to be vague.

"I've given it plenty of thought. Just haven't been talking about it much."

"Because?"

"Oh, you know. End of term. The holidays. And now, with Bob's accident, everything's pretty crazy."

"All the more reason to look ahead." Marlene paused, reaching up to touch a tree growing along the path. "I love these old sycamores. The bark is so beautiful." She turned back to Alex. "Joe's just a wreck over this. He's having his 'oh gosh, we're all mortal' moment."

"Yes. I'm hoping we'll be able to just talk through things but he's so ... quiet."

"Funny, isn't it." Marlene glanced at Alex. "You've been waiting for him to just pause and let you get a word in edgewise, and now you're paralyzed because he won't talk enough."

"Well, if you put it that way, it sounds ridiculous. I should just tell him what I'm thinking."

Marlene agreed. "It's not going to get easier by waiting. And he has no idea, honey, that you have your own ideas on sabbatical. Trust me. You haven't said a peep and so he assumes that means everything's great."

Alex frowned. "A person would have to be unconscious to think everything's great. He lectures me about my stress. What does he think?"

"He thinks exactly what you've let him think. That it's just work, or Sandy being an overaged teenager, or Jonah being thoughtless."

"Fair enough." *But it doesn't feel fair*, Alex thought, a bit resentfully. *It's always my fault, huh?* She kept quiet and breathed. Marlene reached over and gave Alex's hand a gentle squeeze, and Alex felt her burgeoning resentment melt. They walked in companionable silence for a long time. "I need a break," Alex said. "Mind if we sit a bit?" They were passing a bench facing the pond.

Marlene sat down. "This is lovely. The sun on the water, the birds. No snow."

"It is." Alex settled herself, fussing with her sleeves. "I think I'll talk with Joe tonight. New Year's Eve, right? A natural time to talk about the year ahead."

Marlene patted Alex's hand, then gave it a squeeze. "It will be fine, honey. You'll see. Joe adores you. He wants you to be happy."

Alex squeezed her mom's hand. They sat quietly for a long time, thinking about good men who want their wives to be happy.

Later, Alex and Joe were finally having a relatively quiet evening. Sandy was spending the evening with Rachel, Gloria, Cody, the twins, Quinn, Matt, and Tim. Jonah and Beth were spending the evening at a fundraising ball for a local animal rescue organization. Marlene had excused herself to go to her room about nine o'clock. She was tired, she said, and she wanted to relax and be well-rested. She always went to the early Mass on New Year's Day. "Anyone who wants to can join me! Leaving at 6:45!" But as it was every year, there were no takers. Marlene didn't miss church unless she was ill or there was a weather emergency, and they'd become accustomed to her habit of going off to early Mass and then making a huge meal for everyone upon her return.

Alex glanced at Joe. He was staring at the floor a few feet in front of his easy chair. "Tea? Some decaf?" she offered. "I could use a cup." She waited a moment. "Joe? Can I get you anything?"

He looked up quizzically. "Sorry?"

She tried to smile. "You're a million miles away! I wondered if I could get you anything; I'm having a cup of chamomile tea."

Joe shook his head.

"Thinking about Bob and Gloria?"

He nodded slowly, pressing his lips together. Sighing, he looked at Alex. "I can't explain it, quite, but this is really hitting me hard. It's as if nothing makes sense." He looked back at the floor. "Like going to the hospital and seeing Gloria—God bless her, she's usually in charge anywhere she goes. She looks like a lost soul."

"Yes, it hurts to see her so ... shrunken. I was there yesterday and she couldn't even pick what to have for lunch. That's not our Gloria. And Bob ..."

"It all feels ... crazy. Wrong."

Alex took a deep breath. "It feels too soon, if that makes sense. God, that sounds awful. But I thought we'd all have more time."

Joe looked up sharply. "He's not dead."

"No, no, of course not," Alex replied. "But let's face it, Bob was a one-man demolition team, health-wise. He completely disregarded any medical advice whatsoever. And those days will have to be over." She moved toward the kitchen. "Can I get you anything while I'm making tea?"

Joe shrugged. "Sure, a decaf would be good. Just plain."

"Gloria said it will be weeks of rehab and physical therapy before he's reliably out of a wheelchair and on his own. And that's not to mention recovering from the heart attack." Alex leaned in from the doorway. "I'm guessing it will be a long, strange process for both of them. All of us. And the kids, too. Cody relies on his mom with the kids."

"When do they go back to school?"

"The week we do. Well, when I do. You faculty have a soft start." She watched. Usually, a little dig about the limited office hours for faculty during the week before students returned could get a playful rise out of Joe, but not today. Today he barely nodded, still staring at the floor in front of his feet.

She brought out their drinks and a plate with cookies. Joe raised his eyebrows. "Those are some cookies."

Alex laughed. "Marta and Sean had a bit of fun with the colored sugars, didn't they?"

"Is there any sugar left? Anywhere in the county?"

"Hardly. Still, they had fun. And the cookies are festive."

"In a Mardi Gras kind of a way. Since when is purple a Christmas color? Or orange?"

"Oh, Joe." Alex smiled. "Don't be such a curmudgeon. That one's a finch. And that's an oriole."

"Not doves?"

"The silver and white ones are doves."

"I sense your influence in the cookie-making department."

Alex feigned offense. "What? A few crazy colored birds and it's my fault?"

They sipped their drinks.

Joe put his cup down. "This whole thing … it has me thinking."

Alex waited.

Joe turned to her. "I'm not really sure. Just bouncing ideas around. But I'm unsettled and … I don't know. I just don't know."

Alex reached over and squeezed his free hand. Joe squeezed back and then withdrew his hand, wrapping it around the still-steaming mug. "I just … Hell, I can't even string words together. I'm as lost as … I feel lost. Like I'm trying to find something and can't sort out where to even begin."

Alex waited quietly. She thought about Dr. Sam and her ability to just be quiet and wait, to not jump in and fill a space with words and activity. She recalled how many times she'd thought it was some sort of therapist cop-out, a pretense when you didn't know what to do or say.

Now she had a surge of admiration; this holding back and listening was incredibly difficult.

Minutes ticked by. Joe sat back and looked at Alex. "What about you? This can't be any easier for you."

Alex shook her head. "No, it's been a lot to process. And busy." She put her mug down and sighed. "Joe, I've been in that place for months now, that weird, desert place, I guess. Waiting for enlightenment, for a clear path. And it hasn't been easy."

"Desert place?"

Alex shrugged and examined the surface of her tea. "It's been a rough time for me. Probably for a long time, sorting out the 'what now' and 'what next.' Sorting out what I ought to be doing besides being on autopilot."

"I didn't know." Joe frowned at his knees. "I guess I wasn't listening. I thought you were just, you know, having a little fun, doing a little this or that. You never said it was serious."

"I've been seeing a therapist. Doesn't that sound as if it's serious?"

"Oh, hell, everyone I work with has a therapist. Half of them can't decide what to have for dinner without asking someone for insight. If it's not a therapist it's a personal trainer or a life coach. Whatever." Joe shrugged. "I didn't take it seriously."

There was another long silence while Alex wondered what to say. She wanted to shout, "Well, take me seriously for a change!" And she also wanted to be kind. Joe was clearly struggling, and it didn't seem useful to launch an attack. *And*, she thought, *use the "and."* She tried channeling Dr. Sam. "Well, I suppose that on the one hand, you weren't really listening and on the other, I didn't do such a good job of being clear about how much I've been struggling." She paused. "So, it makes sense, you not hearing what I wasn't directly saying."

Joe leaned forward, putting his hand on hers. "Maybe. But I'm listening now."

"It's late," she teased gently. "Maybe another day."

"Hey, it's New Year's Eve. We've got a couple of hours to close up the year right."

Alex stood up. "Then maybe I'll make some cocoa. With marshmallows."

Settled in by Christmas tree lights with hot cocoa, waiting for midnight, it was the perfect time for a little heart-to-heart. Alex felt herself freezing up. She wrestled with quiet resentment that Joe had minimized her efforts to make changes into little fun escapades and the self-indulgent use of psychotherapy that some of his academic friends did. She thought in passing of wild-haired Dr. Arnold from the sociology department; was she one of them? She imagined, suddenly, Dr. Arnold with her Pre-Raphaelite curls and flowing, calf-length vests half-reclining on Dr. Sam's small sofa, gesturing wildly and nearly knocking over the lamps, and Dr. Sam sitting there, implacably calm except for her constantly cavorting eyebrows. Having entertained herself, she sat up straighter and focused on the conversation with Joe.

"I've been struggling with feeling ... bored, stuck, wanting to change things," she started. Joe was silent. "I mean changing me, not us. Not the house. Well, maybe the closets," she acknowledged. "But you know, I've been in a rut. I don't think I ever adapted to being 'off duty' with the kids, so to speak, and I'd like to change course a little, maybe with my sabbatical."

"I know what you mean," he said, "about changing course. With Bob's situation, it makes it even more clear to me I have to make the most of things."

"It's an existential moment for all of us."

"That's the thing." Joe leaned forward and put his mug down. "I thought we all had 'this much' time left," he said, gesturing broadly. "Lots of time, but maybe not. Maybe that was an illusion. And I have to get going. I have to start living, doing the things I've been postponing."

"Yes, that's right where I've been," Alex began. But it was too late for her to elaborate.

Joe had begun talking, his stream of consciousness rolling out, flowing through the remainder of New Year's Eve, elaborating on his postponed dreams of fishing adventures, history books and memoirs, his disappointment in Jonah, his frustration with Sandy and her endless doctoral program, his sense that time was spinning past them all, and all of them, himself included, were blinded by the mundane.

Alex was grateful he was talking a little at last. *At least he's talking about life, our life. But I wish he would pause, take a break to listen to me. To take me seriously.* She tried to interject several times, but each time the waves of words just kept coming from Joe, tumbling right over her attempts to break in.

After they had snuggled under the blankets, she lay awake a while, listening to him breathe quietly and ease into soft snoring. She wondered how a person could love someone so deeply and yet feel unable to speak. She rested in the feeling and recognized it as fear.

Chapter Thirty-One

The Brown-Headed Cowbird

The brown-headed cowbird is a bit of a moocher, often using others' nests and stealing their food. It lets others raise its young. It is a very different relationship than that of a bird some people think of as the "cow bird," the white cattle egret, which rides on cattle or walks beside them, eating bugs stirred up by grazing or ticks and other biting insects that prey on the cattle.

Cody was off on Friday, so Alex didn't have the twins. Gloria had asked her to meet for breakfast at the hospital; there was a big meeting that morning regarding Bob's care, and she'd hoped Alex would come. "An extra pair of ears," Gloria had said.

"Of course," Alex had assured her. She switched to loyal best friend duty and tried hard not to think about having a quiet day to read on

Christmas vacation, glancing over at her favorite chair, and the book ready and waiting for her, as she gently hung up the phone.

When she was honest with herself, Alex wondered if her empathy and concern for Gloria was really all about Gloria and Bob's dilemma. The journaling homework meant she allowed herself more reflection, a side effect of therapy she hadn't really expected. It was making her more aware of her flaws, which felt a lot like preparing to go to confession. She had a sinking sense that part of her strong emotions about Gloria and Bob were really about herself, her imagined future with an ailing, or dead, husband, and the fears, sorrow, and insecurity she could imagine having were getting tangled up with the kind, unflagging concern for her best friend.

Hadn't she listened to Gloria and wondered, more than a bit, what she, herself, would do in this situation? How she would handle it? What would Gloria do if Bob died now, so soon, before he'd even fully retired? What would she do if Joe died now? Alex found herself going down dark trails, realizing that she hadn't really considered how much her life would be thrown into chaos. She'd thought of widowhood briefly, of course, after her father, and then Joe's father, had died, but Jonah and Sandy were younger then, and she was able to focus on them. Now her friend, her best friend, was facing the possibilities of widowhood or a life of caregiving for her husband, and Alex pondered how she would handle it herself.

It was too terrifying to contemplate for more than a few moments. She knew she could not afford the house for long on her own, and that her children would not be as valiantly by her side as Gloria's four. She thought grimly that Jonah would scornfully ask how she and Joe could have failed to plan adequately, and Sandy would be full of well-intended advice and overbearing, unwanted help. Jonah would, at best, rifle through their finances and simply pronounce that she'd have to sell the house and move someplace smaller. Did she know any realtors, he might even add, perhaps someone from church? Sandy, meanwhile, hearing about a move, would launch into one of her crusades. It was a great opportunity to simplify and get rid of all this junk, Alex imagined her announcing. Alex gently touched a small ceramic toothpick holder, faded and chipped, that Sandy had bought for her as a souvenir on a childhood outing with her grandparents. Would this be junk to her, Alex wondered, or would she ever mature enough to realize that what looked like junk to Sandy might be an anchor to precious memories for her mother?

She shrugged into a light jacket and headed out the door, turning uncharacteristically to look at their entryway, as if she had to memorize it. Then she shook her head. *Stop being morbid*, she scolded herself. *It's not healthy.*

The hospital parking lot was already crowded, with the only open spaces a few hundred yards away from the building. Alex hadn't walked more than a moment before a golf cart pulled up beside her. The driver, wearing a T-shirt that said General Hospital Volunteer, waved and said, "Can I give you a lift?"

Nodding, Alex stepped in and sat in the back seat. "Thanks; it's a bit of a walk."

"It is. This place is always crowded. Where can I drop you?"

"The main entrance, I guess. I'm meeting a friend. Her husband's here."

The driver nodded. "Front entrance it is." He glanced over his shoulder. "It's good of you to come spend time with her. It's hard being here alone for any length of time." He shook his head.

"It must be." Alex paused. "It sounds as if you've been through this."

He had. He explained how thirty years ago, their little boy, Tommy, had come down with meningitis. As far as anyone could tell, he picked it up swimming at the lake. They'd lived about fifty miles away then. He'd been working, of course, so he couldn't be at the hospital full-time. But his wife came. Tommy was flown here by helicopter and spent weeks in the intensive care unit. The hospital had been wonderful. The social worker had helped his wife make contact with the convent down the street. The sisters had some small spare rooms where women could stay when they had a loved one in hospital. They didn't charge anything for the rooms; it was just a great kindness. Tommy recovered. He was forty now, and liked to be called Thomas. He guessed that a lot of young people did that, want to switch around what they'd been called since childhood and have the adult version. But Thomas was grown and married, and had two children, a boy and a girl. They lived here in town; maybe she knew them? He taught at the local college, in the English department.

"I'm one of the librarians there. Perhaps I do. What's the last name?" Alex asked.

"Ambrose. Tommy, well, Thomas Ambrose. I'm Tom," he added.

"Good to meet you, Tom. I know Thomas, yes; a lot of his students come to the library for help with their papers."

Tom grinned over his shoulder. "I bet they do." By now they were parked near the main entrance. "I just bet they do." He paused. "This place really is wonderful. I started volunteering here after I retired and we moved closer, five years ago. My wife helps out in the gift shop. Betsy. If you stop in there, introduce yourself. We just can't do enough for this place after how they saved our boy."

"That's beautiful," Alex said warmly. "I'm so glad—so glad that we met and so glad that all is well. Thanks for the lift, Tom."

Tom tipped his ball cap and wished her a good visit. As she went in, she heard him greeting someone. "Hello, there! Need a lift to your car or the bus stop?"

Alex headed toward the cafeteria, where Gloria had asked to meet. Gloria was just stepping out of the elevator, coming down from her early morning time with Bob. As it had been since the accident, Alex felt a twinge of distress when she saw Gloria slumped, disheveled and pale. This morning, she looked wilted.

Alex smiled and hugged her friend. "Good morning! How are you? How's Bob?"

Gloria hugged her back, tighter than usual, then straightened up and tugged at her jacket. She pressed her lips together briefly and looked past Alex's face. "Bob's holding his own, they say. He's awake, he's conversant, and he still doesn't remember much of what happened." She sighed. "He's stable now and the team and I are meeting with him later. We're talking discharge plans to a rehab center. Probably later this week." Gloria gave herself a bit of a shake. "Grandpa Quinn's in the cafeteria, holding a table for us already."

They headed into the cafeteria. It had been upgraded since the last time Alex had been there. The lights had been changed to a warmer tone, so that people didn't have that greenish, sickly look from the lighting. The walls were festooned with cheery posters showing happy people eating healthy foods. The flat, uncomfortable chairs had been replaced with curvier ones that had arms. Alex imagined that would make it easier for people with canes or walkers to get up and down.

Alex rubbed Gloria's back as they strolled to the serving line. "That sounds hopeful, that he's going to rehab. Any good news on his prognosis?"

Gloria shrugged. "It sounds like they want to be hopeful that he'll walk again soon, without a cane, but that it's not terribly likely."

She frowned. "Of course, some of that is based on Bob's history as a 'non-compliant' patient. Let's face it, if he'd been following his doctor's orders on his blood sugar and blood pressure ..."

"This is a tough one, isn't it, because it sounds almost like blaming the patient."

"Yes, and—oh, let's talk more after we sit down." They were surrounded by other visitors, mostly anxious family and friends, and medical and administration staff.

Alex agreed. She gazed down the cafeteria line: parfaits and fruit bowls, stacks of pancakes, what seemed like wet, runny scrambled eggs, slices of ham, potatoes, and a lot of baked goods. She thought briefly of just getting a big plate of home fried potatoes and imagined Gloria's disapproving face. She could imagine the helpful comment. "Alexa, dear! Weren't you just talking about needing to lose a few pounds? Potatoes aren't going to help." She sighed, pushing her tray along the counter. She paused in front of the display of breakfast parfaits and smiled at the cafeteria worker. "Good morning!"

The cafeteria worker looked up with mild surprise, using her forearm to push back her hair net, which had flopped over her eyebrows. "Good morning. Can I help you?"

Alex pointed at the parfaits. "These look delicious. What flavors do you have?" She peered at the name tag. "Joanie. Thanks."

Joanie smiled. "We have blueberry and strawberry."

"Oh, a hard choice. They all look beautiful." Alex hesitated, eyes darting between the rows of parfaits.

Joanie leaned forward conspiratorially. "The blueberries are fresher. I'd go with that." She threw an extra dab of whipped cream on one and pushed it toward Alex.

"Why, thanks!" Alex put it on her tray. "Thanks, Joanie. Have a great day!"

"You, too."

Gloria was nearly at the end of the line and turned to see where Alex was, drawing her eyebrows together. "Alexa! What's taking so long?"

Alex tried not to sigh. She reminded herself Gloria could not be expected to be her best self right now and felt guilty for thinking Gloria wasn't actually behaving any differently than usual, except for looking weary.

Grandpa Quinn was standing by a table near the windows, waving and grinning. He'd found a place with four seats and already dragged over an extra chair. Gloria set down her tray and began dividing up her breakfast from Grandpa's while Alex put her tray down and they exchanged hugs.

"Our beautiful little Alexa!" Grandpa Quinn smiled, giving her an extra pat on the back as he released from the hug. "Always steady." Alex smiled and wondered why it felt gratifying and embarrassing, after all these years, that he still called her their "beautiful little Alexa." He sat back down, pulling his plate in front of him. "Thanks, Gloria. A big pile of potatoes. Start the day with energy, that's my motto. At least when someone else is doing the cooking."

Alex thought, briefly, that she should have gone ahead and gotten a big plate of delicious, butter-browned and salty potatoes. She poked at the parfait and uncovered a big, plump berry. It did look delicious.

Gloria announced she needed the restroom and would be right back. Settled in her chair next to the window, Alex wrapped her hands around her coffee cup and discreetly surveyed the cafeteria. She tried to remember the last time she'd been here. Could it really have been when Sandy was born? No, it had to be some other time; she wouldn't have come to the cafeteria when she was an inpatient for childbirth.

The decor had changed, but the activity hadn't. A few tables away, a weary, smiling young man and two far less weary older couples sat.

A new dad and the grandparents, she thought. The women were chattering happily. The older men looked quietly pleased. The father was poking at his food and staring into space. *Overwhelmed with the reality of responsibility, no doubt.* Alex wondered how long it would be before one of the grandmothers decided there was a competition. It was almost guaranteed that one or the other would quietly declare, at best, a cold war against the other grandmother.

At another table, an elderly woman sat quietly with four other women, three in middle age and one younger, and a small girl. The conversation was hushed. They all had the tight, determined smiles of people trying hard to keep from upsetting one another. Their voices sometimes came through, talking about "your father," "Dad," and, "Grandpa." The preschooler, about three or four, seemingly the elderly woman's great-grandchild, was the only one smiling freely, waving and greeting anyone who wandered past the table.

A group of medical personnel wearing drooping scrubs, with caps covering their hair, passed by, discussing the upcoming weekend. They looked tired and very young. "Sleep," a man with a red ponytail said flatly. "That's the plan. Sleep for twenty-four hours. In a bed, not on a chair in the file room." One of his colleagues nodded. "I may not make it to bed. The dog's going to have to surrender the couch."

Across the room, a religious sister in a brown, knee-length habit was sitting with an elderly man. He was weeping and she sat holding one of his hands while he covered his eyes with the other. Her face was gently sad, her presence peaceful.

She caught Grandpa Quinn's eye; he, too, had been taking in the scene. "All of life is here, isn't it?" he said. "That new dad over there, overwhelmed. The man across the way with the sister. The lady there, with her gaggle of girls, worried about the dad."

"It's stunning, how it all fits into this one place."

Gloria returned; she'd neatened her hair and put on lipstick. "This place is filling up!" she announced. "Of course, where else could you go to eat? It's a monopoly." She frowned briefly. "Matt and Tim should be here any moment."

"Oh, lovely," Alex said. "They were able to take time off. They're joining you for the meeting?"

"Us," Gloria corrected her. "They're joining us. I need lots of ears with me and enough people to be sure the right questions are asked." She shook her head. "I can't remember anything this week; I guess it's the sleep deprivation."

"So, as we were saying." Alex hesitated, rubbed her jaw, and looked straight at Gloria. "Have they told Bob they think this was preventable?"

"Not in so many words." Gloria stared into her coffee cup.

"That hurts," Alex offered tentatively.

Gloria was briefly silent. Grandpa Quinn said, quietly, "It's a bitter lesson and we have to learn it ourselves. At least I did. And that son of mine, he's apparently as hardheaded as me."

Gloria took a deep breath. "This heart attack – it apparently wasn't the first. I guess Bob was lucky – not my words, the doctors' – that it didn't kill him. Apparently, there were earlier events." She looked up at her father-in-law and Alex, her face drooping with weariness. "Everything has to change – everything. He could have been gone – gone – like that." She turned to stare briefly out the window, took a deep breath and faced them again, lips pressed firmly together.

Grandpa Quinn reached out to stroke Gloria's face and Alex watched as Gloria blinked back tears. She rested her hand on Gloria's. "Gloria, Bob's going to be alright. Look at Grandpa – he comes from tough stock."

Gloria nodded resolutely and took one shuddering breath. She shook her head and then poked at her breakfast sandwich. "I'm not quite sure what this is supposed to be."

"It smells good," Alex said. *She can only take so much at one time, just like when her mom died.*

Gloria raised her eyebrows. "But you didn't get it. You got the yogurt and granola."

"Yes, blueberry parfait. I guess I'm fussy about how my eggs are cooked. I'm a cook's nightmare when we go out for breakfast. Joe gave up trying to cook eggs for me years ago. It's that bad."

Gloria managed a small laugh. "Oh, you're one of those people. I guess I never paid attention when we breakfasted before."

"When I ordered my omelets cooked to death."

They smiled at each other—and then a whirlwind broke out. A woman burst into the cafeteria, pushing open the double doors and nearly knocking over an elderly man with a walker. Tall, wearing a short skirt and high boots, she stepped a few paces in with the kind of energy that distracts people—it seemed everyone looked in her direction—and she said, too loudly, "Where is she?" to no one in particular as she scanned the room. A cafeteria employee, attempting to be helpful, walked over. "Can I help you, miss?" and then—

"Oh, dear Lord, it's Jenna," Gloria and Alex said in unison, as the tall woman shrieked and waved her arms. They both reflexively looked down. Grandpa Quinn stood up, ever courteous.

"Oh, my gosh! Gloria! THERE you are." She rushed over, breathing hard, chest heaving, and loomed over their table. The fake fur trim on her sweater almost reached their breakfast; Alex slid a hand over her coffee and another over her parfait. "Gloria! I hadn't HEARD until last night. Oh, my gosh! You can't imagine how upset I was to hear the news!"

Gloria looked up. "Jenna. What a surprise."

Alex added, "Good morning, Jenna. How nice to see you."

Grandpa Quinn smiled as if everything were perfectly fine. "Jenna, how nice to see you. You're looking lovely this morning."

Jenna spared a quick, toothy smile for Grandpa Quinn. She barely looked at Alex. Ignoring the two empty chairs on the far side of the table, she reached over and grabbed a chair from a neighboring table without asking the table's residents, pulled it over, and sat down between Gloria and Grandpa Quinn with an emphatic plop. It was a relief to have her sitting; she was less obvious that way. She was not quite a fit with the staff scrubs and daytime visitor garb at the hospital. Jenna tossed back her hair, crossed her legs and gave her skirt a desultory tug toward her mid-thighs. "So how is he? Bob, I mean? The kids told me all about it."

"Oh, how nice. You've seen the children today already," Gloria said stiffly.

Jenna made a face. "This early? Please. No, I've got such a busy day. You know how it is. But I did call last night, we had a little video chat." She turned toward Alex. "Apparently they've been having such a lovely time at your house. How kind of you to pitch in for us during these incredibly difficult times."

Us? Alex wondered, and rubbed her jaw. Aloud she just said, "That's what friends are for." She glanced past Jenna's fur-trimmed shoulders and her eyes widened just a bit.

Matt and Tim had just strolled in. She watched as Tim pointed toward the line. Matt nodded and headed toward their table. "It looks like Matt and Tim are here," she said to Gloria.

"Ah, the boys," Grandpa Quinn said, smiling. "Wonderful." He turned to Gloria. "I'm over to their place this evening for a few nights, is that right? Giving Veronica a break." He winked at Alex. "Apparently I'm the third kid that makes life too much for these modern parents. They can't handle more than two without a bit of a crisis."

Grandpa Quinn usually stayed with Bob and Gloria and spent a few nights here and there with his grandchildren and their families, but this year the sharing was more extensive due to Bob's hospitalization. Gloria had concerns about rearranging the house for a long-term convalescence, possibly a hospital bed and accommodations for wheelchair and walker. Matt and Tim were looking forward to Grandpa Quinn seeing their new home and meeting the neighbors, and he was anticipating some quiet time with "the boys."

Alex knew the "boys" and Grandpa Quinn had a kind of mutual admiration society. "Oh, no, Kevin," she said. "I'm sure everyone wants a share of your time."

Gloria was watching Matt and Tim. She gave a satisfied nod. "They're early, but that's like them. I wanted them here for the team meeting. An extra set of ears. Well, two sets," she added, apparently forgetting she'd already told Alex this, or perhaps for Jenna's benefit.

Matt came up to the table, kissed his mom and then kissed Alex's cheek as well, and hugged his grandfather. "Good morning, Jenna," he said, and then, "Tim's coming over with our coffees."

Jenna resumed talking. "So, the children said it was serious. Why didn't anyone tell me? I've been so upset since I heard." Alex rubbed her jaw and looked past them all. She glanced over toward the serving line. Tim was making his way along the line, and she smiled a bit to herself: Tim was being Tim. Every cafeteria worker was smiling after Tim went by. She watched a female medical staffer, with a stethoscope around her neck and a tousled, end-of-shift bun of curly dark hair, lean in toward him, smiling and pointing at something in the buffet; the woman was attempting to be flirtatious. Tim smiled serenely and nodded, picked up the tray and headed their way. She turned her attention and caught Matt's eye.

"Tim's being Tim," he said quietly, smiling. "He's like you, Aunt Alex. Everyone has to talk to him." He tilted his head toward the serving line. "It's always like this, everywhere. Well, you know how it is."

Alex looked at Matt, befuddled. Her and Tim? Similar? She shook her head. She would not, in a million years, have ever put herself in any category with Tim.

"And Alexa has been such a help," Gloria was remarking. The sound of her own name cut through Alex's distraction.

"Oh," Jenna said. "The twins have been having a lovely time." Then her face froze.

Tim had arrived with two coffees and one of the largest blueberry muffins Alex had ever seen. He kissed Gloria and Alex, hugged Grandpa Quinn, and gave Jenna a cheerful, "Good morning, Jenna. Looking well! How are you?"

Jenna smiled tightly. Alex watched surreptitiously, absent-mindedly stirring what was left of her parfait. Jenna was scanning Tim. Alex recognized the look: It was the same assessing gaze women gave to other women they perceived to be competition for attention. Alex shook her head in wonderment; Jenna was jealous, somehow, of Tim.

If Tim was aware of her inventory of his appearance, he gave no sign. Wearing old jeans and a worn sweater, he was his usual, relaxed self. *Tim is comfortable in his own skin*, Alex thought, considering that as something more to be envied than his physical beauty.

Gloria said, "Thanks for being here, guys. I really appreciate it."

"Mom, of course," Matt replied, hand on her arm. "What time is the team meeting?" He glanced at Tim, who was cutting the muffin in two. Tim shifted half onto a napkin, kept that half, and pushed the plate toward Matt. Matt broke off a piece and popped it in his mouth. "That's some monster muffin. And good."

"Marcella gave it to me. She said they'll just be tossing them at the end of the morning, anyway."

"Marcella?"

"The lady at the bakery section. She's worked here for thirty years today; isn't that amazing?" Tim looked over toward the serving line. "There she is." Tim waved. An older woman, with dark hair and an apron over her uniform, waved back. Tim smiled and gave her a thumbs-up gesture.

Matt smiled, shook his head, and turned back to his mother.

Gloria was poking at her breakfast sandwich. "Not until ten thirty, up in Dad's room. We have a little time to go over some things."

Jenna glanced from face to face, frowning. "What's going on here? What do you mean, a team meeting?"

"Jenna, I'd rather not go into all this right now," Gloria said quietly. "We have some things to discuss that I would rather keep within the family."

"I'm family," Jenna said flatly. No one responded for a few moments. The table was quiet. Around them were the soft sounds of other people talking and eating.

Jenna pressed her fingers onto the edge of the table and tossed back her hair. *Oh, no,* Alex thought, *not now. Not here.* Alex inwardly cringed. Jenna sat up straighter, throwing back her shoulders and projecting her voice outward. "Excuse me? Aren't I family? I mean, my poor children! Almost losing their grandfather! You cannot imagine." She looked around at their placid faces. Jenna's face was turning an unflattering shade of pink. Alex wondered if Jenna had any idea how she looked. At this moment, she seemed to have forgotten how to curate her appearance.

"Oh, I think we can all imagine, Jenna." Gloria frowned, pressing her lips together and drawing in her brows. For a moment, Alex saw her eagle friend back in the game.

"I mean, of course, Matt's family," Jenna continued, her voice climbing an octave.

"Mighty big of you," Matt said cheerfully.

"And Grandpa Quinn, of course."

Grandpa took a sip of coffee and said nothing.

"But what about them?" She thrust a shoulder and her chin in Alex's direction, then nodded toward Tim. "I'm the mother of your grandchildren. Aren't I more your family than him?"

Alex glanced at Tim, worried that whatever came next would be horrible, and felt a wave of relief. Tim caught her eye, shrugged, and smiled, shaking his hair off to one side. It wasn't going to matter how dreadful Jenna was. It would roll off Tim like raindrops off duck feathers. Matt gazed placidly at Jenna, breaking off a piece of the massive muffin, and popping it in his mouth.

Gloria reiterated, "I wanted my family with me, or at least some of them. Grandpa Quinn is here for us. Alexa is my best friend and I trust her entirely, and Matt and Tim are my sons and I need them by my side right now."

Jenna shoved herself away from the table, forgetting to toss her hair back. "And aren't I your daughter? The mother of your grandchildren?" She paused, waiting.

Seconds ticked by.

"Well! Fine, then!" Most people around them were assiduously pretending not to look, but a nearly six-foot tall woman in a mini skirt, high boots, and fur-trimmed sweater was hard to avoid noticing, even in a busy hospital cafeteria at nine thirty in the morning. "I just can't understand it." Jenna's voice rose over every other voice in the cafeteria.

Then, the clear, high tones of a child's voice rang out over everything.

"Her's mad," announced the preschooler, to no one in particular, from the nearby table. Up until now her voice had been soft and singsong; now it was strong. The youngest woman, apparently her mother, tried to quiet her, but the little girl added, "Her's mad because them don't like her best." A middle-aged couple at a nearby table raised their eyebrows and gave a half shrug, in silent concurrence with the child. Grandpa Quinn craned his neck to look toward the family and smile at the mortified young mother.

Gloria looked up impassively. "Jenna, my husband is upstairs. He has had a major heart attack. He may never walk again without a cane. He may not go home for a long time. He may not live. I have some serious information to absorb and hard decisions to make." Her hands pressed the edge of the table, the whiteness of her fingertips the only sign of the strain to maintain calm. Matt reached over and rested a hand on his mother's forearm. Gloria placed a hand on his, smiling briefly at him before turning her flattened gaze toward Jenna again.

"Her doesn't like the boys," the little girl asserted. She was another Sandy. Alex briefly imagined the tot as some sort of on-the-scene reporter. Her mother was shushing her, while two of the middle-aged women were giggling almost uncontrollably, albeit silently. They were shaking in their seats and one of them had her legs crossed, her wrist shoved between quivering thighs, and was shaking her head, the universal sign of a potential bladder leak.

"I don't understand why you're leaving me out of this." Jenna's voice was not quite so strident, and she seemed to be a shrinking just a bit.

Gloria shrugged. "Of course you don't understand, Jenna. That's always been the problem, hasn't it?"

Jenna briefly resembled nothing more than a gaping-mouthed fish. She smashed her mouth shut and stormed out, nearly plowing over a group of residents. One of them, a young man, said, "Hey, watch it," and Jenna reflexively paused and looked at him, tossed her hair, and then, realizing it was a rebuke rather than an invitation, stomped out.

The five of them looked at each other with bemusement.

"Well, Mom," Tim remarked, "it's reassuring to know that some people never change. A little consistency in an uncertain world." He added, "It doesn't seem that sandwich is working for you; want some of Marcella's muffin?"

"Thanks."

The cafeteria was a little hushed. The little girl was standing up on her mother's lap, gazing toward the doors. "Her doesn't act nice," she announced to the cafeteria, pointing with her spoon toward the doorway. "Them doesn't want her to play 'cause her's not nice." This time, her mother just rubbed the child's back gently and nodded.

"Doesn't that little girl remind you of Sandy?" Matt asked.

Chapter Thirty-Two

"Happy New Year," Alex said as she settled in. "Did you have a nice holiday season?"

"Absolutely. I love my work but a break is nice." Dr. Sam smiled at Alex. "You know how that is!"

"Amen," Alex said. She sighed. "There's been so much, I hardly know where to begin."

"Just start with the synopsis and we'll break open what seems most useful today."

Alex tried to summarize it all: the fishing trip, the accident, the grim prospects and the slowly shifting good news of possible true recovery, the children's many days with her, and Joe's seemingly darkening mood, even as they returned to the college for the spring semester.

"And maybe that's the most important part, in terms of our conversation," Alex finished. "I don't know what to do and there's really no one I can talk to about this."

Dr. Sam nodded. "When you've tried to talk to Joe, what's happened?"

"It's uncomfortable, that's for sure. I mean, you couldn't get him to shut up about the sabbatical, to tell the truth, and now asking about it just gets nothing, like he's gone flat." Alex sighed. "I used to wish he would just plan the damned thing and stop talking about it, and now he won't even discuss it except to say it's not important, or he doesn't know, or maybe he's going to skip it, or worst of all, what's the point."

Dr. Sam's eyebrows shot up.

"Well, we had a good talk on New Year's Eve. Or at least he talked."

Dr. Sam leaned forward, eyebrows drawn.

Alex caught the look. "I know. I think he's depressed. Frankly, I think the wrong one of us is here. He's having some sort of crisis but he's a bit old for a midlife crisis."

"Well, midlife goes from thirties through retirement. It's a stage thing, not an age thing. Whenever people start wondering about the big questions, the 'what's the point' questions, it's a kind of crisis. Not necessarily a bad thing, though."

"A crisis is a crisis."

"It's also the only way growth happens, in this case. If Joe has somehow been merrily going on as if nothing in life is changing, then yes, Bob's having a health crisis smacked him into reality. Optimally, he digs out of this with a greater commitment to doing what he ought to be doing at this point, rather than being on autopilot."

Alex nodded slowly. "He has been on autopilot. It's so easy, the rhythm of the teaching year after all this time, the nice breaks."

"But ..."

"But?"

"I heard a silent, 'but, only,'" Dr. Sam offered. "Sometimes people say something powerful and then negate the whole thing with a 'but only.'"

"Well." Alex sighed. "We're not getting any younger."

"That's not a but. It's an and."

"Hmm?"

"The real issue is an 'and,' like this: The rhythm of the teaching year makes it easy to go on autopilot, *and* we're not getting any younger." Dr. Sam raised her hands, as if holding two objects. She lifted one. "Easy rhythm, and autopilot routine." And then the other. "We grow older, if we're lucky." She looked back and forth from one hand to the other. "Two concurrent truths, not a 'but' where one negates the other. You need to, I need to, we all have to deal with concurrent truths."

Alex tilted her head.

"So, for example. If you say to your kid—'I love you, but you have to stop harping on organic farm to table at dinner every night,' does she hear 'I love you'?"

Alex grimaced. "No, she'd skip right to an argument on pesticides, social justice for farm workers—all important things but—"

"AND you get my point." Dr. Sam smiled. "Once we throw in the 'but,' to ourselves or others, we are picking which truth matters, when maybe they both do." She paused. "For Joe, this is a powerful opportunity to pick the life he wants to have. Based on what you're describing, it sounds as if he's resisting autopilot and absolutely terrified of what happens next."

"I didn't see this as fear." Alex looked straight at Dr. Sam. "Joe's not the fearful type. That's my specialty."

Dr. Sam shrugged. "Perhaps you underestimate yourself, Alexa. You're the one who's dealing with things right now." She paused. "You pretty much have the same challenge as Joe, don't you? Proceed on autopilot or make something happen."

"Making something happen isn't exactly my thing." Alex sighed.

"*And* maybe it's time to do something new," Dr. Sam finished for her.

Alex stared at the landscape painting behind Dr. Sam. She wondered, briefly, for at least the tenth time, if the art was there just for that purpose: to give clients an excuse to stare into space and focus on something. "I guess I've been doing new things, but ... and ... I'm not sure what to do with this."

"Well, actually, I think you are sure about some things. Maybe more that you think."

Alex looked back at Dr. Sam. "Well, everyone's sure about some things."

"I think you know what I mean. I mean, you know what you want to do. You're sick of your job. You'd like to plan the sabbatical you want. You'd like to study and learn more about things that interest you, and to spend more time in nature." Dr. Sam paused. "I think you'd like to spend more time with family—extended family—like Cody's children, or Matt and Tim, and less with students who care less about their studies than you do."

There was silence.

"Alexa, what do you want your life to look like in a year? Five years? Obviously, we can't see the future, but perhaps having an idea of what you hope for then will guide some reverse-engineering for what needs to happen today. Tomorrow. Next week."

Alex shifted, looking at her hands and then at the landscape painting. She sighed, grimaced, shrugged.

"There's a lot going on over there," Dr. Sam said gently. "How about putting all that into words? The seat wiggle, the looking around, the sighing and shrugging?" Dr. Sam did a little enactment.

"It wasn't that bad. Was it?" Dr. Sam shrugged a little and Alex rubbed her jaw. "It's that obvious, huh?"

Dr. Sam smiled. "Yeah, all that fidgeting doesn't fool anyone. That says something, loud and clear." She paused. "Either say what it is or let people guess, and maybe get it all wrong." She sat back a little. "You know—hmm, that Alexa always seems cranky. Alexa's a thousand miles away again in her head. Or, it looks like Alexa had too much coffee or has hemorrhoids, with all that wiggling in the chair."

Alex couldn't help laughing. Then she took a deep breath. "I love my life, our life. Joe's and mine. I really do. I want ... I want ... I want to clear things out. Stuff, responsibilities. I don't want to walk other people's dogs or be lectured. I want to figure out how to make time for my hobbies. I want to take classes. I want to get outdoors and not have people talk at me constantly."

"Sounds good. Keep talking."

And Alex talked, surprising herself as the words kept bubbling up: her frustration with Sandy, her shame and guilt over Sandy's unwillingness, or inability, to take any responsibility for her situation, and Sandy's irrational pride in her research, part-time job and incessant activism. She poured out her anger at herself for failing, over and over, to stick up for herself to Gloria, or anyone else for that matter. She was sick of the perpetual overflow of stuff in their house, sick of her clothes.

"Do you know what happened Monday? I got dressed for work and went out to the car and actually looked down at my slacks for once. My gray slacks. They are terrible! Almost threadbare. Well, not almost. They are. And pilled where they're not threadbare. And I've been wearing them to work. For fifteen years. Without noticing I look a wreck. And no one said anything. Do you think Joe would say anything? Or Sandy? Someone? For God's sake, surely Gloria should have said something. She doesn't filter anything else."

"A wake-up call." Dr. Sam nodded. "Yeah, those can sting. Did you toss the slacks?"

"Ugh! I wrestled with the decision after work. Can you believe it? I had the 'Are they still good?' conversation in my head."

Dr. Sam laughed. "Yeah, well, I can help you with that, Alexa. *They're not still good.*"

Alex grinned. "Yes, I tossed them. It turns out, a lot of stuff is not still good."

"So, you've got some work to do."

"Yes. And maybe it will be sort of fun."

"I wouldn't be surprised."

Alex paused and looked off to the side of Dr. Sam's head. "There is one other thing. I probably should have said something right away, but, well. I didn't. I go by Alex. Not Alexa."

"Thanks for letting me know." Dr. Sam tilted her head. "Any particular reason you didn't tell me? Besides not wanting to be rude?"

Alex shrugged. "It's sort of a whole story. My name is Alexa, and Mom calls me Alexa sometimes, and so does Gloria. And Bob's dad. Just about everyone else calls me Alex."

"And the story? It sounds as if childhood was Alexa, and then ..."

"It was sort of by accident. I had some art in the student show at college. End of freshman year. There were four visiting artists who judged. Two of them misread my signature as 'Alex A. Companeri,' which I found out when I read the critiques. The judges who thought I was a guy—Alex—wrote all sorts of positive things about my use of color to convey mood and the expressive use of line 'Like Matisse in his later years,' one of them actually wrote. The ones who thought I was a girl—Alexa—wrote about the 'sentimentalized use of color' and the 'too-careful, too-precious use of line.' Then I found out that if I wrote research proposals as Alex I got better results, too." Alex rolled her eyes. "By sophomore year I was just Alex and it worked out fine."

Dr. Sam took a moment before replying. "I'm sorry you had those experiences, and I'm really glad you found a way to draw good out of it. I hope things have changed." She caught Alex's eye, then grimaced a little. "But maybe not so much, huh?"

There was a long silence. Alex picked at the loose threads around a button hole on her shirt before she finally looked up. "I guess I could try being more ... blue jay, right? Is that the assignment?"

Dr. Sam shook her head slowly. "No, I don't think so. Not this time." She took off her reading glasses and gave Alex a long look. "I think this time, a sparrow. One of those chirpy, cheeky ones at the park, the ones who let you know what they want without being obnoxious."

"A sparrow."

"Yup." Dr. Sam sounded amused at herself. Maybe, Alex thought, it was the idea of purple-haired Alex hopping around chirping until she got her way. "A sparrow. A cute, chirpy, slightly pushy sparrow." She wiggled her eyebrows. "Have fun with that."

Chapter Thirty-Three

All the way back to the college, Alex thought about being a sparrow. Sparrows are small, quick, and responsive. They were pretty cheeky at the park; they would hop right up, pecking at your feet for crumbs and giving you a long, curious look while you ate, until you dropped a few tidbits their way. *How could I be like a sparrow?*

She went through the library to the staff office area. Suzanne was leaning against her desk, facing away from it with a large mug of tea. Suzanne almost never sat when she could stand, and when she had to sit, she was just as likely to be folded up cross-legged in her chair as sitting like an adult. She smiled broadly at Alex.

"How are things going?" she asked. "Bet you're glad you'll be on sabbatical next year. Well, in about five months. Lucky girl." She sighed. "I have a few years to go. It feels like forever."

"I am looking forward to it," Alex replied, draping her jacket over the back of her chair and straightening her name tag.

"So, what's the plan? Just stay home and do research here?"

"No!" Alex was surprised at her own sharpness. Suzanne's eyes widened a bit. "No," Alex said, more quietly. "Really thinking of getting back to my roots—nature and art."

"Right, you were a bio and art major. What are you thinking?"

Alex shrugged. "Not thinking enough, probably." Inner sparrow, she told herself, and then added, "But I'd like to take an online ornithology course, some art classes for refreshers, and spend a few months away, closer to nature. Maybe a cabin in the mountains. That's the dream, anyway." She was surprised that it all tumbled out so easily. "That's the basis of the project."

"And the project?"

"Kind of a combination art show and educational display, combining artwork of the environment in which the birds and other wildlife live and brief educational essays. Something that could be a standing exhibit after the initial opening, where I'd be talking about the whole process." Alex was surprised at her own words. *Where did that even come from? I don't even remember thinking that before.*

"Sounds great. Do you have a place picked out?" Suzanne asked. "Because if not, we have that place in north Georgia. Maybe twenty minutes out of Helen. Three bedrooms; one could probably make a nice impromptu studio. Lots of trails nearby in the state and national parks. Helen's a sweet little place, very pretty. We'll be there for Thanksgiving but if you wanted the three months from mid-August to mid-November, we could work something out." She poked at her phone. "Here are some pictures."

Alex swiped through several photos: a porch that looked out over a creek and a valley beyond, a roomy kitchen, a loft with a perfect reading nook. "It's beautiful. How much?"

"I'll check with my husband, see what we can work out. Definitely less than it usually goes for, since you'll be there for three months and we won't have the usual heavy-duty commercial cleaning each week. If you don't mind doing your own laundry and basic cleaning, I can deduct that, too."

"No problem," Alex said. "Frankly, it's 'yes' to just about anything you come up with."

"Well, we'll crunch the numbers and try to do right by you," Suzanne said firmly. "I'd be happy having you be there." She paused. "By the way ... no dogs. I hope you don't mind. I mean, I know you enjoy walking your son's dogs at lunch and everything, but, well ..."

"That will be more than fine by me." Alex smiled. "No worries about that."

During the rest of the afternoon, Alex kept thinking about the beautiful cabin in north Georgia. Three months! Three glorious months. No dogs. Hiking. The fall colors. The migrating birds. Perhaps even an early dusting of snow. Frost on red and gold leaves, crunching under her feet and glistening in morning sunlight. She thought about buying art supplies and hiking boots and a portable easel. She wondered, suddenly, if she would be strong enough to carry art supplies and an easel more than about twelve feet from her car, and made a mental note to start doing real exercise to train for sabbatical. Maybe she should talk to George and get some tips about the early stages of Appalachian Trail training.

Then she began picturing herself walking through her neighborhood with a backpack on, gradually making it heaver as the weeks progressed, and felt foolish. George was doing that as part of his training, and one early morning, before dawn, the local deputy on patrol had stopped to see what he was up to. Was he homeless? Needing a ride to the shelter? They'd had a twenty-minute talk about hiking the trail;

the deputy had thought about doing that someday, too, and had all sorts of questions. But that was George. *I'd look like a crazy person*, she thought, and then she pictured Dr. Sam shrugging and saying, "So?"

"So what?" she said aloud, and then looked around quickly. She was at the front desk and fortunately the only student nearby was nodding his head in rhythm to the sound in his headphones. No one was staring at her. *What if I do look crazy to some people*, she thought. It didn't matter; what mattered was being able to get the most out of this sabbatical year. *And after that*, she added. *After that, too.* It suddenly occurred to her that sabbatical was the beginning of doing things differently, that she wasn't supposed to just "do sabbatical" and go back to the way it was before. She was supposed to be different.

She thought, suddenly, that they probably couldn't afford Suzanne's best offer on the house in the mountains, and that maybe it was all just a stupid, silly dream, like growing up to do wildlife illustration had been. Then she thought about how much Joe's plans were going to cost, driving up and down the coast for a year. He wasn't planning on sleeping in the car at rest stops. Surely her plans could find a way, but how could they afford both?

Still, the thought circled around, along with the homework to be a sparrow—to just make her wants known, to go after what she wanted without being obnoxious. She decided, during dinner that night, that she would just wait until she had actual information from Suzanne; perhaps the property manager had already rented it for part of that time or maybe the cost would be just too much. As she and Joe settled in with their reading after dinner, she idly flipped through the week's accumulation of catalogues. A whole catalogue dedicated to clothing for dogs—into the recycling pile. She wasn't even sure how she got on that mailing list. Another dedicated to jigsaw puzzles. *Who has time for all those puzzles?* Alex wondered, adding it to the recycling. Then she thought about long, lazy, rainy afternoons at a mountain cabin, needing to step away from the easel and get a different perspective, and pulled it from the recycling pile to add it to the basket of her magazines. Next was the company where she bought their sweaters, when she did break down and buy something new; this small catalogue was dedicated to outdoor clothing, jeans and jackets, sweaters, hiking shoes, warm socks. She folded over the page of women's hiking shoes and tucked it carefully back into the magazine basket. *Maybe*, she thought, *maybe this weekend I'll give that another look and just go for it.*

She flipped through the art center catalogue. The late spring courses were listed, too, and she lingered over a Monday night drawing class. Beginner to intermediate, it said, but she figured enough time had passed that she qualified as intermediate at best. A nice refresher, anyway, Alex told herself. *Maybe I will.* She folded over the page and put it with the hiking shoes. The next thing in the stack was the art magazine she had faithfully subscribed to for years, although she rarely read it and usually just ended up donating it, barely opened, to the library. In the back were the listings of workshops by professional artists. Usually she glanced at those pages, rolled her eyes, and tossed it aside; today she let herself range over the options. A much-admired pair of landscape artists was offering a five-day course in north Georgia in early October. *As if I could*, she thought, and then suddenly remembered Suzanne's house in the mountains and felt her heart flop.

"It could actually happen," she whispered.

"Hmm?" Joe's voice broke through the trance.

"What, honey?" Alex asked.

"You said something," Joe said. "What could happen?"

"Oh," Alex said slowly. Sparrow, sparrow, sparrow, she reminded herself. "I'm thinking about sabbatical. I was just looking at a landscape course. Two of my favorite landscape painters will be offering it—the lady from Maine, the one who was at the local center a few years ago, and another woman who usually works in the Southwest. It's in early October."

"That sounds great. Is it local?"

"No, up in north Georgia. Near Suzanne's place, Suzanne from the library."

"Oh, nice. Maybe you could stay at her place. Save some money."

Alex nodded. "Maybe." No need to share her hopes without the information to possibly make plans. She folded over the page and put it with the hiking shoes and the drawing class, and then pulled all three out and placed them in a neat stack on top of the side table. There was a porcelain bird figurine next to the lamp. Not quite a sparrow, but good enough. She set it carefully and deliberately on top of the stack. *See you this weekend*, she thought.

Chapter Thirty-Four

January 22

Back at school for two weeks. A nice slow start—not many papers due these first weeks so students haven't been stacking up at the help desk.

And, not but.

I'm glad to be back at school and I wish I had more time off.

I'm grateful for my job and there are parts of it I can barely stand.

I'm glad I can help Gloria but, no, it's and, and I'm afraid she's going to bleed me dry. She's so lonely and every evening it's the same long conversation. Monologue, really.

But that's okay. AND that's okay because Joe is still too quiet. I feel like a fool. I can't get my husband to talk to me.

January 27

I'm starting to enjoy these lunch breaks without walking the dogs. Jonah and Beth seem to have figured it out. And they have the little guilt trip words from time to time. Too bad.

Follow-up appointment with Cody tomorrow—no pain in a while. Odd how that happened.

Went for a walk at lunch two days in a row and brought my binoculars. I never realized how many birds are around the pond on campus.

January 31

Sandy's hardly home these days. Which is nice, but it just underscores how quiet Joe is.

I'm afraid that he'll skip the sabbatical he's worked so hard for.

I'm afraid that he's going to sink into some sort of depression and not come back.

I'm afraid that somehow I'm doing or saying something wrong and it's making things worse.

I'm afraid. Silence with pain in it frightens me.

Chapter Thirty-Five

A blue baby buzzard. That's what she felt like. Like a blue, baby buzzard.

Well, that sounds crazy. Can't very well tell that one to Dr. Sam, not without the whole story. A few summers ago, Sandy had come up behind her while she was feeding the birds on the deck. Alex tensed, as always, waiting for the criticism about learned helplessness and disrupting nature, but that day Sandy just took a startled breath, pointed, and asked, "What's wrong with that one?"

"Which one?" Alex had asked ingenuously. Sandy had sounded horrified.

"That one. By the water dish. The one that looks like a little blue baby buzzard."

"Oh, the one with the molting head feathers." Alex paused, considering. "Yes, I guess they do sort of look like little blue buzzards. But it's fine, it's normal. Happens to all of them. In a week or two you won't be able to tell it happened. It will have nice, bright, full feathers again."

"Huh." Sandy shrugged. "But wow, it looks ugly. And ... vulnerable. It seems naked and its neck is so scrawny without the feathers."

Alex studied the bird. She was used to the annual molt and hadn't thought, until now, about how much these molting jays looked like little blue baby buzzards. "You're right. I was so used to it that I didn't even notice the similarity."

Sandy turned to go back indoors. "Well, it looks weird, that's for sure. I wonder if they feel embarrassed until they're back to normal."

I wonder if they feel embarrassed, Alex thought. Shaking herself out of memories, she stared at her reflection in the mirror inside the closet door. She saw a middle-aged woman, a little heavier than she used to be. Even with the extra pounds, there was the beginning of a turkey neck, and the weird eggplant color still clung, barely, to most of her hair. She cringed; her sweater was hitting in the wrong places, accentuating a bulge over her waistband. She pulled the hem away from her body. *This used to be a tunic*, she thought grimly. *And I have to stop pretending everything suddenly shrank.* She stuck her fingers up through her hair and pulled it straight out from the sides of her head, wondering about cutting it off, getting layers, shedding more of this stupid beet juice. She had a wild thought of doing it herself—just pulling her hair away from her head and hacking away at it. She briefly imagined it would all fall loosely into soft layers and then assured herself it would certainly not. More likely she'd look as much like a baby blue buzzard as she felt. "Well, maybe an eggplant baby buzzard," she said aloud.

"Mom? Are you okay?" It was Sandy.

Alex smoothed her hair and stepped away from the closet. "Sure, fine. Why?" She went out to the hall, where Sandy was standing.

"Buzzards? What are you talking about in there? Who are you talking to?"

Alex shook her head. "No one, just muttering about stuff. Thinking about cleaning out my closet some more."

Sandy looked skeptical. "You said buzzard."

Alex looked at her with almost no expression, and barely blinking, said, "Oh. I don't know. Must have been complaining about my clothes. It's been a while since I did any real trying stuff on, shopping, you know. Not my thing."

"Clearly," Sandy said, heading toward her room. "Nothing personal, Mom. But you are the queen of ruts." She paused in the doorway. "Not that I haven't tried, of course, but wow, you are resistant."

"Oh, resistant. Interesting," Alex replied. She felt a mix of annoyance and hilarity that Sandy, who had never had a real full-time job and only hung out with her best friend from childhood, was judging her resistance to change.

On the other hand, Sandy was right. She sighed. She thought of Dr. Sam and her own "still good" slacks that were so threadbare they barely held together. She thought of hiking and the wind in her hair, and she thought of Aribeth and her pottery wheel, Chen and her freedom, George and his endless training and research for his Appalachian Trail adventure.

Then she thought about a long, lonely year fending off Jonah, the dogs, and Gloria while Joe went off on a fishing adventure.

And then Alex decided to go for a short drive to the store to buy hairstyle magazines.

She bought two, and a bag of dark chocolates, because it was important not to run out of them.

"Need a bag?" the cashier asked lazily, not looking up.

Alex thought of strolling into the house carrying undisguised hairstyle magazines and having to deal with Sandy's enthusiastic helpfulness. "Yes," she said firmly.

It was pleasantly warm in the car, so she sat in the parking lot and tried to figure out which hairstyles, shown on very young, slim women with long, smooth necks and perfect makeup, would translate to fifty-five-year-old her and her awkward relationship with eyeliner and mascara. She wondered if she could still sketch well enough to sort of work out her general facial shape and features and then plop various hairstyles on them. She pulled an old grocery list out of her purse and gave it a shot, as best she could, using the rearview mirror. She picked something called a layered bob with soft bangs, sketched it on the loosely drawn Alex head, frowned, crumpled it up and stuffed it in the console cupholder. *Maybe another day.* She considered giving herself a couple of stars in her journal just for thinking about getting a haircut and buying the magazines. Thinking about things was the first step, she assured herself.

She was able to slip into the house unseen. She stuck the hairstyle magazines in the basket with the art and bird magazines and catalogues that no one else was likely to disturb.

The next day she'd promised Sandy a coffee date—just the two of them—to catch up. Sandy had selected a vegan café, which meant nondairy creamer and no real whipped cream. Still, it would be nice to catch up, away from everything, and have some quality time with Sandy. They weren't in the car two minutes before Sandy fished the crumpled grocery list out of the cupholder to put her water bottle in place.

"What's this?"

Alex barely flicked her eyes in Sandy's direction. "What's what?"

"This." Sandy tilted her head, holding up the list. "You were drawing. Hey, this sort of looks like you. With a different haircut."

"Oh," Alex began.

"You were thinking about a new haircut!" Sandy marveled. "Mom, yeah, about time. A new haircut? That would be great." Sandy held the paper a little further away and then turned to study her mom's profile. "I don't know, your hair has a lot of waves. Are you going to try to have regular bangs or go loose?" Sandy frowned. "Bangs are sort of passé. Well, except for older people. It's a dead giveaway they're trying to hide wrinkles."

"Oh. Really." Alex controlled an urge to roll her eyes.

"But maybe on you it could work. Because the bangs would be sort of messy and not lay flat." Sandy nodded approvingly and carefully folded the paper.

Alex sighed. "Sandy, I have no idea. It was just a little ... flirtation with the idea, really. I haven't even talked to your dad."

"It's not Dad's hair and I bet you a biscotti he won't even notice," Sandy challenged. "Not until you say something." She folded the paper carefully and tucked it into the other cupholder. "How long did it take him to notice the beet juice? Like, a week?"

Sandy had a point. "It was actually, well ... he didn't notice, really. I finally complained that he hadn't noticed, and he just made that face."

Sandy pointed at her mom. "See? So, who cares? He's not even going to notice! Let's go see if there's a walk-in appointment available at the salon after coffee. Or maybe first. Come on, Mom. It'll be fun."

"Sandy, I really was hoping to just enjoy time with you."

"And I want to enjoy time with you. This would so much fun! You've had the same hairstyle since I was in middle school."

Alex fluffed out her hair with one hand. She felt torn between wanting to change—she'd wanted to do this, hadn't she? and giving in to Sandy. But doing something she actually wanted, when Sandy happened to agree, wasn't really giving in, she told herself. Sandy was more like a catalyst than the driver here. "Let's go see about a walk-in first," she said, with more conviction than she felt.

Their salon was a certified animal-friendly salon, with a certificate on the wall asserting that they neither used nor sold any products that used animal testing. This made it Sandy-approved. She was still unsure about the sourcing for their coffee, and the receptionist didn't know, but Sandy poured herself a complimentary cup and handed Alex the grocery list with her sketch on it. "Good luck, Mom!"

Olivia was the stylist who usually gave Alex her precise trim every eight weeks. Olivia would always stand behind Alex, fluffing her hair and meeting her eyes in mirror, asking hopefully, "So, what are we doing today?" and then nodding with a tight little smile when Alex said firmly, "Just the usual. Just under an inch all over, please." Today, it turned out that Olivia's ten o'clock client had the flu, so she was available, and delighted. "Sure! A change would be great." She was effusively enthusiastic. *A little too enthusiastic*, Alex thought; she wondered what was behind that. "Let's go get you shampooed."

Back in the chair, in front of the mirror, Alex tried not to actually look at herself. The overhead light was garish, and it hurt to think she actually looked that old: baggy eyes, saggy jaw. Olivia, however, was busy snapping a purple cape over Alex and combing out her hair. Olivia paused, put her hands on Alex's shoulders, grinned at her in the mirror and said, "So, my dear! What are we doing?"

Alex ferreted out the crumpled grocery list. "I was thinking something a little shorter, layers, kind of soft." She paused. "Something super-low maintenance. Maybe no maintenance, except washing and conditioning."

Olivia looked skeptical. She pulled Alex's hair away from the sides of her head and let it fall. "You're going to have a lot of waves in your hair. So that means either products to minimize frizz or the hair dryer and flat iron."

"Waves it will be," Alex said. She couldn't see herself signing on for even more work on her hair.

"Okay," Olivia agreed with a slight tone of relief. "It's really a messy, layered look. Your bangs won't behave, anyhow. They're going to go quirky. So, I'll trim it up, cut some layers, and show you how to put some stuff in it, easy-peasy. Good?"

Alex started to feel more queasy than easy-peasy. She had the urge to just leave—apologize, give Olivia a tip and pay for the shampoo, and just leave with wet hair. Under the cape, she gripped the arms of the chair so hard her fingers hurt. She thought of her threadbare gray slacks and wondered if her tired hairstyle was in the same category.

Aloud, she said, "Good. Let's go."

For what seemed like an eternity, Olivia's shears snipped. Bits of purplish hair—some four inches long—fell into Alex's lap and on the floor, curling softly as they dried. Olivia chattered about the weather, her children's activities, and occasionally commented on something to do with Alex's hair.

"So, you'll be able to do this mostly wash-and-wear, but also you could blow it out if you wanted to, use a curling iron or a flat iron." Olivia sounded pleased, and Alex tried not to look at the mirror.

Olivia finally stopped snipping and said, "There!" She turned to her countertop and held up two containers. "Okay. Here goes. Curl cream," she said, holding up one, "and a little bit of oil. I use argan. Watch." She put a squirt of the cream into one hand and carefully added a few drops of oil. "Rub this together and just massage it through your hair. Like this." She ran her fingers through all of Alex's hair, over and over. She stepped back, tilted her head, and gave a few pieces a twist. "You can experiment with how much to encourage the curl, or just let the waves do what they will." She stepped back, hands on hips. "What do you think? It's still damp but you get the general idea." Olivia smiled with satisfaction. "It will fluff up more when it dries but try not to mess with it once you're done."

Alex sighed and looked straight at the mirror. It looked like most of her hair was gone; the longest pieces were above her shoulder, the bottoms of her ears showed, and bits and pieces of hair stuck out. The cape made her look bigger than usual, and the bags under her eyes were huge. *Dear God*, she thought, *I really look like a baby buzzard*. Aloud she said, "Well, it's a big change. I guess I have to get used to it." She blinked back tears and smiled. "Thank you. Really."

"Are you crying?" Olivia asked. She peered at Alex's reflection from behind her chair. "Oh, my God. You are. I'm so sorry. But it looks great. Seriously." She looked into the mirror and fluffed up some pieces. "Would you feel better if I dried it with the diffuser so you can see that it's pretty full, actually—just hanging flatter because it's still wet?" Olivia looked anxious.

Sandy came wandering over. "I heard some hubbub and wanted to see ... Oh, Mom. It looks great. Love it. You look five years younger." She paused and with unusual sensitivity added, "I mean, not that you needed to. Look younger, that is."

Alex met Sandy's eyes in the mirror. "You think so?"

Sandy nodded. "I do. It's a great change. You had that helmet hair thing for way too long."

Olivia looked down and rubbed the side of her face. Alex sighed. *Helmet hair; purple helmet hair.*

"Okay, then. I get it." She squinted with feigned sternness at Olivia. "Were you actually in cahoots with Sandy all along?"

Olivia grinned and said, "No ... but only because she didn't ask me. Come on, let's go get you set up for six weeks, shall we?"

Chapter Thirty-Six

"And that's how I ended up like this." Alex pointed at her head. "Like a blue baby buzzard."

Dr. Sam's eyebrows shot up. "Okay, this is a new bird metaphor."

Alex shook her head and felt the strange way the shorter hair moved around. "I was only sort of thinking about doing this. Well, more than sort of. I'd bought some hairstyle magazines and sketched one sample haircut and the next thing I knew, Sandy had bulldozed me into it."

Dr. Sam leaned back, folding her arms and grinning. "Oh, come on, Alex! Stop blaming Sandy. Or anyone else. You wanted to make changes, you decided to make a change, and you're looking for either sympathy that it was a mistake or approval. Be honest."

Alex pulled back. "Ouch."

Dr. Sam nodded, softer. "Yeah, I have to do that sometimes."

"Still," Alex said, a little indignantly, arranging herself on the loveseat and pulling the edge of her sweater. She sighed. "Yeah, I had been thinking about it and honestly, when Sandy found the sketch, I debated in my head whether to do what I sort of wanted to do, or not do it just because she wanted it, too."

Dr. Sam rolled her eyes in exaggerated horror. "Oh, the dilemma! So, do you like it?"

"I sort of do, actually. I mean, it's easy. It's different but not crazy different. I mean, I didn't get it completely chopped off. But it's a lot different and sometimes I see myself with my neck naked and feel like a ... blue baby buzzard." She caught Dr. Sam's eye. "That's what Sandy called molting blue jays a few summers ago. They lose just about all their head and neck feathers at once and sort of look like ..."

"A blue baby buzzard," agreed Dr. Sam. "Okay, I see that. So, what does that mean? What is it like to be like a blue baby buzzard?"

"Naked. Vulnerable. Like I can't hide."

"Hide from what?"

"Everything," Alex blurted and then said, "Whoa." She looked up at Dr. Sam, wringing her hands. "Didn't expect that."

"Why do you have to hide?"

"All this fear work, all that journaling, and it comes down to this. Hiding from everything. Everyone. Myself, I guess."

"And if you can't hide from yourself, or anyone, then what?"

"Then ... I don't know." Alex paused and it was silent for some moments. She thought about all her journaling, all the long one-sided conversations with Gloria, Sandy, and even Joe, and her own simmering resentment. She thought about her mother, gently pushing her to wake up, and the soft encouragement of Matt and Tim with their kind, watchful eyes. She thought about tired-looking Cody, encouraging her to come here in the first place. A parade of the events of the past months went by, and she realized how she was fearful, yes, but also angry in a mean, quiet way.

"Oh, well," she began. "I think I just realized I'm trying to have it both ways. I complain about no one paying attention to me and get angry about it but, boy, do I try to be invisible." She shook her head, sighing and picking at imaginary lint on her sleeve. "I'm like some sort of resentful martyr. 'Oh, poor little me! No one pays me any mind. Now watch me disappear and sulk!'" She grimaced. "It's embarrassing, really." She looked up and met Dr. Sam's patient, gentle smile.

"Good job, Alex. Now we can start getting some real work done." Dr. Sam tilted her head. "So, how do you like the new hairstyle? Is it working for you?"

Alex reached up and fluffed her hair and then gently twisted a wave around one finger. She felt herself grinning. "I love it. Yes, it's working great—no fuss." She sat up a little straighter. "Funny, almost everyone at work noticed right away. Including a bunch of students. All good comments."

"How about Joe?"

Alex shook her head. "He took a week or so. Well, after a week or so Sandy couldn't bear it and she told him."

Sandy had been examining a forkful of rice, and had interrupted her father's comments on the meal with a kind of urgency, as if she had just remembered something of critical importance. "Dad! Haven't you noticed?"

Joe had turned and looked at her with an owlish, perplexed gaze. "Noticed what?"

Sandy pointed at Alex with her fork. "Mom! Haven't you noticed Mom?"

Joe looked from Sandy to Alex and back to Sandy, still perplexed. "Yes, of course I notice Mom."

Sandy rolled her eyes. "Her hair! Have you even noticed her hair? Mom got a whole new haircut and you haven't even noticed, have you?"

Joe turned and gazed at Alex, blinking slowly a few times. "Oh. No, I guess I didn't. You look great, honey. Very ... lively."

"Lively?" Alex repeated. "Oh. Thank you."

Sandy turned to her mom, nodding and gesturing with her fork at her father. "And *you* owe me a biscotti."

"So he didn't really notice at all." Dr. Sam said. "And are you okay with that?"

"Not surprised, not mad, not entirely okay."

"So, let's talk about this not surprised, not mad, not entirely okay."

They did.

Chapter Thirty-Seven

Alex stood at the sliding glass door, open to let in the late February air. Late winter in Florida—always more spring than anything else, with the crazy concurrence of falling oak leaves and pollination. She inhaled the steam rising from her morning coffee and smiled at the brightening morning sky.

She turned at the sound of shuffling socks behind her. "Good morning, honey. Can I get you coffee?"

"Thanks." Joe stepped up to the open door. "What a beautiful day. Nothing like late winter in Florida."

"Amen." Alex replied. "Sleep well?"

Joe nodded. "Much better." He paused. "A nice change."

Alex handed him a steaming mug. "Here goes."

"Thanks." He looked outdoors. "I see the cardinals are back."

"I just love them. The way they sing even while they're eating. What a joy."

Joe glanced at her. "I envy you that," he said. "Not in a bad way. Just that you can actually be that happy about, well, small things." He looked back to the birds. "It's a gift, I guess."

Alex made a skeptical face. "I guess it is, and it's a choice." She pulled her head back a little, feeling as surprised at herself as Joe apparently was. Her remark had come out in a sharper tone than she'd expected. He turned to look at her closely. "I mean, I decide to let myself enjoy these things."

Joe shrugged, considering. "I guess."

Alex paused. *Don't do this*, she thought. *Don't just stop talking.* She took a breath. "I decide to not dismiss them, not look past them." *Not like you not even noticing I cut off my hair.*

"Well, yeah. I see that."

"What about you? Isn't that how you feel about fishing, anyway?"

"I suppose. With fishing it's the doing it, it's the quiet, the water, the companionship." He sighed. Alex briefly held her breath, and breathed out gently as Joe continued. "This whole thing with Bob. It really set me back."

She nodded and put a hand on his arm, standing at his side, facing outside with him.

Joe went on. "I'm sure you noticed. I know it hasn't been exactly easy, putting up with me." He glanced at her and she looked up, smiling gently. "I've just been thinking. I mean, what actually matters, right? What am I even doing?" He shook his head. "I don't mean you, or our home, our life. I mean, what the hell? What am I doing with my job, letting it eat my life? The whole sabbatical thing—there's no real reason to turn it into a work function. Who am I kidding? I'm a few years from retirement. I could retire right now if I wanted."

"And?"

"And I'd like to have the sabbatical be about me. And you."

Alex looked up quickly. "Me?"

"I'm not even sure what I'm thinking, or what makes sense here, but ... I don't know. I think we've been kind of on autopilot. And I'd like to change that."

"Getting off autopilot sounds good." She wasn't ready to offer a buy-in on the sabbatical. She suspected it was all fishing and history, and being a tagalong for that didn't sound particularly enjoyable. *I have my own ideas, my own project to complete.*

"Really?"

Alex feigned offense. "Really? He asks me! I guess you haven't noticed a few things around here."

Joe swiveled his head, owl-like. "Noticed?"

Alex laughed. "I've been going for walks and bird-watching at lunchtime. NOT walking Jonah's dogs. I'm sure I mentioned that. God knows Jonah and Beth mention it regularly, the little whiners. The hair. And perhaps you haven't noticed Sandy stopped lecturing us about our food sourcing?"

"I thought that was because she was so busy helping Cody."

"Well, that hasn't hurt."

"Who knew she liked kids so much?"

"She's always liked kids and I don't think it's just about the twins." Alex nudged him. "You're changing the subject."

Joe grinned. "You caught me." He paused. "I guess I've been doing that a lot. Avoiding things. What else have I missed?"

"I've been painting again on the weekends. Instead of talking about getting back to it someday."

"And?"

"And remember that big pile of stuff in the driveway for the thrift store? Finally tackled the closets. All of them."

"Yes, I remember."

"And the cabin in the mountains? Suzanne's place? I mentioned it, making arrangements for fall."

Joe looked sheepish. "And I've been in a two-month-long funk, having a pity party. I guess you're not the autopilot problem here."

"Oh, I have my moments." Alex pointed. "See the indigo buntings? They're passing through again."

"Beautiful." Joe paused. "After New Year's, it seemed like I had a little direction, a little clarity. But autopilot comes so easy. And I want to stop."

"So, what's turning off autopilot going to look like?"

"I'm not sure," Joe said. "But it's going to happen. I am going to take that sabbatical. I'm just not sure what I'm going to do." He breathed deeply. "But I'd like for you to be with me for part of it, even though I don't know what that means yet. For me, anyway."

"Sure."

"Sure?"

Alex scoffed. "Could you at least not look surprised that I said yes? Do I say no that often?"

Joe gave her the owl look. "I don't know what I'm asking you to do with your time off."

Alex shrugged. "You're going to go somewhere to fish. And talk about fishing. And read about fishing. And write about fishing. So that means nature, and water, and quiet time. And those things mean time for me to look at birds, read, and make art. Or at least try to. What's to not say yes to?"

Joe shook his head. "It's been thirty-two years and you can still surprise me. And that sounds ... perfect."

"But I'm not going to just be tagging along. Seriously, I'm not going so I can be den mother to a bunch of men having fun fishing. I'm entitled to my sabbatical, too. And I'm not going along for the whole trip. I have other plans."

"Who asked you to be den mother?" Joe looked indignant. "What's that supposed to mean?"

Alex sighed. She found it incredible that he didn't know what fishing trips were like for her, as if he were completely oblivious to what had to be done. "Joe, honey. You know. You know what fishing vacations are like for me. Cooking. Cleaning. Packing lunches. Running errands." She paused. "Driving when the other adults are too hungover." She tried to mask how shaky her insides felt. "That's not my idea of fun. I love being with you. But I don't want to be the mom all the time. Not this time." She paused and added, "At least, not until there are grandchildren involved."

It was quiet for what seemed like an eternity but was probably only a couple of moments. Alex focused on breathing and thought about Dr. Sam sitting there, serenely gazing at her during what always felt, to Alex, like awkward silences.

At last, Joe cleared his throat and looked down. "I guess I never thought about what those trips were like for you. And then you fold in the times we had the kids with us, or you were stuck with Gloria while Bob and I were at the water ..."

"Right." She shrugged. "Not much fun." She glanced up. "How would you like to spend all day on a vacation with Gloria? Obviously even Bob can't take it, that's why we go together and you both farm her out to me." Alex was surprised at herself. Gloria was her best friend, and best friends weren't farmed out to each other. *Still*, she thought, *there it is*. The ugly truth.

"This will be different," Joe said firmly. "This time, no den mother. No Gloria. Your sabbatical, too."

"So, it's where and when, not 'what' for us." Alex smiled. "The late summer and early fall are pretty set for me; I have places I want to go, things I'd like to do. Taking a class myself. Well, two classes, actually. Three, if you count the workshop in Georgia."

"Classes?"

"You know you've become the crazy bird lady when your newsfeed includes an alert about an ornithologist position. So, an online class about birds is in order."

"Sounds good," Joe said. Alex couldn't help but notice he didn't comment on the 'crazy bird lady' remark. She said nothing; it was good to hear Joe really speaking again.

"And the landscape course in October in Georgia, and the classes here," she began, but then the phone rang, jangling them out of their peace. Alex stepped over to see the display. She sighed. "Gloria. Already." She looked up at Joe, grimacing.

He shrugged. "Might as well get it. She's going to call at least once. Maybe you're getting it over with early."

She half frowned. "That sounds terrible." Then she picked up.

"Gloria? Good morning!"

"Alexa, I know it's early but—well, Bob's coming home this afternoon. And I'm just so anxious. What if I can't handle things? What if he falls?"

Alex took a deep breath and rubbed her jaw. "Gloria, you've gone over everything. Weren't Matt, Tim, and Cody over a few times this week, making sure everything was set up? The ramp, the bathroom bars, the shower chair?"

"Yes, the boys were all here," Gloria said. "Well, not Kevin, but he's holding down the practice."

"So, everything's ready, and you won't be alone. Someone will be there every day—one of the kids, and probably the home health people and the physical therapists. Bob, me."

"I know, but—" Gloria's voice cracked. "I'm afraid. I'm afraid I won't be able to handle it."

"I'm sorry." Alex looked at Joe helplessly, shrugging. "I don't know what to say, Gloria. But you've got this, and you're not alone. You have a whole army of us behind you. With you." She paused. "How is Bob coming home? Are you getting him? Do you need a hand?"

"Matt and Tim are driving me and they're planning on staying until Bob's in bed for the night this first day. And Cody and the twins are coming for breakfast tomorrow."

"That should be nice," Alex replied, wondering if that would include Sandy. She tried to remember if Sandy had mentioned breakfast plans for tomorrow. "Maybe I could come by the next day? And visit a bit, help out with whatever you need?"

"That sounds good," Gloria said. "I'll look forward to seeing you."

"Give my best to Bob and the boys," Alex said. "And let us know if there's anything we can do. Please check in tomorrow to let us know how things are."

"I will," Gloria said.

After their goodbyes, Alex put down the phone and shook her head. "She's so worried she'll break Bob, basically, drop him, I guess, or let him fall." She looked into her coffee cup. "I understand. I'd feel the same way."

Joe nodded. "I think we're all afraid these days, one way or another. At least Gloria has something to focus on. Maybe she's the lucky one. Not having Bob be so hurt, but having a task. A clear task."

Alex just sighed and looked out the sliding doors. "See how the sunlight glints on the new leaves." *Why doesn't he see that he has a clear task? Why don't I always feel that I have a clear task?* She watched a mockingbird perch and launch into its repertoire of songs. *The mockingbird seems to understand its tasks better than either of us. At least, it's not afraid to take on its tasks.*

Chapter Thirty-Eight

The evenings were longer and quieter than they'd been before. Sandy was gone almost constantly. She'd found a nearly full-time tutoring position at a charter school and, when she and Rachel weren't protesting something or marching on the beach to protect sea turtle nests, she was either working on her research or, most often, was at Cody's house. When Sandy was home, she was less combative; as Alex had noticed, Sandy rarely complained about their food sourcing.

The bad part was, Sandy wasn't around to poke Joe out of his near-constant silence. Alex began to realize how much she'd allowed Sandy to carry the burden of conversation for her.

Alex dried her hands, hung up the dish towel, and made her way to the living room, where Joe was holding a book and pretending to read, with that thousand-yard stare. "Honey? How about some tea? Or a walk? It's a lovely evening." She pushed the drapes open wider.

"It won't be really dark for another hour and if we get out in time, I'll have a legitimate excuse to not pick up Gloria's call."

"Is she going to call?"

"Joe. You know she calls every day. I got out of walking the dogs and instead I listen to Gloria."

"It's a rough time for her," Joe protested. "And she's your best friend."

"It is, and I'm glad to be there for her, but sometimes I need a break, too."

Joe gazed at her quizzically. "What's going on with you?"

Alex turned and stared at him, mouth slightly open, and waited.

Joe shrugged. "I mean, you've always been right there for Gloria. She's your best friend, she needs you."

"And Bob needs you. But you're not going over there every other day, or calling." Alex sighed. "So I need fresh air. And I need to keep breaking in these hiking shoes."

Joe put down the book. "I wasn't reading anyway. Let's go for a walk."

The evening air was cool and smelled of plumeria. "Perfect," Alex said. "Just perfect."

They strolled in silence; enough silence, and perhaps Joe would start talking.

It took thirty minutes before the walk worked its magic and Joe started talking. "I'm sorry."

"Thanks." Alex squeezed his hand. "I know, it's not like me to just go ahead and say I need a break. But I do."

Joe squeezed her hand back and they strolled a while in more companionable silence. After a few minutes, Joe said, "I've been thinking."

"Hmm?"

"I really have to decide something about this sabbatical. And a lot of other things." Joe shook his head. "I had this dream, this crazy, boys-on-a-road-trip dream."

"It sounds wonderful."

"And Bob was all in. At least that's what he said. God only knows how he was going to get it past Gloria. The woman runs things with an iron fist. At least she used to."

"She's having a dreadful time of it," Alex agreed. "It's been a shock, actually. I never would have expected Gloria to be the type of woman to just fall apart this way."

"Well, with this version of Gloria, maybe Bob could have gotten his way. But the old Gloria—never. Maybe it was all just a silly escapist fantasy. Two old guys getting away with an excuse to fish to their hearts' content under the pretense of academia."

"It always sounded as if you did intend to write it up. No pretense."

"Yes, I did. Maybe I was really thinking memoir. Some humor. You know."

Alex squeezed his hand, patting it with her free hand. "It will be great, either way."

Joe looked down at her sharply. "You think so?"

She nodded emphatically. "I'm sure."

Back at the house, they found Sandy perched on a stool eating a plate of leftovers. "Hey, Mom. Dad."

"Hi, honey." Alex kissed her on the cheek. "How was your day?"

"Great." She turned her face for Joe's kiss. "Have you talked to Aunt Gloria yet?"

"No. Did she call?"

"I didn't look. Hasn't she called every day since Uncle Bob's accident? Unless you call first? So, anyway, I was over there picking up the twins and she said that Veronica and Kevin are pregnant again! Isn't that great?"

"Wonderful news," Alex agreed. "What do the twins think of another cousin?"

"Marta's excited about a new baby to play with and take care of. Sean said it will be boring until it's big enough to do anything much, but he'll change his mind. Cody said Sean fussed more over Bobby and Gina than Marta did." She put down her plate. "This was good. See, the organic legumes really make a better side dish, don't they?"

Alex thought about lies of omission. "How's your uncle Bob today?"

"Better." Sandy took a sip of water. "He's doing all his physical therapy work. Aunt Gloria's a real drill sergeant about it. But he's able to get around the house without the walker most of the day. So that's a big improvement. Cody thinks he'll be done with the cane within the month."

"How is Cody doing?"

"Oh, he's great. The dental practice is super busy. He's off Sunday so we're all doing a beach cleanup together. Jenna's supposed to have the twins this weekend, but that won't happen," she said confidently.

"You sound sure."

"She's an idiot. There's some sort of club opening downtown and she's going to be there. You know that. With her stupid camera guy 'friend' filming her every move so they can edit it into her little videos about her wonderfulness." Sandy snorted. "It's pathetic." She hopped off the stool. "But it all works out great for me that she's an idiot." She then abruptly changed the subject. "Dad, you're super quiet. Is something wrong?"

Joe shook his head like someone startled awake, turning toward Sandy quizzically. "What?"

"You're quiet. Everything okay? Students making you crazy this term?"

"Well, that's just normal—the usual blend of excellent students and the ones who pretend they can't understand the syllabus, much less the textbook. No, that's nothing."

"Dad and I have been thinking about our sabbaticals," Alex explained. "We've been bouncing ideas around. It's a big decision—taking a year off and how to handle that. So, it takes a lot of quiet thinking time." She paused and added, "I was planning on having you and Jonah and Beth over for dinner soon to formally announce it. So please try to keep this quiet."

Sandy crossed her heart. "Absolutely. Yeah," Sandy said. "I get that. Sabbatical, huh? Is that the big fishing expedition Uncle Bob talks about?"

Joe's head jerked up. "Bob's talking about it?"

Sandy nodded matter-of-factly. "Gosh, constantly. He's determined to get back to walking without a cane so he can go along or at least meet up with you for part of it. 'Without being a burden,' he says. Aunt Gloria tells him to stop being a fool and just do his exercises. 'Be grateful you can walk at all,' she says, 'instead of daydreaming about fishing.'"

Joe tilted his head and raised an eyebrow, catching Alex's glance. "It sounds like Gloria, at least, is getting back to normal."

Alex gave a short laugh. "I'll believe that when a day goes by without her needing to vent." The phone rang; they turned and looked at it in unison. "That's Gloria. I'll take it outside." Alex stepped out the glass doors. "Gloria? How are you?" She slid the doors shut behind her.

She tried to keep one ear on Joe and Sandy, and the other on Gloria.

Joe and Sandy looked at one another before Joe asked again, "So, Bob's talking about the sabbatical?"

"Every day," Sandy said. "It sounds fun. Matt and Tim are all over it. They figure they could join you for a couple of weeks, as long as it's not the end of a quarter or tax season. Cody said he'd like to meet up with you guys for a week or two, but he needs to figure out what to do with the twins. I said I could help out."

"I'm sure the twins would like that," Joe said. "But how do they feel about kale smoothies for breakfast?"

"Dad. Seriously." Sandy put on a fake frown. "Kale smoothies are for after-school snacks. It's organic muesli for breakfast."

"Ah, my mistake." Joe grinned. Alex watched and listened to them through the glass doors and smiled to herself.

Gloria was talking full speed. "Alexa, we really need Joe to come over and talk some sense into Bob. He's talking about going with Joe on the fishing trip! What could he be thinking? It's obvious that he won't be able to do that—he can't even go back to work yet. He's still learning to take more than a few steps with the walker. How could he go fishing?"

"It's not for months, Gloria. Things could change quite a bit."

"You don't understand. He's as helpless as a baby. I'm up and down tending to him from morning until night. And then all night. It's too much."

"It must be exhausting for you." Alex felt a twinge of pity for Gloria. She couldn't imagine that level of responsibility, even with the boys and Rachel to help.

"Yes, that's it. I'm exhausted. And him rambling on about getting better and going fishing—well, let's just see if he can graduate to a cane on time. The physical therapist thinks he should be able to do that in a couple of weeks, but I'm not seeing it."

"You don't trust the physical therapist? I thought you liked him well enough. And you said Bob seemed to get along with him well."

"Bob? Bob gets along with everyone. Yes, Will is pleasant. But a cane? In two weeks? The man looks anxious with his walker. Oh, I tell you, my nerves are shredded."

Alex eyed Joe and Sandy, who were laughing uproariously. "Sandy mentioned Bob was looking pretty well," she offered cautiously.

"Oh! Sandy and Rachel. Don't get me started. They think they're Florence Nightingale, running and fetching and fussing over Bob like two little mother hens." There was a short silence. "Well, it is a nice break for me. But too much fussing keeps Bob from trying to do for himself."

"Yes, I can see how that would be worrisome." She gazed at the kitchen. Now Sandy was acting out some sort of scene. She looked rather like an eagle, gesturing with tight-lipped disapproval, and Alex realized with horror that she was mimicking Gloria. Alex stepped further into the backyard so no sounds from the theater in her kitchen could accidentally reach the phone.

"I just don't know what to do. I lie in bed at night and stare at the ceiling, waiting for Bob to need help getting up to the bathroom and wondering how I will manage. What if he doesn't graduate to a cane?" Gloria's voice climbed higher. "What if he has another heart attack? What if he never gets back to doing his normal routine?"

"It must be frightening for you," Alex said soothingly. "And yet the medical team is so optimistic."

"They don't understand what this is like for me!"

"No, I'm sure their main focus is Bob."

"Well, I can't deal with this. Not forever. I don't know how to cope."

Alex briefly rubbed her jaw. "Gloria, you know we're all here for you. You don't have to do this alone."

"I know but ... I feel overwhelmed. And like this is turning me into a burden, too."

Alex took a breath. "Gloria, have you thought about a caregiver support group? Or a counselor? Maybe you should talk to someone."

Chapter
Thirty-Nine

"So, I recommended she see a counselor. Obviously, she can't see you, since you already see me and her son."

Dr. Sam raised an eyebrow. "Will she find someone on her own or does she want you to give her a name?"

"Oh, she's on her own. I mentioned someone who works with a colleague at the college—Suzanne's very free with discussing her therapist—so that is someone separate from this loop."

Dr. Sam nodded. "And you? How are you doing?"

"Better, I think." Alex pressed her lips together briefly. "It sounds funny, but for me to even recommend Gloria talk to someone, that I can't be the be-all and end-all for her support, that was a big step."

"Yes, speaking up for yourself hasn't been your strong suit."

"I'm doing better, generally. And Joe seems to have started to snap out of that funk he's been in since Bob's accident."

"You'd mentioned Joe wasn't himself for a while."

"No, not at all. Usually, Joe is a mix—he's quiet, but then starts talking and it's a lecture. In a good way, I mean," she added hurriedly. "Like a college lecture." Dr. Sam nodded helpfully, and Alex continued. "You know—he gets going on something that interests him and that's it. You can barely get a word in edgewise."

"And that's been absent for a few months now, generally?"

"But Joe went to see Bob the other day and they had a long talk. Now Joe is energized about the sabbatical and the possibility of quality time with the guys, and with me, and writing about fishing and history. That's a relief."

Dr. Sam laughed. "Would most wives be relieved that their husbands wanted to immerse themselves in fishing for a year?"

Alex smiled broadly. "Well, there's something in there for me, too. I've got that sabbatical coming up—and I've been dragging my feet about it. Well, sort of. I have arranged to rent a colleague's cabin for three months. She's giving me such a break on the cost it must be hurting them, but she assures me not. Apparently having the place cleaned each week between tenants is almost half the cost, so me being there for three months really is a savings in cost and aggravation. And I did order hiking boots, which I've been wearing for longer and longer walks. But I dillydallied about signing up for a plein air course next October, up in the mountains. I'm not even sure why. But I finally did it."

"And you've been journaling on being stuck, so ..."

"So, it's fear. Of course. What is it always, with me?" Alex shook her head in disapproval. "And I'm afraid about, well, goofy stuff. That I'll waste the time, or not take advantage of it, or something. All things within my control. Well, within my influence, anyway."

"Right."

"So, well, I began thinking, maybe I need to just do things and ride out the anxiety." She paused. "I know you were encouraging me to just do stuff, anxious or not. I'm slow. But, you know, I started a while ago, and now I've cleaned out just about every closet in the house and got rid of a lot of stuff. The veterans' group made a few pickups for their thrift shop. I'd been postponing it, feeling afraid."

"Afraid to clean out closets?"

Alex sighed. "See how crazy it is? I was worried. Worried I'd find something that made me emotional, worried I'd throw something away or donate it and then regret it, worried I'd make more of a mess or that Joe would be upset with me. Of course, Joe didn't even notice I was clearing out. I don't know how he missed the piles of stuff going out the door and waiting in the driveway for pickup."

"And you? You've done a lot of work in the fear department. There's the hair, and the gingerbread house class, the art classes, the cabin rental ..."

"I started doing art again instead of just talking about it. And of course, I'm using my lunch hour for myself, usually nature walks around campus, instead of scampering over to take care of the grand-pups."

"Nice. How is the art going? And the walks?"

"It's been great. It's scary, to dip back into art after a long absence. I signed up for an art class, an ongoing one. Eight weeks, every Monday."

"Painting? Drawing?"

"A drawing class. I'd like to sharpen my drawing skills. It might come in handy." Alex looked down at her hands and took a deep breath. "No, it *will* come in handy. I'm finally putting together my own sabbatical plans." She looked up at Dr. Sam, who was smiling. "I'm not required to come up with some major published research, but I need to do a project for the school. I want, maybe, to do a collection of art and writings, around birds. And to have the time to really study them, draw them, paint them, paint their environments—well, doesn't that sound great?"

"It does."

Alex frowned. "I really think so. But I haven't talked about it much yet. I've told Joe about every part of it so far, but I don't think he's got the big picture. At least, as a whole plan," she added, surprised at the resentment in her voice.

"And you haven't made sure he understands your whole plan because ...?"

"Because I am afraid everyone's opinions will poke it full of holes. It's not just Joe. That one way or another, they'll descend on it all like a flock of vultures. Well, maybe buzzards, and tear little pieces off."

"Mm-hmm."

"You know—Sandy will invite herself along and turn it into an ecology research project. Or Joe will have all sorts of good ideas—really, they are good—but they won't be my ideas, what I want. He'll just bulldoze over me without realizing it. Like I said, I've told him about almost every aspect, just not altogether. And he's been too preoccupied since Bob's accident to follow up on anything. Jonah will complain I'm not available to do whatever he needs doing. And I don't even want to think about my friends—Gloria disapproves of everything, anyway. So as soon as I start talking about what I might want to do, Sandy will try to steer it somewhere else, Jonah and Beth will start griping, and Joe will just hitch it to his project and the next thing you know, I'll be doing all my art in the fringes of his sabbatical instead of having my own."

"Yes, that's been the pattern for you. And yet," Dr. Sam said gently.

"And yet?" Alex echoed.

"And yet your friend came through with a great offer on a cabin, you enrolled in classes, you've worked out plans for yourself, and everyone outside of your inner circle is enthusiastic." She paused. "Didn't you even get tips from that guy who's training for the Appalachian Trail?"

"Yes, George." Alex smiled. "I'm walking the neighborhood in the mornings with a weighted backpack. Everyone I see out walking their dogs or exercising knows what I'm up to and has been checking on me, seeing if I'm carrying more weight as I go along. But I haven't really gotten support or interest from my family."

"That doesn't sound accurate, Alexa. Didn't Joe show some interest lately?"

Alex sighed. "Well, yes. And Sandy's been annoyingly enthusiastic about me doing things that get me out of a rut."

"So, the support is in bits and pieces. And you act as if this is just the 'usual' for you. And inevitable." Dr. Sam paused. "It seems like you don't step back and see how many things are going well, and how much encouragement you are getting from Joe and Sandy."

"Oh." Alex started twisting her hands, and then pretended to study the diplomas on the wall. "Yes, I guess. I'm just starting to figure out how to have my own lunch hour, never mind my own sabbatical. I get a little bonus point for that, don't I?"

Dr. Sam nodded. "It's hard to change, and you've been making a lot of changes these few months." She tilted her head, her gaze fixed on Alex's face. "What change would you want to make next? Not what seems doable, Alex, but what do you *want*?"

"I want ... I want." Alex hesitated and found herself tearing up. Her voice was thick. She looked down at her hands. "I want to be allowed to want what I want without everyone else taking it over. It shouldn't be so hard."

Dr. Sam sighed and leaned forward. "Alex, I'm sorry this is difficult. But listen to yourself. You're wanting something that already exists. You are already 'allowed' to want what you want; you didn't need permission for that. It's entirely interior, isn't it? You do know what you want, and the fear is, you want permission to go after it. So perhaps you need to figure out what that means and who counts."

"Counts?" Alex wiped her suddenly damp cheek, feeling foolish.

"Whose opinion counts. How much can Gloria's count? She's your friend, not your parent or your ruler. Sandy's opinion is interesting but not that important. She seems to have her hands full getting her adult life together, based on what you've shared—she's hardly one to manage yours. Jonah and Beth are fine; they seem to be able to cope without you serving them every day. So that leaves Joe."

"He's my husband, of course he counts."

"Right. Of course. And you count to him, too." Dr. Sam sat back. "Don't you?"

"Yes. That I know."

"You say, yes, you know, but it seems you actually assume—without really thinking about it directly—that he matters more to you than you do to him. That his dreams are more important to you than yours are to him."

It was silent for a few moments. Alex cleared her throat. "I didn't really ..."

"Yes, really. Listen to yourself. Think about how you decide almost anything. It's not just through a filter of what's fair, what's right, what's considerate. It's always hoping for permission to be granted."

Alex tried to study the landscape painting and defaulted to her lap, wringing her hands. She shrugged; her voice seemed to be missing.

"Which sounds, to me, like you've decided Joe doesn't really care what you want."

Alex sighed and blinked hard. A tear splashed on her hand and she wiped it off on her slacks. "Well, yes. I guess I am assuming that."

"Are you giving him enough credit?"

"What?"

"Do you really think he's that selfish, compared to you? That you're really that much kinder and more generous than Joe?" Dr. Sam shrugged. "I mean, I don't know. Maybe he's actually a jerk. Maybe he doesn't notice haircuts because he's so selfish, not because he's a busy guy. Or just a guy who loves his wife. Perhaps he's simply not a loving person. You've never actually said so, to me, anyway. That's not what you've described. A little personally preoccupied, perhaps, but not a selfish monster. But that sounds like what you're assuming here."

"I guess I didn't think about it that way."

"Maybe you should give it some thought."

Chapter Forty

April 10 was only days away, and the deadline to submit the paperwork for her own sabbatical was closing in. Alex wished the college didn't need to make arrangements for the fall term already. *What is the hurry*, she thought with annoyance, chopping a pepper with extra fervor. She smiled to herself; she knew she was not annoyed with the college but with herself for being a coward. She still hadn't had a real discussion about her own sabbatical hopes with Joe. *I really have to stop taking everything out on the vegetables.*

It was good to hear him talking again, she rationalized to herself. She didn't want to break the bubble. It didn't feel as reasonable an excuse as it sounded. She put the knife down, a little harder than necessary.

Joe looked up at the sharp sound. "Everything okay?"

"Hmm?"

"You okay? You seem a little ... I don't know. Preoccupied? Upset?"

Alex pressed her hands hard on the countertop before resuming chopping, this time an onion. "I guess so."

"Guess so upset? Guess so preoccupied?"

"Both." She glanced up. "Have you submitted your sabbatical paperwork?"

Joe turned his best owl look on her. "Yes. Is that what's upsetting you? My sabbatical?"

"I'm not upset."

"It's about my sabbatical?"

"No." A slice of onion bounced away and landed on the floor. Alex kept chopping. "Not yours. Mine."

"Yours? Have you given it any more thought?"

Alex put down the knife, pressed her lips together and raised her eyes to the ceiling, offering a quick prayer for patience before turning to Joe. "Of course I've given it a lot of thought. It's all planned out. I actually told you all about it. It's just, the paperwork is due in three days." She turned back to salad making, frowning.

"It's all planned out?"

"Yes. I've told you about it." She took a breath and tried to sound less angry. "I know there's been a lot going on." *And no one's bothered to ask me about this in days*, she added silently.

"Yes, Gloria's been asking a lot of you lately. It's been tough for her and I know you being there means a lot to her."

"It's not just Gloria." Alex sighed. "It's everything. You realize that this is the first time you've *asked* me about it since I first mentioned it months ago? I bring it up and you just kind of skate by it, if I even get a word in edgewise. Everyone else is all atwitter about your sabbatical and no one has even thought to ask a question about mine. For God's sake, it seems our whole family—and Bob and Gloria's—is part of your sabbatical and no one seems to even remember that I'm planning one, too."

"I'm sorry," Joe said, looking perplexed. "Why haven't you been talking about it?"

Alex's mouth hung open in brief surprise. "I have been. Suzanne's cabin. The art classes. The ornithology course. The big plein air course in Georgia in October." She lifted one foot. "The hiking shoes. I have been talking."

Joe's shoulders slumped. "Oh. Yes, yes you have. Honey, I'm sorry, I didn't get it." He paused. "You didn't really push the conversation. How come?"

Alex shrugged. "Honestly, I thought I did. Many times."

"It didn't seem that way to me."

"It's hard to explain."

"What? What's hard?"

"It's hard because one of you—you or Sandy or Gloria or who-ever—always takes over the conversation. I actually have tried talking about it. Dozens of times. But it's always like now. You're not asking me about my sabbatical plans, you're asking me why I didn't talk about them enough until now. Sandy's going to do the same thing. And Jonah—Jonah won't care as long as he's not inconvenienced. Which is what is going to happen, by the way. And Gloria—well, she never approves of anything."

Joe shook his head. "I'm not taking over, honey. You're reading this wrong."

"Would you please listen to me? Instead of telling me what I'm doing wrong?"

"I'm listening." Joe looked down and then back up at her.

Alex took a deep breath. "I'm sorry I sound angry. But I am. I'm frustrated. And it's partly my fault for letting everyone seem to think it's all fine when it's not. But I have my own things I'd like to do, and I wish I could talk about it without it being taken over or commandeered or criticized." Alex realized she was being redundant but was too angry to care.

Joe nodded and stayed quiet.

Alex continued. "I want my year, too. I'll just get this one chance for a sabbatical, and then it's on until retirement."

"And?"

"And I want to focus on what interests me."

"Which is?"

Alex felt stunned and said, not angrily but in surprise, "Art and birds." She looked at Joe's befuddled face and smiled. "Seriously? Haven't you been listening? I have it all planned out. There's a summer ornithology course, online, from the university. Very doable. I want to take a few art courses, and I could—or we could—stay for three months up in the mountains. I'm thinking August through October. I could do art, write, focus a lot of content on birds." She paused. "Suzanne from work—you know Suzanne—she and her husband have a cabin up in north Georgia, near a lake—lots of hiking, hardly any people, and the rent would be very affordable. She and I discussed it already. You remember, I mentioned this a couple of months ago and again last month. I'd be doing art work and hiking and taking that plein air landscape course. The one I told you about, with the two famous artists. And then I'd be back home, doing more art, studying, writing. Unless I hop a plane to meet you somewhere on the road." She paused. Joe opened his mouth and she held up a hand and continued. "And then put together a presentation – writing, art, a talk, and then an ongoing exhibit for the usual month or so."

Joe nodded thoughtfully. "You've been talking about this some. Just not to me."

"That's not really fair, Joe." Alex took a deep breath and let it out slowly and quietly. *Don't huff and puff,* she told herself. "I've been mentioning things I want to do, in bits and pieces. But yeah, I guess you're right that I haven't sat you down and made you listen and just laid out the whole plan to you. Or to Gloria, or Sandy, or almost anyone." Alex shook her head. "It's like incubating an egg with me. I guess I have to sit on it until it's ready to hatch." She shrugged. "I'm just afraid to bring things up because ..."

"Because I get excited and start managing it." Joe's face twisted. "I know. Sandy just told me the same thing yesterday." He paused. "To tell the truth, she complains about that quite often. I can't give her any advice without her fussing about my 'taking over,' which always seemed unfair. But maybe not, huh?"

"Joe." Alex hugged him. "I love you, and I love how enthusiastic you can be. And I wish you would sometimes hold back a little and let me take my little baby steps before you launch a plan for solving everything or fixing one of us, or sweeping us all off on adventure."

Joe was silent. Alex tried channeling Dr. Sam's gift for patient silence. Finally, Joe said quietly, "Fair enough." He thoughtful. "When would you be leaving?"

"The ornithology class is online, so I can be wherever there's reliable internet and a printer. The art classes start—well, one of them is the Monday night class. I'll be well into that process before the end of term, wrapping up the first course by then. The cabin is from mid-August until mid-November."

"Then in theory, you could do part of this on the road?"

"With you, you mean? Yes. But not with the whole bunch of boys." *I already told you that*, she thought. Aloud she said, "You'll have to entertain Bob, Cody, Matt, and Tim on your own. I'm not signing up for more mother hen duty."

"And Grandpa Quinn. He'll catch us for a week or so when we're up in New England. And Aidan," Joe added. "He wants to join for part of the summer, before school begins."

"Aidan. That sounds nice." She thought about Rachel's possessiveness, wondering how she'd handle her boyfriend off with her father and brothers. "But then Rachel will be jealous of you, too."

"Your sabbatical plans," Joe went on, seemingly oblivious to Rachel's insecurities. "They sound great." Joe caught himself, pausing. "Maybe later we can look at the calendar and the map and figure out where you'd like to do some birding and writing and art along the fishing expedition, and put the beginning of a plan together. If that sounds okay?"

"That sounds perfect." Alex wrapped her arms around his waist. "It will be quite an adventure!" She leaned her head on his shoulder. "I'm looking forward to telling you more about it."

"And I'm looking forward to listening." Joe stroked her hair, resting his head on hers. "What a year it will be!"

Alex smiled. "Sandy knows a little Now we just have to figure out what to tell Jonah and Beth."

She felt his smile against her forehead. "I think they'll manage."

Book Club Conversations

1. What did you think of Alex when you first met her? Did anything she did, or didn't do, surprise you as the story progressed?

2. With which character(s) did you most identify? Why? In what ways do you feel similar to, or want to be like, that character?

3. Alex uses ornithology as a shorthand to understand others. What kind of bird, or another animal, might she assign to you, and why?

4. What is your impression of Alex and Joe's marriage? How do you imagine it being after the book ends?

5. What are your impressions of Jonah and Sandy? What about Alex's relationship with her children? How did Alex deal with her feelings towards each of her children?

6. Were any characters unlikable? If so, what brought you to dislike them, and how would you have wanted the people around them to respond?

7.   Alex is skeptical, and sometimes judgmental, about some of the life changes her colleagues are making. What do you think underlies her reaction to their actions?

8.   In therapy, Alex is challenged to face up to her fearfulness. How did her fearfulness evolve over time? What factors seemed to either increase, or decrease, her fears?

9.   Have you known people ruled by fear? Have any of them broken free, and if so, what did that look like from the outside?